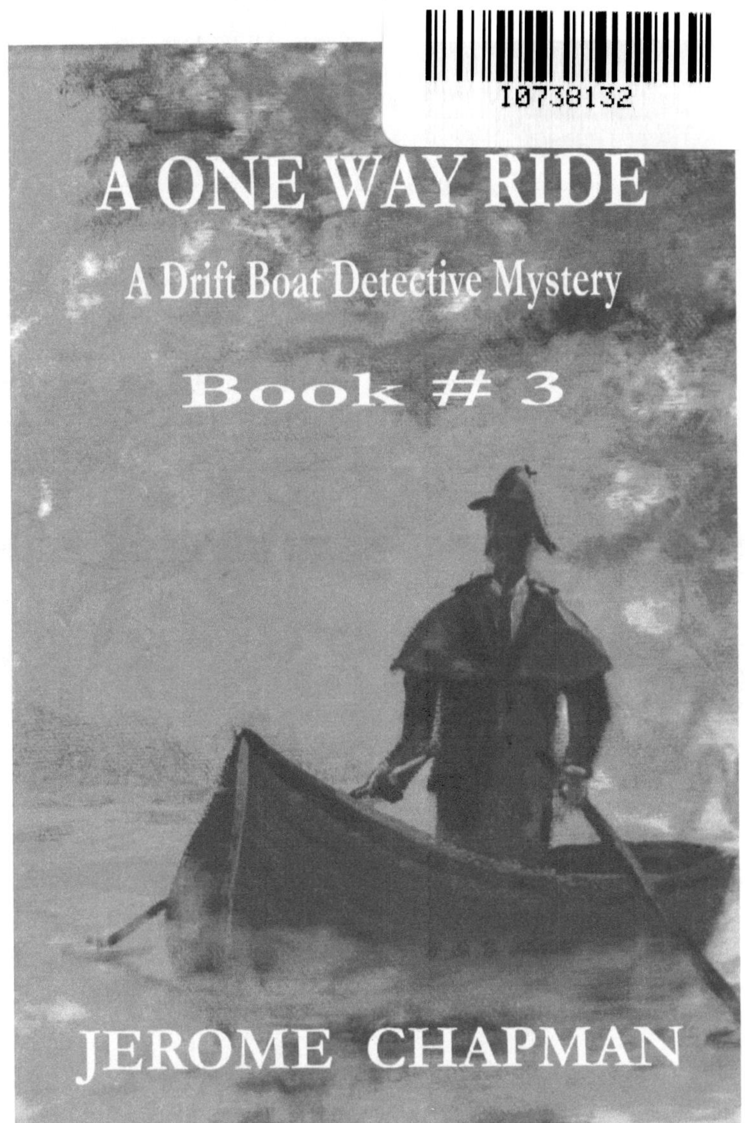
A ONE WAY RIDE
A Drift Boat Detective Mystery
Book # 3
JEROME CHAPMAN

Published by Jerome Chapman
Smyrna, GA, USA
WWW.Driftboatdetective.com

Book design by Jerome Chapman
The Drift Boat Detective Image by Chuck Renfroe
Cover photo is used by license: Shutterstock -Artist:: Unicus Road to the Mountain. - 282643964
© Jerome Chapman 2022
Editing by S.C. Lauren

Printed in the USA
ISBN : 978-0-578-39048-2
1.Fiction/Action & Adventure
2.fiction/mystery & Detective/General
22.01.04

For all those that are, or have been, victims of human trafficking. And to all those who are trying to find a way out, or may have been fortunate enough to do so.

While this is a book of fiction, the story of human trafficking is all too real and current. This is a real problem with real victims and real human tragedies. One that is seldom talked about.

Human trafficking is a real story of loss of personal freedom, dignity, and hope. One of worldwide scope. But, also, a criminal activity that goes on in the cities and towns where we live. Often unnoticed and unreported.

To learn more about human trafficking, to seek help, or to report suspected human trafficking, please call the National Human Trafficking Resource Center, Toll Free. 24 Hours a day. 1-888-373-7888.

Or, call your local authorities or the FBI.

You may save a life.

JC

A One Way Ride
A Russell Baker
Drift Boat Detective
Novel Book 3

By
Jerome Chapman

Chapter 1

Russell Baker walked down to the boat ramp and saw his guide pulling the truck away to the parking lot. Zack Rozier acknowledged Russ with a quick wave of the hand. It wasn't hard to spot the boat and truck as they proudly displayed the name and all the contact information for Captain Zack Rozier Fishing, Islamorada, Florida. Russ had driven up from the in-law's condo in Marathon, about 25 miles away, to the marina at Matecumbe Key.

The sun was high, and it was getting sultry hot. Not unusual here in Florida. The water off on the Atlantic side was shimmering with a smoothness you would seldom see. You could see for miles from where Russ stood overlooking the still water. Zack ran a one-man fishing guide business. It was all he was really good at having tried the nine-to-five life in an Atlanta architectural firm and found it not to his liking.

Florida was a different animal compared to where Russ would take clients down the Madison River out in Montana. Zack's flats boat had a 150 HP motor and could come back to where it started compared to Russ's drift boat that was only good for one direction, powered by a strong back and two oars; and a shuttle driver was required to move the truck from the put in to the take out.

Going out at one o'clock meant they would be in the heat of the day, but Captain Zack wanted to be fishing as the water was falling and approaching the afternoon low tide. According to the charts, that would be as early as five thirty today.

Russ was anxious to try out his new 4-piece rod and reel he'd bought for the occasion. Catching a trophy tarpon, or *Silver King* as some called them, was something that had eluded him for years, and this was his last day in the Keys and his last shot for a while to attempt to wrangle in the tough fish.

The guide came back to the boat and looked at the rod in Russ's hand. "What do you have there?" Zack asked as he nodded toward the rod.

"It's a 12 WT, 4-piece," replied Russ, quite proud of his pricey purchase.

"If you don't mind too much, I have a one piece 11 Wt. set up for today, ready to go. It will be better for landing a 'poon if you manage to hook one. It has a tapered leader and shock tippet set up, and it will lay out well for you. I suggest you secure your rod in your car."

Russ had paid a handsome price for his rod and reel and was not happy with the suggestion. But he knew that he would be better off taking the guide's advice. Anyone who called the beastly tarpons *'poons* usually knew what they were talking about as it was a local fisherman's term.

They had been fishing three days in the same boat over the past week. He supposed the boat to be about $60,000 or more but had not asked. Russ stepped in as Zack gave a shove, and the boat floated out as the motor was lowered with a low whining sound.

Russ sat down on the bench seat beside Zack, and with a brief whirr of the starter, the motor fired up, and they eased out. The quest was on.

The center console boat would skim easily over the water and could go in water as shallow as about five inches: far too shallow to run a motor. Zack would push the boat silently toward any fish they saw with a 20-foot graphite push pole while standing on an elevated poling platform that was built up over the motor: something that took a little practice otherwise the person pushing would undoubtedly wind up in the water.

As soon as they reached the channel, Captain Zack was up on the poling platform looking for the tarpon that had eluded him and his client for the past few days. In a channel just off shore at Matecumbe, the currents looked good as the tide was going out.

There were some tarpons there that locals believed stayed in the area all year and then there were some migratory fish that came through. Russ did not care where they lived; he just wanted to hook up and get one of the boney mouthed monsters to the boat.

"I believe this is going to be the day," Captain Zack said.

Russ seemed to remember that same statement being proclaimed the past few mornings as well. But, ticking off the guide on your last day before you catch that trophy tarpon was not a good idea, he reasoned. So, he just replied, "Sounds good to me."

Going on a break to Florida with his in-laws had seemed a good idea. His in-laws were his only family now, and he was theirs since their daughter Sarah, his late wife, had died. But his father-in-law was not up to fishing every day, and the prize tarpon had yet to be caught. Today it was just Russ and Captain Zack.

Sharks, goliath grouper, and a variety of others, both off shore and in the back country, had been accounted for. Lots of snook. No tarpon

Standing up front with the 11 WT fly rod felt a little unusual for Russ. He was more a 5, 6, or 7 Wt. guy when he fished for big trout in Montana or Georgia. An 8 Wt. for bone fish. He'd even been known to use a 2 Wt. or a 3 Wt., but a big tarpon was not easy to handle or a sure thing even on the big fly rods or spinners that a lot of folks used. Quite different than he was used to.

And, there was that plane ticket on his dresser in the guest room at the condo which was scheduled for tomorrow. It was now or never, at least for a while.

"Heads up, Russ, there are some fish headed straight for us at twelve o'clock! Get ready! Do you see them?"

Russ had not liked the casting platform, choosing instead to fish on deck of the boat and did not have the angle that Zack had standing on the poling platform. "Not yet!" Russ yelled.

"You have to cast now before they see us! Lay it out as far as you can and get it in front of them! Hurry! If they see us, they'll turn and run!"

Without really seeing the fish, Russ lifted the fly rod and started his back cast of the yellow streamer fly called *The Tarpon Toad* on a 50-pound shock leader. Metal wire leaders were not used as the tarpon could see them and be spooked more easily than using the nylon. It took a heavy leader to withstand the grinding on the fish's boney mouth. And, even then, landing the fish once hooked was not a sure thing.

After a couple of double hauls, Zack was yelling, "Drop it in front of them, now!"

Russ would have liked one more back cast but instead dropped the fly into the blue green water, relying on the guide's instinct.

"Let it sit a couple of seconds!" Zack called as he watched the school of fish. "Now, strip…strip…strip. He's coming to it. Strip. He's turned off but there's one behind coming to it. Strip…strip. He's coming. He's on it!"

Russ had caught lots of fish in his day. Lots of big browns, lake trout, and rainbows. Near record size trout in the White River and Little Red. In nearly every state. Big bass and red fish in Louisiana and South Carolina. But he had never felt what he felt when the tarpon hit the fly on the end of his line. It was a powerful hit, and as soon as the fish felt the hook in his jaw, he went airborne for what looked like three or four feet with a shake of the head in defiance. Russ could only hold on to the quivering fly rod that was tested with the full energy of the angry, massive fish. A fish that wanted no part of the hook, the line, or the fisherman.

"Get him on the reel, Russ. He's gonna want to run," said Zack.

Zack was trying to keep the boat up with the fish using the push pole. The fish was now headed away from the boat in leaps and bounds. The line was coming off the reel. The fight was on! Would 250 feet of backing and 100 feet of fly line be enough?

Again, the fish went airborne. The line was peeling off the reel. The fish surged and jumped, shaking his head violently, and the rod looked like it was bent to the max.

Then, the line went slack.

Just as fast as the action had started, the fish was gone. Russ couldn't believe it. Usually not one to use much profanity, he yelled, "Hell fire! The damned fish is off!"

"Reel it in fast and take a seat," said Zack who was already putting the push pole in the brackets and starting up the outboard. "They're headed up the beach. We'll go to the other side of that line of floating grass and try to cut them off and see if we can get another shot at that group."

Zack could do something that could not be done in Russ's drift boat: chase fish.

Zack ran for about a quarter mile and started a wide turn in toward the beach to try and see if he could pick up the school again. Suddenly, he cut the throttle, shut the engine, and hit the button to raise it out of the water. It had all seemed like one motion to Russ.

"Get up and get your line out there. There is another group coming at us just like last time. We won't have many more shots like this. Get up on the casting platform."

This time, standing on the casting platform, he could see the fish with his angle and the light, and he made three double-haul back casts and dropped the fly into the path of the oncoming fish.

"That's perfect, Russ. Start stripping. "Strip…strip…strip. You have one looking. Strip…strip. He's on it!"

Russ had thought the first fish hit hard and with a lot of power. This second (and much bigger) fish took him by surprise as it tried to rip the rod out of his hand with tremendous raw power. Russ's heart was pounding.

It went into the air, and Russ heard Zack yell, "That's what we came for. That's a monster!"

Russ could only agree by shaking his head. He had his hands full, and he didn't want to break his concentration. The power of the tarpon was coming through the line and reverberating in the state-of-the-art fly rod. He could feel the hate and anger of the brute in his hands.

The fish stripped line off the reel, Zack poled the boat to help Russ keep the fish from using up all the backing.

Russ would reel in, and then the fish would leap and run again. Reel in, leap, and run. Over and over, and every time the fish went into the air it was heart pounding, and Russ was afraid the fish was coming off again. Just as he thought he had the fish whipped and he was coming toward the boat, the fish would see the boat and Russ and away it would go.

Finally, after twenty long minutes that seemed like an hour, Russ was able to pull the creature alongside, and Zack got a gloved hand on the fish. Success, at last. An 81-pound tarpon on a fly rod. While there were bigger tarpon, this one would do just fine. This was his first big tarpon on a fly rod, his biggest tarpon, and maybe his last tarpon for a while.

A rare quick picture and a little reviving of the fish and the tarpon made an angry slap of the water as it was released and just like that it was over. Mission accomplished. An experience to remember.

Russ gave Captain Zack a high five as he sat down. Exhausted. He couldn't wait to tell his father-in-law.

Now he could go back to Montana.

Chapter 2

It had been a long day of traveling. Russ had accompanied his in-laws from Key West to Atlanta and then had travelled alone from Atlanta to Denver. Finally, at a few minutes past ten, he had made it to Bozeman with the drive to Ennis still ahead. It was twelve o'clock in Florida. With the time zone and plane hopping, it was turning into a long day. Mr. Ted Turner used a personal jet when he came from Atlanta. No messing around with security and flight schedules for the mega wealthy.

The rented house, just outside Ennis, Montana was cold as Russell stepped inside. The car thermometer had shown 33°, and it felt just as cold in the house. It could likely get a little colder by morning and a line of rain, sleet and snow storms was moving in. With the river's high flows, it would probably be a good day to sit home and catch up on household duties. Rain and snow, he could take ordinarily, if necessary, but fishing in those conditions after just returning from the sunny weather in Florida had no appeal.

Montana was a big change from the fishing he had done in the Florida Keys, the Everglades, and the Ten Thousand Islands. In his years, he had traversed some of the country's best fishing spots.

He had a stack of mail that had been delivered today, and his phone message light was flashing. The messages would have to wait until tomorrow.

Marta

A few days earlier, in New Orleans, Marta Andruko had made a fateful choice.

Her father and mother wanted to return to Ukraine, but Marta and her sisters did not want to leave the US. When the day to leave was fast approaching, at almost 18 now, she felt she could make it on her own somehow. Marta had put a few things in a duffle bag, prepared to walk away with little money and no place to go.

She had a passport, green card, and a school ID, but they all had her real name. She knew that once her father found out she was gone, there would be people looking for her. She had to get out of town fast and be miles away before they knew she was even gone.

So, when her father left for his part time job at 6:00 AM, she left with $48 in cash and headed for the Amtrak Station at Union Passenger Terminal in New Orleans. This would give her a day's head start before he realized she was gone. She was thinking either Los Angeles or Atlanta. She refused to return to Ukraine.

She had come to the US with her family with the assistance of a Baptist Missionary group in Louisiana following the 2014 revolution. Her father had been enrolled in the National University of Pharmacy in Ukraine and was about to be called up for the military when he had fled with his family to Poland. He was met by a US aid group and had gotten an educational visa to come to the US and continue his training in a Louisiana school of pharmacy. Marta and her sisters had been enrolled in a school run by the same church.

The adjustment for Marta and her two sisters had been hard at first, but they had soon settled into the school and a house had been provided for them. They had come to love it in the US, and her parents wanted to strip that away from them and uproot them once more.

Marta got her first shock when she walked in to the Amtrak station and found that she did not have enough money to buy even the cheapest ticket on the Amtrak to Atlanta. The agent suggested she try the Greyhound bus counter which was in the same building. A ticket on Greyhound to Atlanta was $37. The first leg of her one-way ride was about to start.

She boarded a bus headed to Atlanta and nine and one-half hours later, Marta stepped outside the Greyhound Station on Forsyth St. in Atlanta at 11:30 PM, and she had no idea what to do or where to go. She knew she would not get far on the eleven dollars she had left. For a moment, she let the reality of her plight sink in, and a slight fear gripped her.

As she walked out to the street and stood looking around in awe, a black late model Mercedes pulled up to the curb and a young and handsome man in his thirties stepped out.

"Do you need some help, young lady?" he asked as he motioned toward Marta.

Somewhat startled, she replied, "Eh…no. I'm waiting on someone."

"This isn't a safe area for you to be in alone this time of night. I know because I work just down the street. I can wait with you 'till your ride shows up," he suggested.

"They should be here shortly," she said.

"Do you want to call and make sure they're coming? I am going to stop at a Waffle House a couple of blocks over, and you can get something to eat there with me and wait for them if you like. Are you hungry?"

She was, and he did seem nice. But she was wary of getting into the car with a stranger.

"I don't think I should get into the car with someone I don't know," she said.

"I totally agree. It pays to be cautious. But you don't feel safe here on the street by yourself, do you?"

"No."

"You can walk over to Waffle House, and I'll watch you 'till you get there if you want. I just don't feel right leaving you here alone. Or, you can just hop in, and we'll go over. I won't bite. I promise."

"I guess that will be okay," she said.

"Great. I'll put your bag in the back seat. What's your name?"

"Marta."

"Really? That is the name of our transit system here in Atlanta."

"That's my name," she said. "What's your name?"

"I'm Max. Max Johnson."

They drove to the nearby Waffle House and went to a booth.

"Should you make that call?" he asked.

"Yes. I'll step outside and call."

She walked out to the side walk and took her phone and listened to her voice mails. All from her dad and sisters wanting to know where she was. She pretended to call. She did not know what to tell Max when she went back in, but she was starving.

"Everything okay?"

"They're just running late."

"Well, let's order," he said.

She ordered waffles, eggs, and a piece of steak. It was the best meal she'd had in a while.

"Marta, I have to be going, but why don't I drop you at a motel somewhere? I don't want to go off and leave you here by yourself."

"I don't have any money for a motel," she said.

"Do you have any money?"

"I have about ten dollars."

"Marta, you aren't really meeting anyone here are you?" he asked in what appeared to be a sympathetic voice.

She hesitated.

"I believe you are running away from home. How old are you?" he asked.

She pulled out her Ukraine passport. "I am almost eighteen," she said.

"Tell you what. I'll drop you off at the hotel up the street, and I'll pay for it for tonight. And, I'll give you some cash for tomorrow. They will have a free breakfast in the morning, and you can decide what you want to do."

"I can't pay you back," she said.

"We won't worry about that. I'll give you my number, and if you need anything, you can call me. Do you want me to buy you a bus ticket back home?"

"No! I'm not going back home!" she said in an emphatic voice.

"What do you say? Should I drop you off?"

"I guess so. You aren't going to report me, are you?"

"No, of course not. I just want to be sure you are alright. But you might give me your number so that I can check in on you."

They drove up the street to a motel near I-75, and he went in and rented a room. After escorting her to the room, he wrote his burn cell phone number down and gave it to her and two twenty-dollar bills as well. He said goodnight and left.

What a nice man, she thought, perhaps a bit too ignorant to realize it was just enough money to appear helpful without it being enough for her to easily leave town.

Marta had a room, a TV, and about fifty dollars. She was ahead of the game from when she had left home.

She texted her father. It said that she was fine, not to worry, and that she would get back to them again soon.

While her parents were still frantic, the local police didn't treat this as a kidnapping or abduction. To them it was just another teenager who had left home on their own. She had a visa and a passport and was old enough to go if she wanted to go. Law enforcement had no reason to pursue her.

Max

As Max Johnson, as he called himself, drove away from the motel, he pushed the call button on his car's blue-tooth. A voice answered, "Have any luck tonight?"

"Yeah. I picked up a cute seventeen-year-old blonde runaway from Louisiana. She is actually from Ukraine. She'll bring a good price. I have her stashed at the usual place. If she doesn't call me, I'll get back by there tomorrow. She likes me."

"Of course, she does. Okay, but don't wait too long. Can you send me a picture?"

"I'll send it when I get to a stopping place. Where do you have in mind for this one?"

"I have some folks out West that are looking for European blondes. They will go thirty grand for the really pretty and clean ones." He sounded like a man selling a used car – not that that bothered Max.

"Call you soon."

Max Johnson was a spotter, or locator, for a network of criminals that were in the human trafficking business in one of the hottest cities in the country for that enterprise. He regularly checked the bus stations, Amtrak, hospital emergency rooms, and places where homeless and hopeless people, or people looking for a drug fix, hung out. He searched for people traveling alone that appeared vulnerable and in need of help. Soup kitchens and parks.

Young, pretty girls and boys were on his radar. With his charm, nice clothes, nice car, and non-threatening approach and a little money, he could win their confidence.

Then would come drugs and dependency, and he could start controlling them. They used quaaludes and date rape drugs – harder drugs if needed. The victims would then go to strip clubs, prostitution groups, sweat shops, shop lifting rings, and some would even become high end sex slaves. And, for people like Marta, there was usually no way out and no way back. It was a one-way ride.

This had been a big night for Max Johnson. Marta would bring top dollar. And, he would introduce her forcefully to prostitution and pick up a few bucks in the bargain to cover his costs. He was on a hot streak this week with two other young ladies staying at the same motel.

Max would treat Marta nice: he would buy her clothes, offer to send her home, and begin showing her affection and persuade her to start experimenting with drugs and sex. He would tell her she would need to pay him back for the money he was spending on her.

In a few days, he would have control over her and be ready to move her to a buyer who could make over $120,000 a year with her. Little or none of which she would receive. His targets were often promised a movie role, acting lessons, or a high paying job as an au pair and made to believe they were bound by law to repay the money spent on them. Acts of physical harm, drugs, and threats of deportation or jail would be resorted to if necessary. And, there were threats against the victim's family if she or he ever failed to comply.

A network of spotters, groomers, and distributors had evolved using low tech communication methods that kept them off the internet and highly visible sites. Mail boxes secured using fake ID's and fake home addresses were common, and the victims were moved using a variety of methods. A simple letter with a date, burn phone number, and the name and color of the RV being used for transport would be mailed to a mail box, and there might be a picture and a price.

Max had come to rely on rented motor homes to move two, three, or four of his products at a time from Atlanta to cities mainly up and down the east coast, eliminating the need for restroom stops, motel rooms, and going in and out of restaurants – allowing him to keep them under control by drugs and intimidation.

Bulletin boards at RV centers, truck stops, building supply stores, and even trail heads often had a simple message that was understood by certain movers and buyers.

Men like Max had to have no remorse to make it in this world.

Max Johnson called Marta the next morning, "Good morning, Marta. This is Max. Everything okay with you?"

"Yes, sir; the room is nice. I'll be checking out soon. Thank you for dinner last night and for the room."

"It was my pleasure. What do you plan to do today?" he asked.

"I guess I'll start looking for a job. I saw where there are some movies being made in the area. Maybe I can find something like that or get a waitressing job."

He smiled. She would be easy.

"That sounds pretty risky to me. Why not stay with us, and we will see about finding a steady job for you? It may take several days to find something, and you have no money," he said.

"Won't I have to pay you back?" she asked.

"Yes, but we can do a little contract, and you can pay me out of your money when you start working. Or, I'll find something for you to do to work off the money. You need some clothes and pictures for your headshots if you want to look into acting. I can get the photos done, too. I have a house down in College Park where some other folks like yourself are staying. If you're interested, we can move you down there, and we can do the photos there," he said and added, "I can act as your agent. I've got some connections in the industry."

"Do you think this will all take long?" she asked.

"Probably will take a while. I may can get you something in Las Vegas. I have some connections out there, as well. I'll work on that, too. Maybe a casino job, but that might require some new ID papers."

"How will I get to Las Vegas?" she asked. "What would I do in Las Vegas that I couldn't do here?"

"There's lots of different types of work for a girl like you in Vegas. I could arrange travel when the time comes," he said. "We have to prepare you for working so that you can make some real money if that's what you want to do."

"Can… can I think about it?" Marta questioned.

Max had been doing this long enough to know when he had someone's interest piqued. "Of course, sweetheart. After all, I'm just here to help."

Chapter 3

Morning came early for Russ. His body was still on East Coast time, and the early May morning sky was still dark when he woke up at 4:00. After getting his mental bearings, he realized he was back in his bed in Ennis.

Going fishing was out for today. The weather was just too bad. He had several days of mail to go through. And, who knows how many voice mails? And, there were a few calls he needed to make. *Coffee first – then work,* he decided.

As he got the coffee pot going, he looked at the weather station on the kitchen counter. It still said 33°, and it was raining pretty hard. With lightning in the forecast, it would be a perfect day to drink coffee and catch up on more miniscule tasks. There would be more good fishing days ahead, hopefully.

He needed to call Nancy Freeman. That was a priority. He had called several times while he was in Florida and had never gotten her. He had left her numerous voice mails, and she had not responded. He and Nancy did not have any sort of official arrangement, but they had been seeing each other now for some time. He suspected they might be headed to a more serious commitment that both had avoided up to this point.

Russ had finally come to grips with the loss of his wife, and Nancy had put the loss of her soldier fiancé behind her. Maybe they could both move on now?

He also needed to call Nancy's brother, Chad. Chad worked as a fishing guide and had become a good friend and someone he could rely on to keep him up to date with Nancy. Chad should be back from Belize where he had been working as a guide in the off season.

Coffee in hand, Russ sat down by the phone and hit the *message waiting* button: "You have sixty-one messages. To hear your messages, push 2."

There were messages from stock brokers, burial plot sales people, home security firms, the pest control company wanted to set up an appointment, and a number of people warning him that his computer was seriously infected and to call at once. There were a couple of calls asking about fishing, but they were too old to matter now and did not need calling back.

Then, there was one message from Nancy Freeman. Why had she called his home phone to leave a message when she knew he was in Florida and had not called him back on his cell? Strange. Then he hit the *play message* button.

"Russ. This is Nancy. I'm sorry that I have not returned any of your calls, but I did not have the courage to talk to you in person. You have meant so much to me these past months, and I guess I had once thought we could make this work. But we just don't seem to get beyond our past histories. I recently started seeing Dr. Carter at the school, again. He has stopped drinking, and, Russ, I really do like him. I guess I love him… and… so, I won't be seeing you again in any sort of dating situation. Hopefully we can still be friends. Also, I plan to stop doing the fishing shuttles. Elanor Wills is taking over that for me. I don't have her number in front of me, but you can get it from Chad. Again, I'm sorry I did not have the courage to tell you in person. I did not want to spoil your visit with the folks in Atlanta."

There was a long pause before she softly added, "Goodbye, Russ," and the message cut off.

The voicemail asked if he want to save the message or delete it. Russ hit the delete without thinking about it. He was erasing a lot more than a voicemail.

Then, there was silence. All Russ could hear was the closing of a slamming door. Metaphorically. Somewhere. Not since his wife had died had he felt what he was feeling right now.

Russ wanted to call Nancy, but it was too early. And, it seemed, too late as well. Friends? Maybe someday. But not right now. Nancy had never been able to get past the cop in him; that part of him scared her. Nothing he could do about that. But he had not expected this.

He needed to catch his breath. He felt he had just been sucker punched right in the gut.

The last time Russ had heard anything from Dr. Carter, the man had made an ass of himself and embarrassed Nancy at a party. She had called her brother to come get her. Dr. Carter? Russ would have never guessed this on his best day as a detective with the Cobb County Police in Marietta, Georgia.

Maybe, Russ thought, *it's time to go back to the real world.* Go back and see if he could get his old job back as a detective with Cobb County or one of the surrounding areas. His mind was whirling.

He had been living off of the life insurance income, the sale of his house, and the investments his father-in-law had made for him plus a fair amount of guide trips on the Madison and surrounding areas. He had also helped the local sheriff out at times when they needed extra assistance. He had played a key role in solving a couple of big cases. Financially, he did not need to work.

But, maybe his trip into this fantasy life had hit a dead end? If Nancy had been trying to spare his feelings, she had failed miserably. The big once-in-a-lifetime tarpon on the fly rod was quickly a distant memory. The big catch in his life had just gotten away.

Russ laid down on the sofa, and in a few minutes was asleep, and his dreams were a far cry from pleasant.

It was nearly eight o'clock when Russ reawakened. The large clap of thunder jarred him out of his uneasy sleep, and he sat up only to hear heavy rain and see bright flashes of lightening. The coffee that he had poured at four AM was still in its cup. He took it to the kitchen microwave and warmed it up. He was now facing a grim reality: he was a long way from home and very much alone.

The same place he was when he had first arrived in Montana months earlier. This was not working out well at all.

On top of everything else, he had been gone so long that everything in his refrigerator was on the putrid side. He could not even eat breakfast at home and hide away from the harsh realities outside.

Russ picked up his phone and sent a text to Chad Freeman: *Are you up?*

Awake. Dreading getting up, came the reply.

How about I buy you breakfast at Perkins in an hour and a half?

Sounds good. If they are slammed, we can go to the bagel place, replied Chad.

Since when did you start eating bagels?

Alise says if you are buying, she's coming too. Her mom is here and can see about the kids. Russ liked Chad's wife a lot.

Hour and a half, replied Russ, and he put the phone down. He would have to hustle to get a shower and dressed and get to Bozeman in an hour and a half. He really had not wanted Alise along, but he decided it best not to rock the boat.

Russ wanted to see what Chad could tell him about Nancy dumping him for Dr. Carter. He expected Chad had already figured that out. With a 70 miles per hour speed limit and applying the universal fudge factor he could do the shower and make the 60 miles from his house in time, hopefully.

Although he knew the locals, he might not know the Montana Highway Patrol trooper he might encounter on his way. He did not feel like a speeding ticket right now.

Russ made it to Perkins with about five minutes to spare. And, no MHP encounters.

Alise was pretty as ever and greeted Russ with a hug.

"Easy, there, woman!" joked Chad. "He might get to liking that."

"He already likes it," she said with a devilish grin. Russ just shrugged as he shook Chad's hand.

"I hope you brought plenty of money, Russ. I think I can eat two breakfasts," she teased.

The breakfast and small talk about their recent trips went well, and the Perkins coffee was great. He showed them a picture of the big tarpon he had on his phone. They had not mentioned Nancy and the professor during breakfast once, and he was growing impatient at walking around the subject himself.

"I guess Nancy told you that she dumped me on the voicemail while I was gone," said Russ.

They looked at each other in amazement. No, they had not been told anything about it.

Russ had just blown thirty bucks and broken several traffic laws to get no answer about Nancy. It would have to come from her if he was to get one, and he wasn't sure how to go about that.

Chad seemed to sense that a change of subject was a good idea. "I start back taking clients out Monday. John called me from the fly shop yesterday and said bookings are great. Are you ready to get back at it?"

"Maybe after this next week. I need to catch up on some things. I'll call John and let him know. In fact, I may just go by while I'm in town."

As he left breakfast, Russ drove by Nancy's clothing store and resisted the urge to stop as he headed toward the fly shop. Another time, maybe. He needed to think about what he would say.

Chapter 4

Teresa

Over in Butte, Teresa Walker was just getting off her 3:00 to 11:00 shift at *Wayne's Truck Plaza* which was located on I-90 near the I-15 intersection. Recently paroled, Teresa had found it impossible to find a job that came anywhere close to the career she had once had at the Montana DCI (Department of Criminal Investigations). Her involvement with drug runners had gotten her fired, jailed, and almost killed. The thrills, pay-off money, and sex ended up costing her a lot. But her assistance in the prosecution of the ringleaders and a lenient judge had gotten her a short sentence and early parole. Waiting tables at a truck stop and living at home with her mother were not what she had planned for her life.

One of over 330 truck stops on I-90, *Wayne's* was an

incredible operation catering to the big rigs that hauled freight of all kinds on the longest interstate road in the US.

Stretching 3020 miles from Route 1A near Logan Airport in Boston to State Route 519 in Seattle, the drivers that stayed within the rules needed four 11-hour days to make the trip with cargo of all kinds. A river of concrete and asphalt crossing the US with ships rolling on 18 wheels or more. Some with multiple trailers and tons of freight.

Wayne's had hook-ups for the trucks that provide heat and air, internet connections, and TV. There were showers, bunks and restaurants. There were truck wash stations. They even had a full-service garage that could rebuild or replace the powerful 400, 500, and 600 horsepower engines in the Peterbilts, Kenworths, Freightliners, Macks, Volvos, Western Stars and Internationals. And, of course, they had dozens of fuel islands. Gas was also available for the folks driving cars, campers, and pickup trucks. Coming soon were recharging stations for the electric cars and soon, who knew when, the big rigs.

They even had a national eye glass company there to examine eyes and fit new glasses and a drug store that was part of the big convenience store operation. There was a western wear section selling boots, jeans, cowboy hats, and denim jackets.

Out in the huge lot, trucks could be parked while drivers took advantage of all the services, eat, shower, and rest. In spite of the security patrols in the lot, the lot lizards were always at work knocking on the doors of the big rigs trying to sell their services of various sexual favors. And, there were others that came and went using the lot as a meeting place to exchange certain items of value for money. Not all legitimate.

Old and new rigs parked side by side. Some looking as though they had seen better days while others modelled new and expensive dual bunks and creatures' comforts. Chrome and lights galore. Most of their cargo was given a one-way ride.

But old or new, the trucks in the regular freight hauling business generated about the same revenue per mile, often not leaving the owner operator a lot to live on considering the time away from home. On average, by some estimates, independent drivers earned about $32,000 per year, net. Owner operators who did some specialized hauling earned a little more. So, some were often tempted by the fast buck opportunities when they come along. Especially when the pay was off the books and in cash.

A driver, wearing a cowboy hat and boots, sat in the booth in the far corner of *Wayne's* and was the last of Teresa Walker's customers. She needed to close out his bill so that she could settle her tickets and leave, but he seemed to be waiting on someone and kept looking toward the entrance of the restaurant area.

The young girl wearing a PINK baseball type cap sitting with the driver looked ill at ease. Teresa imagined she was spaced out on drugs as she seemed incapable of making eye contact when she was taking their order or serving their food. She looked to be about sixteen, and Teresa assumed her to be the trucker's daughter. Her blonde hair was tucked under the cap.

A man who was also wearing a baseball cap pulled down low over his face came into the restaurant and stopped and looked back where the two were seated. He made a quick nod toward them and walked back to their table and sat down.

Just what Teresa did not want was someone to delay them from leaving. She walked over with a menu, but the guy waved her off. Having worked with a lot of cops, he looked like a cop to Teresa, but that was a quick assessment. He did not look directly at her.

She walked to the register to start checking her tickets and turned to see the new man walking out with the young girl, holding her hand. The driver in the cowboy hat put some money on the table and quickly left the restaurant. *Curious*, she thought.

The driver walked across the long parking area, looked to see if anyone was following, and climbed up into the cab of his old KW truck and was soon moving across and out of the parking lot toward the I-90 West ramp.

He took a quick look at the $2500 in the envelope. He would not see the young girl again. She didn't know his real name and he did not know hers. She was Marta Andruko from Ukraine via New Orleans.

She was someone's daughter, but not his. And, she was not his problem or concern any longer. She had been given a one-way ride, whether she knew it yet or not, thanks to Max Johnson, the man she had wanted desperately to believe was her friend and benefactor. Sexually abused, drugged, and physically hurt, she was now under his control. Photographed in the most embarrassing poses and situations and threatened by them. All her innocence and self-respect had been lost in a few days.

And now, Marta was in a rented Chevy Impala with California plates headed South on I-15 driven by the man wearing the baseball cap. Her one-way ride was not yet over. Not 'til Las Vegas.

Max said he had a modeling job lined up for her, and a new identity would be set up. He was really a nice man, she had thought.

She was warned that she would be deported if picked up. Keep quiet and do as she was told.

Teresa Walker picked up her money from the table and was happy to see a ten-dollar tip. Her day was over. Finally.

When Teresa drove into the driveway at her mother's home, she sat looking at the dark house. A little glow came from a nightlight in the hall through the window in the front door, and Teresa knew there was a small light in her mother's room. Her mother had a hard time sleeping alone since her father had died. And, now, her cancer treatments had not been going well with the local oncologist and he had referred them to a cancer center in Helena. They were trying to get her an appointment.

Chapter 5

Darin

The man in the baseball cap drove close to the speed limit on I-15. Attracting no attention was the key. No unexpected encounters with a law officer while he had the young woman in his car. He had a meeting in the parking lot of a big super store in Murray, Utah 424 miles down the road. Halfway to Las Vegas. He would turn over the *package* to another person waiting there. A person he did not know but who had his burn phone number and a description of the car he was driving. Much was built into making the tracking of these packages difficult if not impossible. No paper trails. No phone tracking. No internet IP addresses.

This was always a nervous time. There was always a possibility of being sold out to the cops. But, if all went well, he would hand Marta over to the driver, get a wad of cash, and be headed back home to Helena, Montana in a few hours. He had the evening shift at the Helena Police Department where he was a patrol officer. His job as a transporter would be done for a few days, and he could catch up on his sleep.

Darin Marchman had grown up in South Carolina and had gone into the Air Force following two years at the community college near his home. His money had run out. He had then been sent to Malmstrom Air Force Base near Great Falls, Montana, where he had met a young woman airman, and they had gotten married.

When their enlistments were up, Darin had applied for a lot of jobs and had gotten a job offer in Helena at the police department there. Eight years and three kids later, money was tight, and a contact had suggested he could make a lot of tax-free money if he did not mind being a little on the shady side.

The pressure at home had been getting higher and higher, so he had listened. And, after listening and looking at the money potential, he had accepted the sketchy side job. It was just about the money.

Camps for the kids, daycare, kindergarten, ballet lessons, new clothes and bikes, well, they were no problem now. He did have to make a few late-night trips to Butte and other places. He told his wife he was moonlighting on a security detail. She liked the money, so she did not press it.

Out of the ten grand he would be paid in Murray, he had paid some trucker $2,500, rented a car, and paid for some sodas and crackers. And gas, of course. Cash for the gas. He would clear at least $7,000. Do that two or three times a month, and the only problem was what to do with the money so you would not attract attention.

He thought no-one suspected a thing. He was not aware that he had been noticed by the waitress. He had caught her eye because, with her ex-law enforcement background, she thought he looked like a cop when he had shown up to pick up the girl.

Darin could see the Lincoln Navigator from the description he had been given, and his burner phone started to ring.

"Yeah," Darin said.

"White Navigator, blinking my lights now."

"I see you," said Darin.

He spoke to Marta without looking at her.

"You're going with the guy in that car. He will get you to your new job, and he will have new ID's. Don't cause him any trouble. He doesn't put up with anything."

The exchange took about one minute. Darin did not count the money. He knew it would be correct. He got in his car a drove back to I-15 and headed north. The first dark exit he got to he would stop and put the Montana plates back on the car and remove the California plate that he had stolen off a tourist's car. If anyone was checking the plate on the rental car, they would have some accountant in Burbank, California. Not a cop in Helena, Montana with three kids. He would use another car next time. And, another license plate.

Darin Marchman would buy nice things for his children. His contact, Max Johnson, was already looking for new victims and had not a second thought for Marta or her future. He was working within the law of supply and demand, after all.

Marta Andruko's plans for a glamorous life would have to wait. She was now in a world where she was property to be sold and rented. A life of pain, despair and hopelessness.

Chapter 6

Russell pulled into the parking lot at the *River's Run Fly Shop*. There were a few cars in the lot, and most of the guides and their clients had cancelled for the day with the rain and lightning. Tomorrow was iffy, too. But he needed to let the owner, John, know he was back and could take any overflow of clients.

Russell did not take clients every day, but there were more and more client days that were coming his way. He needed to get Elanor Wills' number, if they had it, to see if she would do his shuttles. She actually lived close to Ennis, and it would be easier for her to help him than Nancy, but he wished it was still Nancy for a lot of reasons.

As he was leaving after his brief visit with John, he punched in Nancy's number and waited as the call went to voicemail. Maybe she was screening her calls? A call to the store, and the clerk said that Nancy was out of the store and out of town.

A trip to the grocery store, he decided, and he would go home.

Russ spent the next few days cleaning up his boat, checking all of his fly lines, servicing his reels, and making a list of supplies he would need to replenish before taking any clients out again. He consistently thought he should clear out some of the dozens of flies he had accumulated over the years but could never seem to bring himself to do it. So, his boat bag was stuffed with flies that had never seen the light of day and probably never would.

His calls to Nancy Freeman were all going to voicemail, and no one seemed to know where she was – that, or they just weren't saying. Even Chad seemed to be in the dark.

He got a call from John at the Fly Shop; a couple wanted to go out on the Madison for a half day. He did not like half days as a rule, but after being off the water for a while, maybe it would be nice to do a half day?

"I guess that would be okay, John," Russ said when John explained no one else wanted to pick up the trip for him. "Where do you suggest I take them? I haven't been out since I got back in town."

"They had actually wanted to go on the Gallatin since they did the Madison before, but it is blown out from the rains last week. The Yellowstone is roaring, so it's out. So, I suggest the lower section down toward Ennis Lake. That would be right up close to you and make life a little easier. And, I suggest the afternoon. The guys have been catching some there."

John continued, "They have been hitting dries in the afternoons lately, so there's no need to get out there first thing. A few hours before dark have been the prime time. BWO's, midges, and caddis have been the best choices."

"Nymphing the holes and weed beds has been producing some good fish, too. Crawfish patterns or soft hackles have been a great setup for all day. And, the clients will meet you out there, so you don't have to drive to town."

"Sounds good," Russ said.

"Elanor Wills was in here a few minutes ago, by the way, and said she could move your truck for you tomorrow. Heck, I've done everything for you but hook up your boat trailer on this one," John said jokingly.

"I would be okay if you want to do that too," replied Russ.

"Hold your breath on that one, partner," was the reply from John.

"Say, John. Are these people experienced?"

"They claim to be, and the lady is a knock out!"

"That can be a distraction, John. You know what a lady's man I am."

"Well, since Nancy is off the market, I guess you have to be looking somewhere," commented John.

"I don't know that she is off the market, exactly," said Russ, still feeling confused about how quiet Nancy was being.

"Well, Chad just told me that she got back from Las Vegas last night and that she and that professor spent the last week there. But I'm sure you probably know that," John said.

For a few seconds, Russ couldn't speak.

"No, John, I didn't know."

"Oh crap! I guess I wasn't supposed to say anything. Chad did say he had to call you this morning about a matter. That was probably it."

"Give the clients my number, and text me theirs. Tell them to meet me tomorrow at 1:00 at Ennis take out, and Elanor can get my truck at Varney Bridge and take it to Ennis. We'll do those eight miles. Thanks, John, I'll talk to you later. I have a call from Chad coming in," Russ said, as his phone was vibrating.

Russ took a deep breath and touched the incoming call button as he walked out to his truck.

"Hello, Chad."

"Hi, Russ. Man, I got some bad news from Nancy, and I thought I should call you. We are still in shock up here."

There was no response from Russ.

"Russ, she went to Las Vegas with that creep Carter, and they spent the week there. Alise and I are really pissed, and I think Mom may have a stroke."

Russ took another deep breath and still didn't speak. He wasn't sure if he should bash his fist through the truck window, cry, yell, or all of the above.

"Russ, are you okay?"

"Sure. I guess, Chad. This is a shot out of the blue. I guess I'm in shock too. The fact that she'd be back with that guy is surprising enough. But to realize she did it without a word to us, especially you and your mom, that is a real downer. And so unlike Nancy. Have you had a chance to talk to her?"

"Only for a minute. She had left us word that she would be out of town for a few days on business. She got back yesterday afternoon and stopped by with her jerk boyfriend. He didn't say too much to me. We were caught completely off guard, and they were here all of five minutes, and she said we would talk later. Are you going to call her or anything, Russ?"

Russ hesitated for a minute.

"I guess there is no point, Chad. Maybe our paths will cross, and I can get a chance to talk, but in reality, she doesn't owe me an explanation. Best to leave it alone, I guess," said Russ. He cut off the call and just sat looking out the windshield at nothing. He could see out the window for miles with his eyes, but in reality, he couldn't see as far as tomorrow.

But he could see there would be no Nancy Freeman in it as he might have thought just a few days ago. Nancy had been a part of his recovery when his life had been in tatters from losing his wife, and there was no doubt there had been some strong feelings between them. But not strong enough, it seemed. He had not seen it coming: the end to that dream.

Russ knew he would wonder, and it would gnaw at him, but he made up his mind that he would not call or ask her why she had made this unseen and abrupt decision. He could do something this time he could not do when his wife had died: he could move on.

Chapter 7

The Ennis boat ramp at Main Street was busy as Russ pulled in to pick up his clients. They would leave their vehicle there and pick it up at the end of the day when the float ended, and Russ's truck and trailer would have been shuttled back by Elanor and be waiting there, too.

Russ pulled through to make the loop of the parking area, and he saw a couple standing by what looked like an airport rental car. He leaned out the window and spoke to them.

"Hello. I'm Russell Baker. Are you the Parker's?"

"Yes. That's us," replied the man. "I'm Reggie, and this is my wife, Barbara," Reggie said.

"We can throw your stuff in the boat and leave your car here. We're going on back up river a distance and put in," Russ said.

"We'd like to use our own rods, if that's okay," inquired Reggie.

"No problem. We'll rig them up when we get to the parking area."

John had been right about Barbara Parker; she was a tall, slender brunette, and both of them looked in great physical condition. Probably hikers and bikers and workout types. Not an ounce of fat, and they both had a confident look about them. They put their boat bag and fishing rods in the drift boat for the drive up to Varney Road. Reggie opened the front door of the Silverado pickup, gave his wife a hand up into the front seat, and then climbed in the back. Russ thought that's how he would have done it with his wife and noted that there was real a connection between these two. He could sense it.

Barbara extended her hand and said, "Nice to meet you, Russell."

Russell said, "Same here. Hope we have a good day today," as he moved the rig around and back toward the road.

Reggie leaned forward and said, "You probably don't remember them, but my uncle and my cousin fished with you. They were with you when you came up on a body on the river. Do you remember? We're all from Knoxville, Tennessee."

Russ stopped abruptly as he was about to pull on the highway. He couldn't believe it.

"That's a day that is a little hard for me to forget," Russ said. "And, I imagine, for your uncle and cousin also."

"It's one of those things where they say: Did we ever tell you about the time we were fishing out in Montana, and everyone laughs," said Barbara.

"I hope we won't have that problem today," commented Reggie.

"We don't have that too often," joked Russ. "Once is enough."

"The cops got the folks responsible, didn't they?" asked Barbara.

"Yes. They got them," replied Russ. He decided to leave it there and not go into the details of how he was the guy that had found them and had killed the shooter.

"I'm surprised we are going out this time of day," Reggie said. "How long is this float?"

"About nine miles," said Russ. "John said you wanted to do some dry flies, and they have been hitting later in the afternoon. We will take it slow and do some nymphing and then switch over to dries unless we see some hitting early. The hoot owl restrictions will kick in before long where we have to be off the water by two o'clock, and we can't do this type of float. They may make them permanent. Some new rules may be coming for the Madison, and we are waiting to see where all that goes."

Russ pulled on to Varney Road, and they were soon at the parking lot.

"Let's get you rigged up before we put the boat in. I'm going to have you using a dropper set up with a strike indicator if that's okay. I think it works better to have the strike indicator when we are drifting. In some of the pools and runs, we may use a streamer. I'll have a rod rigged up with one with a bank robber pattern. What size are your rods?"

"We both have 6 Wt. rods, 9 Ft. They are okay, right?" commented Barbara.

"Should be great."

"Russ, do you mind if we set the rods up and tie on our own flies?" asked Reggie.

"I don't mind as long as they are working and you don't take a lot of time doing them. If we have a lot of pull offs, we will be missing a lot of opportunity. So, let's start with 3X leaders, and we'll use 3X tippet. We may have to downsize if we aren't getting any hits. I recommend you use the screw-on round strike indicators unless you just want to use yarn. The screw-on caps allow us to change depth easily and have less drag on the cast. And, they don't need drying out. Let's put on a bead head pheasant tail and then we'll use a girdle bug for a dropper about 15 to 16 inches down on one rod and a jig head prince on the other to see what might work best. Let me know if you want my help."

It was evident that both of them were very experienced, and they made quick work of their set ups. Russ couldn't resist checking each rod and tugging on the flies to see if they would pull off. They didn't. *This might be a good day.*

Russ backed the trailer down the ramp, slid the boat off, and pulled it up on the sand with a rope. After parking the truck and leaving the key, they were ready.

"Who's taking the front?" asked Russ.

"We'll let Barbara have the front for a while and then we may change, if you are okay with that," Reggie said.
"Besides, you'll have a better view that way."

Barbara shook her finger at Reggie but clearly did not mind the compliment. Russ decided it best not to comment even if he did agree. They were off.

They needed little in the way of instructions and set about hitting the runs and getting good long drifts. When he could, Russe was slowing the boat and stopping in dead water to allow for multiple drifts through buckets and holes and longer seams. The Parkers were covering the water very well; clearly, this was not their first time in a drift boat.

"You folks look like you fish a lot."

"We go somewhere just about every week," said Reggie. "We don't have kids yet, so we try to make use of the chance to go while we can. You probably know how that is."

"I'm not married, but I can see that would make it a lot easier," Russ replied.

He was looking at Barbara strike indicator when it happened: a hard hit, or a snagged bottom. In an instant, Barbara raised the rod tip and exclaimed, "Fish on!"

Since the boat was in slow back eddy, Russ waited to see if she was going to get control of the fish. She was palming the reel to catch up the slack line and get the fish on the reel. Yes, she had certainly done this before. And one jump told Russ she had on a very nice fish.

Russ released the anchor and grabbed the net. She had the fish almost to the boat, and Russ did not want to get out of the boat to land the fish in moving water. Chasing a runaway boat was not on his agenda. He had learned that the hard way. And, just then, Reggie yelled, "Fish on!"

Barbara maneuvered the fish, a big rainbow with its head up out of the water, to the boat, and Russ netted the fish. It was a nice 22", fat, rainbow with beautiful wild fish colors. He got the barbless hook out and held the fish in the net in the water a moment to let it catch a breath and then handed it to her. She held it like a pro, and he took a quick picture with his small Nikon.

"Okay, Barbara, great job. Now ease him back in the water so I can help Reggie."

But Reggie had his fish up and out of the water and was already posed for a picture. His fish was beautiful but not quite as large as the one Barbara had released. A quick shot, and he held the fish over the side of the boat in the water for a couple of seconds and then the fish swam away in defiance. They had scored a double. Both fish had hit the bottom dropper on each line. Several high fives all around, and they were back to fishing.

Now, the competition was on between husband and wife, and Russ could see they loved it. She'd catch one, then he'd catch one. They were having a great day. Not a dead body anywhere.

They moved slowly and had eaten up a lot of clock. Russ's first day back was turning out splendidly. A nice experienced couple and lots of fish. They could tie on their own flies and wanted to. They could land a fish and release it. And, they did not want a picture of every fish. But they did want one of them together with a fish each. They finally managed it.

The late afternoon dry fly action was just as John had predicted. The fish were willing, and the fishermen were grateful and capable. Some of the fish sipped the flies, and some exploded on them as if they hadn't eaten since last summer.

Barbara never did move to the back of the boat, although she weakly asked Reggie if he wanted to swap out. He graciously declined. And, they managed to wade around one section and caught some there too.

At about six thirty, Reggie called to her, "Have you had enough for today?"

There was almost two and one-half hours of sun left.

"How about one more fish, and then we can go. That okay, Russ?" Barbra suggested.

"Sure. If you are happy with that, I am. Barbara, why don't you take this rod I have the big streamer on and fish it around that bucket and the bank over there to see if anything will take it. Then we'll let Reggie give it a shot. You okay throwing a streamer?"

"Sure," she said. And she was.

On about the fourth cast, as she started stripping the fly through the water, she almost had the rod pulled out of her hand. A huge hit and strong pull, and the fight of the day was on. Downstream it went, ripping off line and giving her quite the battle.

Russ got the boat headed after the fish and let Barbara recover some line and then the fish took off again. They were almost to the boat ramp when Barbara finally got the fish close to the boat.

Reggie had put his rod down and was easing by with the net to land the fish. Russ was not happy to see him shifting the boat weight, but he said nothing.

Reggie got the fish in the net and turned to hand the net to Barbara just as the boat bumped a rock. Out over the side went Reggie, and the net with the huge brown trout dropped at his wife's feet.

Russ dropped the anchor and was about to go in after Reggie when he yelled, "I'm Okay! Help Barbara with the fish!"

Russ decided that a picture of Reggie in the water might be the best picture of the day. So, he quickly snapped three or four before helping secure the big brown.

After all the excitement of landing a nearly 30-inch brown and recovering Reggie, they all started laughing all the way over to the ramp.

Russ loaded the boat on the trailer and pulled away from the ramp so that another guide could get his boat out. As he was tying it down, the Parker's said their goodbyes and commented that it was their best day ever. Reggie slipped an envelope to Russ as they were leaving containing two one-hundred-dollar bills and a note reading simply "Thanks!"

A stop by the hot dog shop for some take-out, and Russ was back home. Dinner for one.

The guides all posted their results on the fly shop's website. They could see what other guides were having success with and where they were hitting best to help prepare for the next run. His would be a good report, and it appeared the other guides had a good day as well.

He was finishing with his post when his phone lit up. It was John from the shop.

"Hello, John," he answered.

"Hey, man. I just got a call from the Parker couple. You guys had a great afternoon, they said."

"We had a very good day. It didn't hurt that they were very experienced."

"I got the guy's card and checked him out online. It seems his wife is some heiress, and they are rolling in money. So, they fish all over the world. Her family apparently was in copper, steel, and oil," said John. "Someone said they flew in here on their own jet."

"Well, she sure didn't try to put on any airs. They were both as nice as could be. I got a nice tip, too."

"So… been wanting to say, sorry if I spoke out of turn about Nancy the other day. We are all stunned around here. I hope you are doing okay."

"I'm fine, John. I survived a wife dying. I guess I can handle being dumped. Not good for my ego, though."

"I don't have anything for tomorrow. I guess you still don't want to be on a regular schedule?" inquired John.

"No. But call me when you need me. I may slip over to the Gallatin when it gets back in shape one day. Have a nice evening." Russ hung up.

Russ needed some time to think about where he was going from here. Maybe it was time to head back to Georgia.

Chapter 8

Teresa

It was business as usual at *Wayne's Truck Plaza*, and Teresa
Walker was hustling tables and taking orders as fast as she could.
She had hardly noticed the driver and the young girl that had
come in and sat at another station being worked by one of the
other waitresses. But she *did* notice when the young girl left with a
man in a baseball cap pulled low over his face. She was pretty sure
that she had seen that same man before. She was pretty sure he
still looked like a cop.

Darin Marchman had walked out in less than a minute with
the young lady to his rented Kia Sorento with Tennessee plates.
He was delivering the package in Salt Lake in a few hours,
collecting his check and would be back in Helena for his shift
tomorrow night. His second trip this month.

Paula, one of the other waitresses rung up a driver with a cowboy hat pulled low, and he walked out. "Did that guy come in with a young girl, Paula?" asked Teresa as she walked by.

"Yeah. I guess she left or went to the lady's room. I didn't pay any attention. Is there a problem?"

"No. Just curious," answered Teresa.

"Best to mind your own business," said the older and tough spoken Paula. "Don't ask too many questions. Sometimes men are often meeting women that are not their wives here, if you know what I mean."

Teresa started to snap back an answer, but she just gave a wave of the hand to acknowledge she had heard the advice. Was that a casual reply or words of wisdom? A warning based upon experience? She didn't know.

Teresa didn't have time to be an investigator of every customer that came through Wayne's. She had to make every dollar in tips to help her mother pay for her cancer drugs and trips to Helena to the cancer center. Her treatments would be starting in just a few days, so she could not risk losing the only job opportunity she had found in the area over some lousy husbands.

The next morning at her home, she heard, "Hurry up, Teresa! We'll be late for my appointment." Teresa's mother was knocking on her bedroom door and had a frantic sound in her voice.

Teresa rolled over and looked at the digital clock glowing red on the nightstand. "Mother, it's five thirty. It's only about an hour to get to Helena. It's only about seventy miles, and we are not due in there until ten! I just got to bed at twelve thirty."

"I know how long it takes, but you are not dressed, and we don't know exactly where the Cancer Center is," said her mother.

"Call me at eight. We'll leave at eight thirty. I need a little more sleep."

Teresa's mother had been referred to an oncologist in Helena, and they hoped the cancer center there could arrest her bladder cancer. She was anxious to get there to see if they could offer her hope of a solution.

At about five minutes before eight, Teresa heard a heavy knocking again. "It's time to get up, Teresa. Please, hurry up."

Teresa threw on some clothes and grabbed the keys to her mom's car off the counter and said, "Let's go. Do you have the insurance cards and the image discs that we are supposed to be taking?"

"Yes. I have everything."

They had a short drive to get from their house to I-15, but a large truck was stalled, and traffic was being held up as the wrecker was trying to get it towed away. Teresa's mother was quick to say *I told you so*. When they finally got on the interstate, it was twenty minutes before nine.

Teresa drove above the speed limit and was watching her mirror. Being on parole, she wanted no run-ins with law enforcement. She hit the exit ramp in Helena with 9:40 showing on the clock on her phone, and they still had to find the place, and she did not have a GPS on the old car. She picked up her cell and spoke into the search the name of the cancer center. In a few seconds, directions were coming out from the female voice on the phone.

Then it happened. Blue lights came on behind her, and an electronic siren sounded three short bursts. "Oh my goodness, Teresa, are we getting pulled over for speeding?"

"Crap! It looks like it, Mother."

"We'll never make it on time."

The police officer walked to the car window, and Teresa already had out her license as she rolled down the window.

"I need to see your license, please. You seem to be in kind of a hurry, ma'am. You were doing fifty-five in a twenty-five-mile zone."

"I'm sorry, officer. We are trying to get my mother to the cancer center for a ten o'clock appointment, and we got..."

Teresa stopped in mid-sentence as she turned to the officer and recognized him. She was certain he was the man in the baseball cap she had seen in *Wayne's* on at least two separate occasions leaving with young women. She quickly regained her composure. "We got delayed by some congestion, and I guess I wasn't paying attention to my speed." And in her mind, she added *Officer D. Marchman*, the name on his name tag.

The officer walked behind the car and looked at the license and car plates and came back to the window. "This is your mom's car?" he asked.

Before Teresa could answer, her mother said, "Yes, Officer, it is my car. It is actually my late husband's name on the paperwork."

"Okay, ladies, I'm going to let you go, but don't let me see you speeding again. The cancer center is two blocks down on the right. The parking garage is in the back. It'll be a ticket next time."

Teresa was shaking as she drove off. "Are you alright, Teresa?" her mother asked. "You seem really upset."

"I'm okay, Mother. I've seen that police officer before. I'll tell you all about it later."

They walked into the cancer center at exactly ten. On time, somehow. Then they waited for another forty minutes to be called back. So much for being on time. Patients have to be on time, but doctors don't.

Teresa kept thinking about Officer D. Marchman and her instincts about him when she had first seen him at *Wayne's*. What was he doing at *Wayne's*, and where was he taking the young women? An undercover operation, maybe?

Maybe. Maybe not.

She would keep her eyes open for him in the future. She doubted he had noticed her at *Wayne's* as she'd not had any direct contact with him. And, she would like it to stay that way until she could determine what he was really up to.

As they waited, she tried Googling him on her phone, but there were a lot of Darin Marchman's and none that seemed to match his profile. She'd look further online when she got home.

If she were still with DCI, she'd log in to the system, and she could find out a lot about him as all law officers were in there. But she had no access and was not sure of anyone who would help her or risk being involved with her looking at confidential files.

Calm down, Teresa, she said to herself. *This is probably nothing, and you may be interfering with a major investigation.*

The meeting with the doctor went as well as it could when dealing with such a serious health issue. Some surgery and chemo and radiation, and there was a good chance they could get the cancer under control. Simple to say, but both Teresa and her mother knew they were talking about a lot of trips, lots of discomfort, and lots of money.

The cancer center in Helena was going to be expensive. They would have to come up with the difference.

Teresa had put a lot of cash in her mother's storage shed in a plastic storage container. Her pay for helping the drug dealers was in cash and never deposited. But, when her father had been sick, and her mother needed to have someone come in and help care for him; bills had started piling up. Teresa had used up a lot of the money, then.

Now, it looked like they would need a lot of what was left, if not all of it. Her mother was never in the garden shed anymore since her father died, so she was unaware any money was there. Ill-gotten gain, but she was using it for a good cause. That's how she justified it, anyway.

On the way home, the traffic-stop never came back up as her mother was preoccupied with the doctor's visit and doctor bills. Just as well. Her mother had enough to worry about.

"What are we going to do about the money, Teresa? My savings are about gone. I really hate to get a loan that I can't pay."

"I may can come up with most of it, Mother. Let's take it a day at a time. I may can make some extra shifts at *Wayne's*. The tips are pretty good."

When they arrived back home, Teresa sat down at her computer and started searching for the Helena cop. All she got was the usual lists of people with the same name and possible phone numbers for a price. But nothing that jumped out. He was not on the radar screen and was not high profile.

And, if he was, he would likely not have a job with the police department.

It was not uncommon for local law enforcement and highway patrol to come into *Wayne's*. After all, it was a great place to eat. It was often a place where divorced parents met to exchange the kids for weekends. Who knew what was going on in the parking lot? Probably a lot more than she cared to know.

She took out a small notebook that she had had since her days as a DCI agent. She thumbed through it and tried to think of who might be safe for her to inquire about her concern. Former colleagues, former bosses, former local law enforcement contacts. None that she felt would want to hear from her. Then, at last, she thought of one.

Detective Russell Baker had been a temporary member of the Madison County Sherriff's office when she had met him. He had been the one who broke open the case and had ended up setting up the arrest of her former boss. He had also been the one who had killed her former lover and accomplice. And, it was he who had testified on her behalf at her trial for assisting in the case. It was Russ and the sheriff who had helped get her a reduced sentence.

Russell Baker had seemed like a mild-mannered, easy-going guy. He was most of the time. But she and many others had come to know that he was a great detective and a tough guy that wasn't to be taken lightly. Maybe he was worth a try. If he was still around. She had his cell number.

She punched in his number, but he did not answer the call.

She imagined he didn't want to chat with anyone whose number came up as *Private Number*. It went to voice mail.

Hello, this is Russell Baker. Please leave a message and your number. I'll call back as soon as possible, was the less-than-creative message on Russ's voicemail.

"Detective Baker, you may not remember me, but this is Teresa Walker. Could you give me a call at your convenience? I could use your help with something." She left her number, hoping that he would consider returning the call soon.

Chapter 9

It was a beautiful morning when Russ poured the milk over his cereal and sipped his coffee. No one was looking back across the small breakfast table, but then, there usually wasn't.

The stack of fly-fishing magazines and sales catalogs were in a neat array just waiting to help him waste the morning. He had nowhere to be today. No clients. And, even worse, he did not have any desire to be on the river with or without a client. He wasn't even sure he wanted to be anywhere near here right now. The wind was out of his sails.

He clicked on the voicemail left by Teresa Walker and listened to it for the second time. He had listened to it the day before but had decided to mull it over before returning the call. She obviously still thought that he was with the sheriff's department, or she would not have called him. They had no personal history and certainly would not be considered friends. He had arrested her and was responsible for her going to jail.

It was 8:15 when he touched the button on his phone to call Teresa Walker.

After about four rings, a sleepy voice answered, "Yeah, this is Teresa, who is this?"

"This is Russell Baker, Miss Walker, returning your call."

He thought it best to keep the return call on a formal basis. He did not know who was listening and what she had on her mind.

"I'm sure you remember me, Officer Baker. I was with DCI and ended up on life support before I went to jail."

"Sure, Miss Walker, I remember you. I am not Officer Baker now, though. I'm part-time, Deputy Baker. I only help out at the Sheriff's office when someone is on vacation or sick or something."

"I got out on parole a little early," she said. "I'm back in Butte with my mother. Not exactly an ideal arrangement for me, but she is ill and alone since my father died, so I guess its best right now."

"I'm glad you are out and hope it goes well for you, Miss Walker. What's on your mind?"

Teresa said, "Please, call me Teresa."

"Okay, Teresa. Why'd you call?"

"I got a job waitressing at *Wayne's Truck Plaza* here in Butte. They are a huge truck stop. Are you familiar with them?"

"I've never been in the place, but I've seen it and their billboards," said Russ.

"Well," she continued. "On a couple of occasions, I have noticed truck drivers coming in with young women, girls, actually. Then this guy came in and left with them, and I just thought he looked like a cop. Instinct, you know?"

She continued, "I could be way off base, and it may be nothing. The oldest waitress there has told me to mind my own business, and I really can't afford to rock the boat. Finding a job is hard enough when you have a record like mine. The pay's pretty good, and I need the money since I'm having to look after my mother."

"What about your manager there? Can you ask them about your suspicions? Has something happened to give you more cause for concern?" asked Russ.

"They are a good company, as far as I can see. But, I'm new there and don't have any real evidence. If I get the reputation as a trouble maker, I expect they would show me the door. I was interviewed by their HR person and then the restaurant manager. Because of my record, I'm sure, I also was interviewed by the General Manager. His name is Mr. Renfroe. He's a VP. This place must have a couple hundred employees. Its twenty-four/seven here in all departments. They are owned by an equity group out of Salt Lake that owns several large truck stops and some casinos."

Russ replied, "Sounds like a place where they wouldn't want any illegal activity going on. But just a gut feeling, *instinct* I think you said, probably won't be enough to get them too concerned."

"That's just it, Officer Baker, my suspicions were confirmed about the guy who I saw coming in and leaving with the girls when I took my mother to Helena yesterday; we were running close to being late."

"There had been a traffic problem in Butte, and I was speeding. I got pulled over by a traffic officer, and I just about pee'd in my pants when I looked up and saw the guy from the restaurant standing there asking for my driver's license."

"Did he recognize you?" asked Russ.

"If he did, he did a great job of hiding it. Besides, I never actually waited on him. And, he and the truck drivers wear hats and caps pulled down low, so the security cameras never get a full shot of their faces, and they don't seem to make a lot of eye contact. I would think he didn't ever actually look at me when he came in."

"I guess you've considered calling the police there in Butte and telling them about your suspicions, Teresa?" Russ said in a questioning way.

"I have considered lots of options, including forgetting the whole thing. We get a lot of local and state uniform cops in every day. I don't know who I can trust. I don't need a bunch of cops making life tough for ratting out one of their own if I am wrong," said Teresa.

"What do you expect me to do?"

"I was hoping you might be able to do a criminal background check on NLETS at the sheriff's office on Darin Marchman and see if there is anything on him. I can't find anything online other than the normal stuff, and there are a ton of people with that name."

"Well, Teresa, as I mentioned, I am not a full-time deputy there, and all those checks are done by one person in the office with the sheriff's approval. This is a conversation you should have with him. But I doubt he will do much for you with nothing to go on, Russ said.

He added, "And then, he would want to work with the local authorities since it is not in his jurisdiction."

"Officer Baker, what if there is something going on with these girls? Kidnapped or something? I know you'd want to help them," said Teresa.

"Just call me Russ or Russell, please. I don't know that anything is going on right now other than a suspicion you have. You were an investigator long enough to know we can't make a case on what you have at this point. I suggest you contact the local police and make them aware of your concern."

"Okay, Russell. I don't know who to trust or who is involved. I know I will not get too far right now with just my suspicions and intuition, and if I involve the local police at work I will be probably be out on my ass. Especially if there is some undercover thing going on and I blow it. I won't get anywhere in Helena, for sure, at this point. I really need this job even if it doesn't sound like a big deal. I'm actually making it pretty good here."

"I haven't had any dealings with the police in Butte. What county is that in?" asked Russ.

"That is Silver Bow County, and I did know some people there at one time. They probably wouldn't let me in the door now. Helena is in Lewis and Clark County, and the same is true there. I think all those departments are all well run and first-class outfits, but there may be someone like this one cop who is involved in something."

"Well, Teresa, my only suggestion is you either go to one of them and tell them you are concerned or you bide your time and try to get more evidence. If he comes in again, he may recognize you."

"If not, maybe you can get a cellphone picture of him and the girl without being too obvious. From what you say, it may be best not to discuss this with your coworkers until you get to know them better," Russ added.

"Russell, will you at least ask the sheriff there for his advice? We both know he's one of the best."

"I'll stop by and talk to him in the next day or so, Teresa. That is about all I can do. He may want to call you, or he may go straight to one of the other jurisdictions with your concerns. I have no control or say in that, you understand."

"I understand, but please let him know I don't need to be put on the spot here. This is the only job I have at the moment."

"Sure. And going it alone may be dangerous if there is anything going on, so you need to tread light, Teresa. I'll let you know what the Sheriff says. Have a good day."

Russ ended the call. He was already sorry he had made it.

Russ poured another cup of coffee and touched scrolled to *Sheriff* on his speed dial. After two rings, the familiar voice of Sheriff Barry Steinbrenner answered.

"Good morning, Russell. Good to hear from you. Are you still in Florida?"

"Good morning, Sheriff. No. I got back a few days ago and am getting back in the swing of things here. Back to the grindstone, you know."

"Yeah, you have a hard life, Russ. Go to bed when you want. Get up when you want. Nobody to answer to. And, oh yes, fishing when you want. And, let's not forget: the prettiest girlfriend in all of Montana."

"That's a little bit of an exaggeration, Sheriff. Especially that about the prettiest girlfriend. I'm afraid I don't have a girlfriend around anymore. She gave me the boot while I was gone, and she's seeing somebody else."

"Man! That sucks, Russ. I hadn't heard. Sorry, buddy."

"Well, what did you have on your mind when you called? Or are you just looking for a shoulder to cry on?"

"I had a call from Teresa Walker. I guess you remember her?"

"Sure, I remember her. In fact, I was asked to speak at her parole hearing, and I supported her getting out on parole. I think she was stupid in getting involved with those guys in the drug business, but she paid a big price getting shot up, and she did help us get them all. Was she asking you out on a date?"

Russ went on to explain Teresa's concerns about the Helena policeman, Darin Marchman.

"Russ, I hear nothing but good things about the police in Helena. They are a well-respected department. They have about 30 officers, I would guess. With that many people, there is always a chance one bad apple is in the bunch. But with what you told me, I doubt they would launch a big investigation. And, they just could have this guy coming to help with some undercover work."

"Teresa considered that possibility, and we went over that on her call. All she has is intuition and hunches."

"Russ, I'd be reluctant to open up a can of worms on this with no more information than we have. And I'll bet you a burger that there is no negative information on this guy Marchman, or he would not be on the force in Helena."

"That would seem to be the case to me, too," said Russ.

"If they are running a sting or some undercover operation,

I could mess things up, Russ, nosing into it if I spoke to the wrong person."

Maybe we just see if she comes up with anything tangible that we can take to the chief there in Helena or the sheriff over there. Maybe the DCI."

"If she does spot anything, who should she talk to about it, Barry?" Russ asked.

"Let's see what, if anything, she gets. Then we'll decide where and whom to take it to."

"Sounds fair enough to me. I'll call her and let her know."

Chapter 10

Alejandro

Alejandro Eduardo Torres grew up in the town of Tapachula, Mexico on the border of Mexico and Guatemala. Tapachula was a town of over 300,000 people with a diverse economy based on coffee growing and processing, bananas, sugarcane, distilleries, mining, silver smiths and goldsmiths. Tourism was an important segment with the beaches in the area.

Tapachula was also a corridor of illegal immigrants and a conduit for smuggling and drugs passing from central America. A seaport town, a major airport and land connection to Guatemala made for a prime place to do all kinds of business. Legal and illegal.

Alejandro's father had started trading coffee, farm machinery, and mining equipment in the 50's and 60's, and the business had grown with Alejandro taking over. Now their business was flourishing.

Trucks, people, and goods came and went every day. Things had seemed pretty good until the drug kingpins in the area decided they needed a place to store, transfer and ship drugs in quantity. They had made it clear to Alejandro that he had to cooperate otherwise he and his family would be severely punished. Violence and terror were the groups primary negotiation tactics.

Alejandro knew that he was in the middle and could lose whichever way he went. He could not refuse the drug dealers without major danger. He could not continue without major danger from the federal authorities.

His decision was to accumulate as much cash as possible, get it out of town to someone he could trust, and then, get out with his family before anyone ever missed him. Not easy with him being watched all the time. His destination: The United States.

Alejandro's brother had gotten a student visa when he had gotten out of high school, and, with some money put in the right hands by his father, he had made it to Atlanta and had eventually gotten into Georgia Tech. Once there, his brother had started the process to becoming an American citizen. His brother was now living in East Cobb County in a gated community with a nice job in the Atlanta area.

Alejandro also had several cousins and nephews that had gotten into the US by one means or another. He knew their addresses and phone numbers, and they would be willing to help him if he made the move to leave Tapachula. He would probably arrive with enough money to live comfortably if he could arrive alive, but they might be in danger if he was visibly involved with them. Once he started, he knew there was no turning back.

The services provided by Alejandro's trucks, logistics and warehouses were too important to the drug smugglers, and he knew too much about their operation. He and his family would be in danger if they even learned he was planning to leave.

With a wife and two daughters and one on the way, he had to set things into motion soon. He wanted his third child to be born in the US.

He would have to keep everything a secret, even from his daughters, until they were leaving. There would not, and could not, be any goodbyes. A slip up could not be risked.

The time had come.

Alejandro made some of the regular runs in his large semi-truck hauling goods out. He planned a run to Morelia, some 670 miles to the north. He made this run often and it was common for him to have contraband hidden in the sleeper cab of his relatively new Volvo truck. There would be no contraband this time.

He would not announce his plan of not coming back. The business would be left behind.

His wife would not accompany him in the truck. To avoid arousing suspicion, she and her daughters would make the long, twenty-hour bus ride from Tapachula to Morelia where they would join him at a hotel. He would then call his office and tell them his truck was having problems and had to be serviced at the Volvo distributor in Morelia and that he would be delayed in coming back. This would buy him some time to make it with his wife and daughters by bus on to Monterrey where his wife's cousin was living. They would be able to stay with her temporarily. For a fee, naturally.

He would hire a private car in Monterrey to take him to Piedras Negras on the Rio Grande River, 225 feet from Eagle Pass, Texas. Then, he would use part of his US dollars to pay someone to get him across.

The trip would take four or five days, and the river crossing would still have to be worked out. Though there were bridges across the Rio Grande, there were also border guards and checks of passports, etc. None of which he had gotten yet. Too much chance of being found out.

He would pay exorbitant prices in the US for counterfeit ID's, green cards, and passports that would pass a casual inspection. All readily available if you asked the right people and flashed some US hundred-dollar bills.

There was a lot of activity on the Rio Grande at Eagle Pass and a large boat ramp that happened to have a large sliding gate in the border fence at the corner of Ryan Street and the end of Main Street. This space was long known as an often-open portal to the US.

Two young girls and a pregnant wife and suitcases full of money would require careful handling to avoid being detected and jailed on either side. Or worse. Attracting attention would be very dangerous. He would wait for the right time.

Chapter 11

Russ decided to try a little fishing on the Gallatin River near Bozeman. He knew of a reasonably private spot not too far from downtown Bozeman.

Just by chance, he had stopped at a house one day that backed up to the river. It also had *No Trespassing No Fishing* signs prominently displayed, so one could imagine the look on the guy's face when Russ stopped by to ask if he could go fishing.

But Russ had charmed the guy and had soon discovered there was a little pocket water spot that was great fishing and wading. And all it cost was a trip by a certain pastry shop and a few key lime tarts. The nearly 70 miles was a long drive for a guy from Marietta, Georgia; but to go from Ennis to Bozeman for people living in Montana was considered to just be a hop, skip, and a jump away. But for Russ, a good fishing hole with browns and rainbows waiting to be caught was never too far by any standard.

Russ threw a couple of rods in the truck along with his waders, boots and fishing vest, and he was soon cruising up US 287 toward Norris. He would hit Highway 84 which would take him near the fishing spot.

Russ picked up the key lime tarts at the pastry shop and left them by the side door since no one seemed to be home. They had probably been missing the treats as Russ had not been there in a while.

Russ hoped the fish might take a dry, but after a few minutes he decided to go ahead and put on a rubber legs type fly and a midge dropper. While a lot of guys were doing all kinds of nymphing, Russ still preferred using a strike indicator. And, when none of the other guides were looking, he used the new round balloon type screw-on indicators. Some of the traditionalists used only yarn and he still used yarn some, but the screw adjustment and the fact they could be removed and not damage the leader had won Russ over. And, they never got waterlogged. Much better for most clients.

It was after a dozen casts that he got his first nice brown. A determined 16" fish. That was a fairly common fish for this water. He caught bigger ones there at times. After a couple of hours, Russ had missed a few and landed about 8 nice fish and released them to fight another day. An even split between beautiful rainbows and browns.

Russ liked guiding most of the time, especially when he had nice and cooperative clients. There was the occasional jerk that could make for a long day on the water.

Russ had never really thought of himself as a guide. Certainly not like Chad and the other guides that worked out of the *River's Run shop*. They were real trout bums. They lived for being on the water somewhere all the time. Russ was, at heart, a cop. A cop that liked to fly fish.

He loved Bozeman and the whole Montana scene, but it was his memories of meeting Sarah there for the first time that had really brought him back after she had died. Although they had both lived in the Marietta, Georgia area, they had never met until they crossed paths in Bozeman. Their mutual love for the sport of fly fishing was something they had enjoyed together.

She had made him a complete person. He was not sure he would ever get back to that again, especially since the one person he thought he could be happy with had just dumped him.

Russ hooked his fly on the keeper, waded out and stopped back by the house, but the key lime tarts were still where he had left them. No one seemed to be back yet. They would see his *Thank You* treats that served as his rod fee by the door.

He drove on into Bozeman and rode by Nancy's store. It was hard not to stop, but he was not sure he would keep a calm demeaner, and there was nothing to be said that would change the fact that she was back involved with some bozo professor that not too long ago was drunk and embarrassing her so much that her brother had to come get her. *Unbelievable.*

After a quick stop to see John at the fly shop, he headed home to the empty house in Ennis. He was glad John didn't need him; he was ready for some time at home.

When he walked into the kitchen, he saw on the answering machine that he had some messages. A quick look, and he saw one from Miriam in Salt Lake. She was his close friend and landlady.

What was Miriam calling for? He knew it wasn't for the rent money as he was paid up in advance. Just in case there was a problem, he thought he would call her first.

"Well, hello stranger. It's been forever since we talked," said Miriam.

"Hi, Miriam. You know I was gone to Atlanta and the Florida Keys for several days and have sorta been catching up here since I got back."

Russ gave her a quick recap of his visit and fishing experience with his father-in-law. She was trying to sound interested in his catching a big tarpon, but he could tell that really didn't excite her.

"And how is Nancy doing? Have you set a date, yet?" she asked.

The question really stung, and he hesitated before answering. "It appears that Nancy and I are done, Miriam. She called and said goodbye on voicemail while I was gone to Florida. Out of the blue, she is back to dating a professor from the college. I didn't see it coming."

In almost a whisper, Miriam said, "Oh Russ, I am so sorry. I thought you guys were a perfect match. I don't know what to say." Russ knew she was surprised and genuinely feeling his pain.

"Well, it's done and I just have to accept it. Maybe she'll be happy with the guy. Who knows? But I know you had some reason for calling."

"My stuff can wait, Russ. We'll talk later."

"Go ahead, and let's discuss it now. I'm fine here."

"Okay, if you're sure. Russ, I am not likely to be coming back to Ennis other than an occasional visit. I would like to sell the house, and I wanted to let you know before I do anything."

She continued, "I know you have a little time left on the lease and thought you might want to consider buying it. I would make you a good deal for less than we'd list it for. You don't have to let me know right now but sometime before the lease is out. I don't want to rent or lease it after that. I hope you understand."

"Of course, I do, Miriam. I was surprised when you agreed to lease it to me in the first place. I had thought you'd want to get your money out and buy a place there in Salt Lake. It's been great living here. And, I'll consider the option of buying. Do you have a price in mind?"

"I'll let you know in a day or two. We're talking to an agent about prices now."

"Who is *we*, Miriam? Do you mean the girls?"

Once again, her voice went very soft, and she hesitated before answering.

"That's another thing I wanted to tell you, Russ. I'm engaged. I have been dating a fellow in town who operates several carpet stores and also has a kitchen remodeling business. I hired them to put some carpet in my condo, and he asked me out, and we hit it off. He was married very young and divorced with no children. He's nice, Russ. He reminds me of you a lot. We're getting married next month."

If there had been any air left in Russ's emotional balloon, it had just left in a flash of reality. He couldn't have imagined how the news would hit him right behind Nancy's recent surprise. He sat silent for what seemed like several minutes.

"Russ? Are you okay?"

"I'm happy for you, Miriam. You can be sure of that. I want only the best for you. I hope this will make you very happy."

At one time, Miriam had entertained the idea that she and Russ might get more serious, but she had always known that Nancy was his first choice. She also knew that this was a big pill for Russ to swallow right now.

"He's a great guy, Russ. I will always love you – you know? There will always be a place for you in my heart. I'll wait to hear from you about the house in a few days. And I'll let you know about the wedding. I want you to come. It'll be nothing big. Promise you'll come? Okay?"

"Okay, Miriam. I wouldn't miss the wedding. As far as the house, I'll let you know. Goodbye for now."

"Goodbye, Russ."

Russ sat down in at the table and just stared at the phone.

Please don't ring again, he thought. The bad news just kept coming. Both of the women in his life who had helped him recover from the loss of his wife were suddenly, and without warning, gone. He couldn't decide who he was maddest at or if he was mad at all. Maybe it was all for the best. Time would tell.

But he knew the recent developments had taken care of a lot of decision making. He only had to make decisions for himself.

He would no longer have questions about his future with Nancy nor Miriam. They were moving on without him. And another good day fishing was now forgotten.

Then, the phone lit up again. It was John from the fly shop.

With the luck he was having, he couldn't decide if he should answer or not. "Hello, John."

"Russ, I have a couple who called and want to fish tomorrow. I don't have anyone open. They are in town from Philadelphia and are set up for later this week but want to go tomorrow, too, if they can. Think you might take them?"

"I suppose so. They want an all-day float?"

"Yes."

"Okay. Can they meet me at the Ennis take-out at seven thirty?"

"I will tell them to be there. And, I'll get Elanor to move your truck down. From Varney, I suppose?"

"That's right," Russ said.

He was right on time the next morning, and so was the couple from Philadelphia. The day started out as a normal day. But it went downhill from there.

The man started shouting at his wife and criticizing her almost as soon as they put in, and then managed to miss his first strike. The wife had immediately hooked a decent fish, and they netted it, but she managed to drop the fish after her husband had insisted that she could hold it for a picture. Russ knew better but went along. The husband had then lit into her for dropping it and made an offhand remark about how Russ let her do so.

For the next hour and a half, it was missed fish, hung flies, tangled lines, bad casts, and poor drifts. They were bickering back and forth and generally unpleasant. The husband tried to impress he knew everything, but it showed that he had little actual experience.

Finally, with them both at each other's throats, Russ maneuvered into a slow moving, shallow spot and dropped the anchor. His demeanor went from pleasant fishing guide to the hard-nosed, policeman-like side. The one where there is a good cop and a bad cop, but he was only playing the bad cop role. It startled the couple, to say the least.

"Okay. I've listened to this arguing and yelling all I intend to. This is supposed to be a fun and enjoyable experience. You two are about as bad to be in a boat with as I've ever encountered. Missing fish and losing fish can be frustrating, but we can still make a good time of it if you would listen and stop griping at each other."

The man interrupted, "Hey, man. We're the customers! I think you are forgetting that. We are paying big bucks for this trip."

Russell glared at him. "You are going to reel in those lines, put the rods down, and we're going non-stop to the take out. I'm firing you as a customer. You can get your money back at the fly shop. If I hear another word out of you, I will put you out here, and you can call someone to come get you."

The man, started to speak, but his wife spoke up, "Ron, just please shut up. He's not the only one who has had enough. If you don't watch it, you'll be going back to Philadelphia by yourself. Now, you are going to apologize to this man, and we are going to show him we can be civil human beings. Russ, will you allow us to continue if Ron apologizes and keeps his mouth shut? He's been talking about this fishing trip for months. He really is a nice person. Most of the time."

Russ was still staring when Ron said in a much lower voice, "I guess I've been an ass, Russ. Let's fish on if you will. I'll listen and try to follow instructions and be more pleasant to be around. I think you mean that about putting us out. And, I can't have her mad with me all the way back home."

"Okay," said Russ. "We'll see how it goes."

And, it had gone better for the rest of the float. They both actually started catching some fish, giving high fives and yucking it up. Near the end of the float, the woman asked, "Have you always been a fishing guide?"

"No. I was a policeman for several years. Still am part-time."

"That explains a lot," she said, smiling at him.

The couple made a quick, somewhat embarrassed departure from the take out and drove off as Russ had finished tying down the boat. It was a quick half-hearted thank you, and they were gone. No tip. *Can't imagine why,* he jokingly thought to himself.

Russ had some things he had to get done. He had to let Miriam know about the house. His decision was to rent another place in the area and let Miriam get on with selling this one.

Russ had seen an ad in the classified section of the local area newspaper, and he knew the location and the house. They were willing to take a six-month lease. It would do for him with its wide paved parking area where he could park the boat. It was a smaller house with higher rent than he was paying now, but buying a house at this time did not seem ideal. Perhaps that was putting down deeper roots than he was ready for in Montana.

When Russ finally got back home from the float trip, he got a call on his cell. Since he didn't recognize the number, he let it go to voicemail. A hot shower and some iced tea were all he wanted after being with a quarreling couple on the river all day.

His phone rang again, and he could see it was John at the fly shop. "Hello, John. I was kind of expecting you to call."

"You must have had some day, Russ. Did you really tell them you were going to put them out of the boat?"

"Afraid so, John. If you made them a refund, I'll reimburse you. It looked as though that was going to be the only way to get them to stop yelling at each other. So, they told you about the wonderful first hour or so?"

"The lady came in, and the guy sat in the car. She said she had insisted that they come by the shop to see if they might catch you and leave your tip. She said they left in a hurry and failed to give it to you."

"You must be joking, John."

"No joke. One hundred and fifty dollars is here for you. Then she told me that you had read them the riot act," he said.

"They should be glad I didn't have my nine-millimeter," chuckled Russ. He added, "Thanks for calling. I'll be by in a day or so. I have to be out of pocket a few days. I have to pack up my stuff and move. My landlord wants to sell the house, and I don't want to buy one right now. But I'll check back soon."

A quick call to Miriam in Salt Lake went to voicemail.

"Hello, Miriam. I'll try to call to talk in person later, maybe tomorrow. I wanted to let you know that I have decided against buying the house. I have secured a place to rent out on Shining Mountain Loop, near Varney. The house is available, so I will be moving on over there and will be out of the house here a few days before the end of the month. I will have someone come and do a complete cleaning and try to leave it as I found it. It's been great living here. Call if you need to talk to me."

Then Russ touched the voicemail button to see who had called earlier. He heard an unfamiliar voice.

"Hello, Mr. Baker. My name is Brad Taylor. I got your number from my sister, Debra Taylor. Could you call me back at your convenience? My Dad and I would like to go fishing when we are in the Bozeman area on business next week, if possible. Debra sends her regards."

Detective Debra Taylor had worked on a case with Russ involving some young men who were friends of Miriam's daughters. She was a beautiful, smart, and very tough cop from Salt Lake. And, not to mention, rich.

Russ had met her dad briefly when he was in Salt Lake working the case, and she had been to Bozeman, Ennis, and Virginia City with Russ. He had not heard back from her since she had testified in court on the case.

Russ dialed the number.

"Hello. Brad Taylor."

"Hello, Brad. This is Russell Baker returning your call."

"Oh, great! I know you remember my sister Debra, and I believe you met my dad briefly. Debra speaks very highly of you."

"Well, I have a lot of respect for Debra. She is quite a lady. I hope she is well."

"Yes. She is still a pain in my dad's backside with this police thing. He worries about her and wants her to come into the business. We all do. But we don't seem to get anywhere with her."

"I understand. I suspect she can be right stubborn," replied Russ.

"Mildly put, Mr. Baker. Bull headed is how I describe her, but we love her anyway. Dad and I have to be in Bozeman on business next week, and we were wondering about maybe doing a float trip on the Missouri. Do you guide on the Missouri?"

"Please just call me Russ or Russell. I've been there a few times, Brad, but I'm no expert on the Missouri. There are some other guides that work out of Rivers Run that would be a great deal better. There are also some outfitters up around Craig and Cascade that could do a better job for you, as well."

"Since my dad finally got the whole story about Debra coming down to help you catch the bad guys, he has wanted to come fish with you. Debra told us you did some guiding there. He really isn't concerned about your skill level. He has checked you out. Are you available any next week? Our dates are not firm yet."

"I actually have left next week open on booking trips. I'm going to be moving and setting up a new house. But I can work with you next week if you let me know soon."

Bradley asked, "Would we be driving up from Bozeman with you, or what would you suggest?"

"It would be best if you can find a room in Cascade. There are a couple of nice places there, and there are a couple of good restaurants there too. The places cater to fishermen. It's about two and a half hours from Bozeman. About one hundred and sixty miles. Of course, if you are coming in your plane, you could land in Great Falls and drive down from there. It's only about twenty-three or twenty-four miles. You may have to stay in Great Falls anyway."

"We will look into those options," said Brad.

Russ said, "I would suggest you rent a car and drive up the day before if you are going from Bozeman. It's an easier drive from Great Falls. I'd be driving up there with my boat the day before.Places get sold out, so don't wait till the last minute or you may be out of luck."

"We'll probably know by tomorrow afternoon about our schedule. Should I call you back before I make reservations?"

"No. I'll not be booking anything until I hear back from you. I assume you both have experience fly fishing?"

"Yes. Dad is much better than me, but we can manage okay." To Russ that meant, *I think we are actually pretty good.*

Russ said, "There are a number of people offering guide services in the area and there's a dozen or so places to access the river and wade fish from the Holter Dam up to Cascade. It's about thirty-five miles of good water, so you could fish on your own if you get there earlier."

"Where will we put in if we get this worked out?"

"At Pelican Point. It's just over a nine-mile float to Cascade," replied Russ. "There are some good little maps showing the access points available online. Just look for a Missouri River trout fishing map. And go ahead and get a license the day before, if you can, to save some time. You can book the trip with *Rivers Run Fly Shop* in Bozeman online or phone. Tell them you talked to me already."

"Thanks, Russ. I'll get back as fast as I can."

"Okay. Say hello to Debra for me. Goodbye."

Chapter 12

Maria

Alejandro Eduardo Torres's plan had gotten him and his family to Monterrey and the arrangements had been made for a car to get them to Piedras Negras. So far, he believed they had covered their tracks and left no trail for anyone to follow.

But the trip had taken a toll on his pregnant wife, and she was showing signs of something being wrong. The baby that they had planned to be born in the US was coming, and going to the hospital threatened to expose their escape. The solution that they arrived at was to call a local midwife. Some cash would insure her silence.

The third daughter was born without any serious problems, but she wasn't born in the US. as they had wished. They would be delayed for at least a few days in getting to Piedras Negras and then to the border crossing. Getting an infant across would pose new challenges.

Because of the new baby, the family would be separated, with Alejandro and his oldest daughter slipping across by boats at the river crossing while his wife, new baby and their other daughter would trade places with a family from Eagle Pass that would drive her across the border. They would all meet at a safe house later.

The crossing took place without incident, and Alejandro had also been provided with something he had not expected by the family: a way to get his daughter reborn in the United States.

A small medical clinic in Eagle Pass that was open twenty-four hours had a side business: one of the doctors, along with a nurse and staff member admitted, for a fee, women with infant children in the evenings. The woman was admitted as being in labor, a *delivery* was performed, and the next morning the mother and *newborn* were discharged with all the paperwork showing the address of a vacant house or a mobile home in a mobile home park, and the infant was now an American citizen, duly registered with the State of Texas. Reborn at the *Rebirthing Clinic,* as it had become known by the underground. The clinica de renacimento. The Renaissance Clinic. A place to be born again.

For five thousand dollars, Maria Elena Torres was born May 16th, 2003 in Eagle Pass, Texas and not in Monterrey, Mexico. Alejandro Torres had made it with his family to the US and had managed to get his newest daughter all the paperwork to verify her citizenship. Birth certificates, hospital bills and applying for a Social Security card would be the next step for her when he reached his final destination. He had given out as much misdirection information to everyone as he could so no one knew exactly where he was headed, if anyone was looking.

He had been given counterfeit green cards for him and his wife to keep the immigration folks at bay. But he wanted something permanent and secure when he arrived at his final destination in a little community of Cedar Creek, Texas where he intended to buy a small house.

The folks that had helped him across the border had given him a tip on how to get the more important documents he would need to get a social security card, birth certificates and a driver's license so he could get a job driving a truck. The American Dream was in reach. For a price, of course.

A company in San Antonio, working out of a small suite of offices in a building on the west side of town, Hispanic Family Finders, advertised in Spanish language papers, markets and on various public bulletin boards across the Western US and as far east as Kansas City. They had individuals that worked as agents that could make contact with clients, visit yard sales and other places where contacts could possibly result in uncovering persons and old documents, bibles, and correspondence.

Known also as Buscadores de Familias Hispanic, LLC, they offered various services to Hispanic families. Locating missing family members, tracing family history in families where many times the original family member had little or no documentation and helping members of the community get proper documents.

In some cases, people would just go missing. No apparent foul play. They just left for a trip or a visit back to Mexico or some other Central or South American country and never returned. Sometimes leaving behind a treasure trove of information and documents that Hispanic Family Finders could have for the asking.

Such was the case of Miguel and Veronica Torres in Kansas City, Kansas. Both were natural born US citizens with no children. Miguel had learned the machinist trade and worked for one of the large machine shops in Kansas City. He and his wife had moved around from job to job to find better pay several times and had landed in Kansas City where they rented a nice little home.

They left on vacation telling his company and their neighbors they were driving to Mexico and were not heard from again. Since there was no evidence of foul play and attempts to reach someone who might know them failed, they were soon forgotten.

The owner of the house set about cleaning it out and contacted Hispanic Family Finders for assistance in locating the Torres couple. HFF was very eager to help and had their agent in Kansas City go by and pick up the papers, letters and bills that had names and addresses.

After writing a handful of letters to people who were mentioned in the collection of correspondences, they set about determining what they had. They quickly realized they had hit the jackpot.

A small metal box contained all of the Torres family Birth certificates and social security numbers.

Checking accounts with small balances and a small savings account. The social security numbers were still active and, they were worth a lot to someone who needed a birth certificate and social security number and especially to someone named Torres.

When Alejandro Torres contacted HFF about needing these

documents for himself, they knew they had a customer. One who was willing to pay. And he did. Now, he was able to look for a job as Miguel Torres, give them his Social Security number and there were no questions asked. The same with his wife.

Alejandro, now known to everyone as Miguel, got a job driving for a freight line based in Austin. The pay was pretty good and with the remaining stash of cash, he and his family lived a comfortable and safe life.

Maria Elena Torres had attended school at Cedar Creek Elementary, Middle School, and the high school in Cedar Creek. She had good grades, and her father and mother wanted her to attend either Austin Community College or University of Texas. But Maria had been secretly sending texts and emails to her cousin in Atlanta. A cousin that had been able to get some small parts in some movies being shot in Georgia. Tall, pretty, and smart, Maria could almost see her name in lights.

But her dad and mother had said no to the idea.

Maria had some cash saved back from babysitting and birthday presents, etc. She decided that she would go to Georgia on her own to make it big in the movies with a little help from her cousin who would meet her at the bus station. College would have to wait until after she had made it big in the movies. She had no doubt that would happen.

A little checking on the internet gave her bus schedules and prices. A 3:30 PM ticket with one stop over would get her to Atlanta in a little under twenty-four hours for one hundred and eighty-nine dollars. That would leave her about one hundred to eat on until she got to the movie company office.

Maria left a short note on her bed for her mother to find

When she got home from work at the Dollar General nearby. By then, Maria would be long gone. She told them she loved them, would call soon, and not to worry.

The trip to Atlanta was an hour late arriving due to a traffic back up as they approached the I-285 loop. She called her cousin to let her know, and the call went to voicemail. There was still time to get to the office, but being stranded at the Forsyth Street bus station was not something she had planned for. Several more attempts had the same result.

Finally, she got a text: *So sorry. I got a speeding ticket and my father has grounded me. No car keys. Trying to get someone to bring me down. Maybe by six?*

Maria stood outside at six and tried the phone again. No Luck. "Where are you?" she asked on the voicemail.

A well-dressed man walked up as she was furiously hanging up the phone and politely asked, "Excuse me, young lady, but are you okay? It's not safe to be standing here when it gets dark. I work down the street and saw you standing here. Do you need some help?"

"I'm fine. I'm waiting on someone to pick me up. They're on the way."

"Okay. If you are sure."

"I'm sure," she said.

He turned and walked across to a late model, black Mercedes and drove off. Still, no answer from her cousin. She had her cousin's number but not her address. Maria walked back into the terminal.

Forty-five minutes later, and night was setting in. She'd had several calls from home but had let them go to voicemail, opting instead to send her mother a text: *I'm OK. Can't talk right now. Don't worry about me.*

She walked back outside. and in few short minutes, the same black Mercedes pulled up at a parking spot just past the station. The same nice-looking guy got out and walked toward her.

"I just left my office down the street and noticed you still standing out here. This is not a safe place to be after dark."

"I'm okay, thank you," she replied.

"Look. My name is Max Johnson. I'm going to stop by the Waffle House just down the street for a bite to eat. Why not call the person who's coming to pick you up and tell them to come to the Waffle House on Capitol Avenue? I'll even buy you a meal."

"I'm okay. Thanks anyway."

"I sure wish you'd reconsider. I really hate leaving you here by yourself. Suppose I just wait with you here, then? I just can't stand the thoughts of leaving you alone."

She didn't answer.

He gave a shrug, turned, and walked a few steps. But then he stopped and turned back toward her. "What's your name, by the way?"

"My name is Maria."

"Maria, give your friend another try, and if you don't get them, come on and have something to eat and figure out what you want to do. You'll be safer at the Waffle House."

Maria's phone chirped indicating a text message from her cousin. *Your mom called my dad. I had to tell them you were coming to Atlanta and I was to pick you. He said no. He's coming to pick you up and send you back home or take you. Sorry.*

Maria looked at Max Johnson. "I'll go with you to the Waffle House. My ride is not coming right away."

She would be gone when her uncle arrived.

"That's great. Let's go."

She sent a text to her cousin: *I will be gone when your dad gets here. I have a ride and will get a place to stay. I'm not going back to Texas right now.*

At the Waffle House, Max Johnson was his most concerned and non-threatening self. She began to see him as charming and helpful. He even said he knew some people in the Atlanta area movie scene as well as Hollywood. He might could help her. And, he could help her find a place to spend the night in a nearby hotel. He could make his dreams come true, if not hers.

After leaving her at the motel, giving her his burn phone number and providing a little cash, he promised to start helping her out the next day. It would take about a few days to have her feeling obligated and requiring her to pay back his investment. And, to find a suitable buyer.

In the car he sent a text: *Working on a beautiful girl about eighteen. From Texas I believe. Not a missing person as she has advised her family of her leaving and intentions of being a movie star.*

"Great," read the reply. "We can make her a star. Maybe in Vancouver or Salt Lake. Could you come through Baltimore for a pick up? I have another package or two to go that way."

"Probably," he replied.

"Let me know when you are ready to move," came the reply.

The next morning, Maria received a call from the helpful Max Johnson. "How are you this morning?"

"Fine. Thank you. I appreciate your help."

"Did you get in touch with the folks that were supposed to meet you.?" he asked with a real sound of concern.

"No. It looks like I won't be able to meet up with them. There is a problem, and they want me to go back to Texas," she said.

"Well," he said. "I have a place down at College Park where some young people stay when they are trying to get a start. Some are singers, some are looking for jobs, and some are trying to get into a movie in the area like yourself. It is a secure place with a security guard, and I might can find room for you there if you need a place to stay until you get something going."

Then she said what he was hoping she would say. "You know I don't have any money to pay you?"

"Don't worry about that. I can advance you some money, and you can sign an agreement to pay me back when you can. We'll work that out. I do this sort of thing a lot."

"Are you sure?"

"Absolutely. You may need several days to find something, and you don't want to be on the streets in Atlanta, do you?" he asked.

"No. That's for sure."

"Well, I'll come pick you up, and we'll get some breakfast, and I'll take you down to College Park, and then you can settle in."

"I don't know how to thank you, Mr. Johnson."

"It'll all work out, I'm sure," he assured her.

Maria thought she was headed to College Park when she was really headed to Vancouver through a dark tunnel of lost dreams, lost innocence, and hopelessness. The human trafficking machine was working well. At least, for the traffickers.

Chapter 13

In Ennis, Russ's phone lit up with an incoming call. *Bradley Taylor* appeared on the caller ID screen.

"Hello. This is Russell Baker," he answered.

"Brad Taylor, here, Russ. I wanted to let you know what we see as far as our meeting you for that Missouri River trip and see if it meets with your approval."

"Okay, Brad. What have you worked out?"

"We should be finished in Bozeman Tuesday afternoon. Taking your suggestion, we will fly up to Great Falls, and we got rooms at the Trout Lodge in Cascade. They had a cancellation just before I called, as luck would have it."

"Okay. I'll probably get up there around six Tuesday evening," said Russ. "Will you guys have your own rods?"

"Yes. We both have five, six, and seven weight rods."

"Great. Any of those will do. We might rig one for nymphing and one for dries for each of you. See you Tuesday."

Russ knew then that this wasn't their first rodeo, as they say.

"Russ, plan on having dinner with us if you can."

"That will be fine," said Russ. "Goodbye."

The drive to the Missouri to meet the Taylor's wouldn't normally take Russ through Butte. Taking US 287 from Ennis to Helena to I-15 saved about 50 miles. But Russ thought it might be a good time to just drop in at the *Wayne's Truck Stop* in Butte where Teresa Walker worked.

A phone call confirmed that she would be working the three o'clock till eleven shift on Tuesday. So far, there was not much to go on in her inquiry about the strange goings on with the Helena policeman, Darin Marchman.

Tuesday arrived, and Russ came to see that the truck stop was an impressive operation. There was even a barber shop. A driver laying over there could eat, sleep, receive money by western Union, watch videos, play video games, log into the internet, get basic health care attention as well as about any service for their truck including tires, chrome accessories, and lights.

It was a one stop shop, for sure. It was almost as big as the largest truck stop in the country, the Iowa 80 Truckstop which sat on two hundred and twenty acres in Walcott, Iowa and had 5,000 visitors daily.

He texted Teresa Walker from the parking lot. She told him the area she was working and suggested that he ask to be seated in her section.

When she came to the table, he almost didn't recognize her. Thinner than he remembered and paler. *Prison can do that*, he guessed. No business suit with a jacket to cover the 9MM handgun that she had once worn as a state law officer.

Her hair was longer and pulled back. She was wearing a neat waitress uniform with a pin-on name tag that simply said *Teresa*.

The cockiness he had remembered from their first meeting was replaced with something difficult to describe. A combination, maybe, of humility, resignation, and some sadness. But she showed little signs of the trauma she had suffered at the hands of her former boyfriend who had felt the need to eliminate her when she had cooperated with Russ and the sheriff. It wouldn't take much to have her old attractiveness back, but maybe she wasn't too interested in that right now.

"Hello, Teresa. It's nice to see you again. I hope you are well."

"I'm okay, I guess, Russell. Under the circumstances, I guess I'm lucky to be here at all."

"I am headed up to Cascade and thought it might be a good time to touch base with you. Is anything happening?"

"Look, Russell, I'll be going on break in thirty minutes. Can I come out and talk to you in the car? I'll just say you are an old friend from Bozeman if anyone asks. Maybe you could have some pie and coffee. I don't want Mr. Renfroe to be checking up on me."

"That sounds good. I'll do the coffee and pie, and I'll be in the Chevy pickup pulling the drift boat over on the camping trailer lot," he said before departing for the parking lot.

It was a busy place. People from all over the country coming and going. Back and forth across the miles and miles of concrete.

She came to the truck with two coffees and handed one to Russ before hopping up into the passenger's seat. Here they could talk without being overheard.

"Thanks for coming by, Russell," she said.

"No problem. I don't get up to fish the Missouri too much, but some folks called and wanted me to take them. Coming by here was easy. Anything happening with the Helena cop?"

"He has been in at least two more times since I called you. Once when I wasn't here, but Paula, the head waitress, saw him once after I left one night. I had pointed him out to her, and she was pretty sure it was him."

"Seems strange he would come inside multiple times and risk being seen if he was involved in anything illegal," said Russ.

"Yeah. I agree. It may be a chance to let the females get to a restroom under a somewhat controlled situation. They always sit back in the area where you can access them easily."

"Aren't they off the main lobby?" asked Russ.

"The main ones are, but the restaurant has some of its own since some people just stop for the restaurant and don't have a reason to go to the main lobby. At least that's how it was explained to me."

"And," she continued, "it's possible he's meeting in a public space to keep from getting ripped off if he's carrying a lot of money."

"That would make sense," replied Russ. "Could be a way of keeping each other from seeing what the other is driving, license plates, etc. Have you mentioned anything to the General Manager?"

"No. But now Paula is on board with the idea that there is something peculiar going on. Her opinion really matters around here, so I'm feeling a little more confident about talking to the GM."

"Have you been able to get a picture? One with one of these girls with him would be a big help. Especially one that showed the cop," replied Russ.

"Not yet, but I'll keep my eye out and see what I can do."

"Any chance we can look at CCT footage?" he asked.

"I don't believe I can ask that. Mr. Renfroe is a by the book guy."

Russ replied, "If the cop's doing something illegal, it must be a very profitable deal for him to risk exposing himself like this. I believe this is the same Highway Patrol district as Helena, so he could easily run into an MHP trooper here that he has had dealings with there."

"For that matter, DCI Agents as well," she said.

"Well, until you get more or are willing to go public with your concerns, I guess we have to wait," said Russ.

"Okay. I'll see if I can come up with anything. Thanks for coming by."

"By the way, Teresa, how's your mother doing?"

"We have started treatments at the cancer center in Helena once a week. It'll be a while before we can expect any results. Thanks for asking."

With that, she opened the truck door, stepped out, and sprinted to the side door of the restaurant. Russ sat for a minute and wondered what would happen next.

He pulled out of the sprawling parking lot between trucks of all sizes, motor homes, cars, and pickups and campers and eased on to I-90 for the quick trip over to I-15 North toward Cascade, a drive of about one hundred and twenty miles.

Russ had made this trip a few times, and each time he did he was reminded of what he liked about Montana. He still loved the North Georgia area with its creeks and rivers and beautiful wooded hills and low mountains, the fall colors, and places like Blue Ridge, Rabun Gap, Dahlonega and Helen and all the little communities. Names like Jacks Gap and Sooky Gap, Soque, Tickanetley, Chattahoochee, and Etowah. But this Montana was something all its own to Russ.

Montana, the Latin word for *mountainous,* had been given its name in 1864 by most accounts. The man who had named it was a congressman from Ohio, of all places.

Georgia had its Brasstown Bald at nearly five thousand feet. But on this ride to Cascade you could see The Little Belt Mountains, Black Reef Mountains, Castle Mountains, and Pinnacles. Over a hundred named mountain ranges in Montana with difficulty knowing where one begins and the other ends.

Where does the sky start and the mountain end, or are they all part of the same landscape, simply blended together? Peaks of over eight thousand feet off in the distant horizon and others ranging from four to six thousand very near the valley where the interstate highway and US 287 ran together, twisting and crossing and meandering along the Missouri over and over. Patches of green and brown, ranches and farming land with drift boats and rafts ambling downstream from the dam at Holter Lake. Blue ribbon trout water for the next fifty miles to Cascade. Civilization to be seen but not too much. He wondered if the people living in this valley ever noticed the breathtaking beauty all around or if they were always wishing they were somewhere else. Paris, Rome, or New York.

Drive through it, enjoy it, but don't drive too fast. And, if you are lucky, you get to come back the same way.

Too late. Russ pulled into the parking lot at the motel. Tomorrow he would enjoy the view from his drift boat. Too bad Sarah was not there.

Russ walked in to register and was told his room was being paid by the Taylor's. He was handed a note telling him to join them at the steak restaurant about a quarter mile down the street. It was better to walk than try parking with the boat in tow, and he really did not want to unhook and re-hook if he could avoid it.

Russ halfway expected to see a couple of guys who looked as if they had just walked out of the dressing room at L.L. Bean, Kevin's, or Orvis, with all new, well-pressed creases and the finest in boots and belts and the works. He was surprised to see the Taylor's sitting at a table with long neck beers in hand, scruffy looking jeans that they might have been wearing while working on a tractor. Brad was wearing an old faded Columbia fishing shirt, and his father had on an old Levi's shirt. Neither of which had ever had a crease from the way they looked.

Evan Taylor, whom Russ had met, threw up his hand, "Hello, Russ. Come and join us. This is my son, Brad."

Russ realized quickly that he liked them both. There was a certain confidence about them that came from success and money, but they did not try to act with too high of an opinion of themselves.

A few minutes into the conversation, and he had learned they were both very experienced and fished a lot in Utah on the Provo, the Green River, the Logan, and numerous lakes like the Strawberry Reservoir.

So did Debra, they said, but she had not mentioned it to Russ. Brad tied some flies as well. *Tomorrow might be fun*, Russ thought.

"Russ, are we fishing out of a drift boat or raft?" asked Brad.

"We will be in a drift boat," answered Russ. "A lot of guys are using the rafts, and I have no issue with them, but the drift boat is just my preference for the places I fish and more comfortable to me. Some guys have both, and some have just the rafts. They feel the rafts give them a little more versatility of waters they can fish. They also like them in rougher water and rapids. Drift boats are heavier and will sink. We'll try to avoid that tomorrow," he said with a grin.

Morning was overcast, and the Pelican Point launch only had one boat being launched when they arrived. The Taylor's each had a couple of high-end Douglas rods and a couple of Sage's best rods. The rod cases showed plenty of use, and they needed little help in getting themselves situated with Mr. Taylor electing to take the back seat. They were rigged up for nymphs and droppers and strike indicators with two rods and for dry flies on the other two. There would be several places where they could wade, and they had elected to forego the waders.

It didn't take long for the action to start. The three of them worked well in the boat, and once they hit a lull, Russ moved the boat out of the current, dropped the anchor, and poured a cup of coffee for each of them from his thermos that he had filled up at the hotel. Then, Mr. Taylor brought up Debra.

"Russ, Debra came over to Montana and got into a pretty dangerous situation, I guess. She never talked much about it, but her boss at the department in Salt Lake told me some about it."

"Debra is a tough lady. She came over on her own, you know, I didn't ask her and tried to discourage her, but she persuaded the sheriff that she had SWAT training and could hold her own. And she proved to be very valuable to us."

Mr. Taylor responded, "That's what I hear. But, I really wish she would find another line of work. She can work for me, and we seldom get shot at." He laughed at his own joke.

Russ said with a grin, "I guess that will take some real selling, Mr. Taylor. I wish you luck with that."

"How about you, Russ? I understand you lost your wife some time back. Are you still single? I think Debra said you had a serious lady friend in Bozeman."

Russ really was uncomfortable talking about any of this with the Taylor's, but they were polite enough, so he was gentle in his attempt to change the subject.

"No, not anything happening in that department, I'm afraid. But I think we should get back to fishing."

Mr. Taylor nodded. He'd gotten the message. That was an area of discussion not included in the float trip package.

The day went well. At one point, Mr. Taylor got out and worked his way to the head of one of the slower pools with a dry fly. Russ was watching with the net just in case. As he stood watching, he realized that Mr. Taylor was not just standing in the water, but it was more like he was part of the river. The rod was an extension of his arm, and with a smooth lift of the rod and an effortless cast, the dry fly landed like a butterfly on a flower. Taylor saw nothing but the size 16 PMD fly. Focused. In the zone.

Then the sip of the fly by the large rainbow, a ripple, a splash, and a jump. Away the fish went as Taylor spun up the slack on the reel and took control of the line. In a couple of minutes, Russ slid the net under the catch, and the fight was over. It was nice watching a man close to being an expert, and that's certainly what Taylor was.

As they eased downstream, Russ asked Taylor, "How long have you been fly fishing?"

"Oh, about as long as I can remember. My father made some bamboo rods, tied flies, and fished every chance he could and took me along. I haven't stopped since."

"Was he in the same business as you?" asked Russ.

"My father worked on John Deere tractors for most of his life, Russ. He was manager of the service department for a large dealer in Illinois that had several locations."

A number of large fish cooperated, and the dry fly action toward the end of the float was icing on the cake. The take out at Cascade was now in sight, and he could see his truck waiting.

"Russ, this has been a delightful day. Thank you for taking us out. You might call Debra sometime if you are going to be in Salt Lake. She'd like to hear from you. She'd like to make this trip too, I know. Right, Brad?"

"No doubt," said Brad.

As Russ spun the boat around and headed toward the take-out, Mr. Taylor asked, "Ever consider doing anything else, Russ?"

Russ wasn't sure where he was going with that question.

"Someday, probably. Thanks to late wife's father, I am able to do mostly what I want to do right now. He manages my finances better than I ever would have, and he has done a great job. But the day may come when I go in another direction. I may go back to law enforcement. Maybe sooner than later. This is like a sabbatical that has been extended. I still consider Georgia my home."

"Call me if you ever want to be in the business world. We might have a slot for a good man," said Mr. Taylor.

Russ couldn't help but wonder if this trip was a personal evaluation trip to see what he was like and wondered where Debra fit into this, if at all. And, he couldn't help but wonder why she had not mentioned being an experienced fly fisher when they had once discussed his working as a part time guide.

Chapter 14

Goodbye, Miriam

The invitation came in the mail. It was addressed to Russell Baker, Ennis, Montana; it read:

You are cordially invited to attend
The Wedding of
Miriam Alexander
To
Bruce Whittaker

The Saturday wedding date and the time were all listed, and the reception would follow at the same exclusive country club he had visited with Debra Taylor when he was in Salt Lake investigating a case that he had assisted on with the Sheriff's Department.

That told Russ something about Bruce Whittaker: he must have been one successful carpet dealer if he was a member at that club. *Way to go, Miriam! This might not be such a small affair, after all.*

The actual flying time from Bozeman to Salt Lake City was about fifty-five minutes. Quite a bit more time would have been required to make the four hundred plus miles by car both ways, so Russ decided to fly to attend Miriam's wedding.

He had promised he would attend and was fulfilling that promise, and as soon as he boarded the plane, he was regretting the decision. While he was really happy for Miriam, he couldn't help but feel a little sorry for himself.

This trip would close out another relationship that had meant a lot to him. No matter how you sliced it, she would be moving on, and he would still be in the same place. Better for having known her, perhaps, but still alone in a rented house in Ennis, Montana.

"Welcome aboard, sir," the flight attendant said as Russ entered the doorway of the plane. "I hope you are having a great day."

"Yes, thank you. I'm having a wonderful day. I hope you are too." A white lie now and then never hurt anybody, he figured.

The flight was non-eventful, and the person sitting next to him was reading a newspaper and sending out the *I really am not interested in chatting* signals. That was just fine with Russ. Neither was he.

The Kia rental car was waiting, and a quick ride to the Hilton left him with an evening to kill. He contemplated taking Mr. Taylor's advice from the Missouri River float trip and touching base with Debra Taylor. *Don't expect much, and you won't be disappointed he thought to himself.*

She answered on the third ring. "Well, there must be something wrong with my caller ID," she said without a *hello*. "It's been quite a while since I received a call from this number."

"Well, your father said I should call you if I was back out this way. So, to avoid losing a client, I thought I'd better do as he suggested."

"I'll give you about ten seconds to come up with a better line than that, or I'm hanging up and removing you from my contact list," she said. He thought he might have heard a little chuckle? Maybe not.

"How about the old *I've been meaning to call but have just been so busy* line?" he asked.

"That's even worse!"

"Okay. How about *I'm so sorry I haven't called; I hope you will forgive me for being such a thoughtless oaf?*"

"That's starting to sound a little better. Maybe you need to work on the apology thing."

"I'll make a point of it," he said.

"To what do I owe the honor of getting this call from such a thoughtless oaf?" She laughed.

"I am in town for a wedding tomorrow. I will be in town a couple of days, and I thought I would try to see if you have any time open for a coffee, breakfast, lunch, and so forth."

"Well, that's just great. I don't have anything on my date book for months and then the weekend I do, you decide to call. I have a date tonight, and I am also going to a wedding tomorrow and then a reception tomorrow evening."

A friend of my dad's is getting married. My mother was supposed to go, but she had some surgery and decided to drop out, and my dad twisted my arm to go."

She continued, "Who do you know getting married here?"

"You will probably remember Miriam Alexander, the lady whose daughters knew the guys who were involved in the attack on the sheriff. She's marrying some guy from here who is a local carpet dealer, I think. I think the reception is at your club."

"What? You must be joking. Hold on a moment."

When she returned to the phone she said, "That's the same wedding we're invited to. I just looked at the invitation my dad had handed me. I hadn't looked at the woman's name on it. Bruce Whittaker is a client and friend of my dad's. He is a very successful businessman here in Salt Lake. He owns those carpet stores, apartments, some strip shopping centers, and is a very good investor. My brother and dad do some property development for him. Your friend is marrying well!"

Russ was taken back by the news but recovered quickly. "I suspected something when I saw the reception was at your club. Well, I guess I'll see you at the wedding or the reception or both."

"I'll look for you, and maybe you can sit with Dad and me. I think Brad is coming, too. Are you traveling alone?"

"Yes. I am. I look forward to seeing all of you," said Russ.

"Maybe I can clear my calendar while you are in town," she added.

Coincidence? Fate? It might would be an interesting evening tomorrow. But, *don't have your expectations too high* was written on the caution flag.

Russ decided not to call Miriam, thinking she was busy getting ready for tomorrow. He would get a chance to congratulate her and meet the new husband at the reception, hopefully.

The wedding was nice, sweet, and uneventful. Miriam looked beautiful in a fashionable dress, but there was no wedding gown, veils, and all the stuff associated with a formal wedding. Bruce was a nice-looking fellow who appeared to stay in shape and maybe a year or two older than Miriam.

Russ had not gotten there in time to find Debra before going into the chapel, so he decided to get a seat wherever he could and keep a low profile. There were more people there than he had expected considering it was supposedly just a few friends. Not too many friends from low places, though, it seemed. Maybe he was the only one.

Russ lingered after the ceremony and saw Debra and her father leaving. "Hello, Mr. Taylor. Nice to see you again. Hello, Debra. It is, as they say, a small world. I would have never expected to run into you two at this wedding today."

Mr. Taylor responded, "I guess we are all pleasantly surprised. I have known Bruce for several years, and we have done some projects together. He's quite the businessman. Debra tells me you knew Miriam from Montana and rent her house."

"Yes, I did rent her house for quite a while. Her first husband is a very good builder, and it's a very nice house, and I enjoyed living there. I have recently relocated since they plan to sell it, and I decided I did not want to buy right now."

"Still thinking about moving back to Georgia, Russ? I thought you might be settling down around Bozeman," asked Debra.

"No settling down plans on the table right now, Debra."

"We may want to do that Missouri River trip again with you, Russ. I might can talk Debra into coming next time," Mr. Taylor said.

"That can be arranged, I'm sure. Debra would be most welcomed," Russ replied.

"I guess we'll start over to the club, Russ. I suppose you are coming?" asked Mr. Taylor.

"Yes, sir. I have to speak to Miriam and get introduced to her new husband. I have yet to meet him. I'm looking forward to doing both." Another white lie, maybe.

"Russ, how about I ride over with you, and we can catch up a bit? You won't mind me riding with Russ, will you, Dad?" Debra asked.

"I don't mind. This is twice now I've been abandoned. First your mother and now you," he said with a smile. He extended his hand to Russ. "I'll see you at the club." The man turned, heading off in a separate direction.

Russ handed his car keys to Debra. "Why don't you drive since you know the way. Sorry I don't have a BMW rental for you."

"Well, I do drive the cop car around, so I remember what it's like to rough it," she said, happily climbing into the driver's seat of the rental.

"I enjoyed your dad and Brad coming to fish with me. Why didn't you tell me your whole family was into fly fishing?" Russ asked as they pulled out of the parking lot.

"I didn't try to keep it from you; it just didn't come up, I guess. Dad and Brad went on and on about how great the day was with you, Dad kept saying how I should book a trip with you."

"And, now that we're talking about what should've happened, I wondered why you never bothered to call me once the case was closed over there. I guess you were involved with someone at the time. How's that going, if I may ask?"

"Well, I guess I will allow you that question since you've made me feel like a heel, now. Truth is, I did think I was in a serious relationship, but neither she nor I could ever really make the kind of commitment that was required to go to anything more permanent. I was a mess when my wife died, and she had lost a fiancé in Afghanistan or Iraq or some place, so we had issues. So, she left me a goodbye voicemail while I was on a recent trip to Florida with my late wife's parents."

"Well, that stinks," Debra replied. "No chance of you getting back together?"

"Not likely. She left the message and then went to Las Vegas for a week with the college professor she had gone out with some in the past."

"Oh my. I guess that does make it unlikely."

"Surprisingly, Debra, everyone thought I would fall apart over it, but I didn't. I guess it will work out for the best for both of us. She didn't like the idea of me being a cop and maybe going back to that someday."

"Well, let's go in here and eat some free food and mingle and say hello to the newlyweds," she said as they pulled up to the valet at the country club.

As they walked in, Russ could see Miriam and her new husband greeting the guests, hugging, shaking hands, and looking very happy. For a moment, Russ felt a wave of sadness, but he recovered by the time they had reached the couple, displaying a huge smile.

"Oh, Russ! I am so glad you came," she said as she gave Russ a kiss on the cheek and a big hug. "Please meet Bruce. I told him all about you!"

Then she whispered in his ear, "Well, not really all, Russ."

Russ shook the outstretched hand of Bruce Whittaker and couldn't help but think about some old saying about winner take all. "So nice to meet you, Bruce. Congratulations."

"Thank you, Russ. The Taylors had told me about their fishing trip on the Missouri, but I only learned a few days ago that the fellow they were fishing with was the same person renting Miriam's house. Maybe we can make that trip with you sometimes. I have never done much fly fishing."

"I would be happy to have you over. Just call me when you can come."

Miriam mouthed to Russ as he started to move on, "We'll talk some more."

Russ couldn't help but think there was not much left to be said. They could still be friends from a distance. But what they had had once would never be again. But he knew she had made a good decision in marrying Bruce.

The reception affair was very nice, and Russ could see that Bruce had spared no expense. Nothing came cheap at this place with dues close to $100,000 a year with assessments. *Having some money sure looks nice*, Russ thought. *Having lots of money, well, that's even nicer!* Russ hoped he'd get a chance to talk one on one with Miriam, but her new husband was hanging on to her and she to him. Their time for private talks were over, and Russ knew it.

Miriam made no effort to break away, either. *Don't get off on the wrong foot* seemed to be the rule.

People started saying their goodbyes and thank you's, and the crowd got smaller. The newlyweds were off to Hawaii for their honeymoon, and Russ knew they wanted the event to draw to a close.

Russ walked over and said goodnight cordially. He turned to see where Debra was, and she spotted him, gave a wave, and started toward him. She said a quick goodbye, and they headed to the car together when her cell phone started to ring.

"Detective Taylor," she said.

She listened for a moment. "I'm not on duty tonight. Don't you have someone else available?"

A short pause, then, "Okay. I'll be the one in the Giorgio Armani dress." She hung up the phone and then turned to him. "Russ, I'm so sorry, but I have to go in on a call. Seems it's a busy night. I'll call Uber to come get me."

"No need to call Uber. Just drive us over, and I'll let you out," he said with a smile. "Do you have your badge and gun?"

"Of course. I never go to a wedding reception without them. You never know how quickly the fireworks might start."

"You don't seem to have a high opinion of marriage, Miss Taylor."

"On the contrary, I would love to be married someday. If the right man came along and asked me."

"I can't imagine you having any trouble finding the *right man* as you call it," said Russ.

"Finding the right man is a lot like fishing, Russ. Sometimes the good one gets off the hook, and you don't get the trophy."

Sometimes the one you want isn't interested and doesn't take the bait." She gave him a do-you-know-what-I-mean look as she pulled up outside the crime scene.

They both got out as he had to move to the driver's side. In the front of the car, she embraced him, kissed him and said, "I know you have my number. I have a rare date tomorrow night, or I'd ask you out to dinner."

"Goodnight, Debra. I really enjoyed seeing you. My flight is at 12:30 tomorrow. You have my number, too".

Debra flashed her badge to the patrolman and crossed under the crime tape, and heads turned as she started up the steps to the apartment.

Russ drove back to the hotel, lay across the bed, and turned on the TV. A quick check of voicemails and texts showed nothing that couldn't wait his return to Ennis.

He found a fly-fishing show on and propped up on the pillows to watch. They always showed them catching big fish and plenty of them and never seemed to put on a show where the fisherman got skunked. No demand for that on TV, he supposed.

The next thing Russ knew, his cell was chiming loudly, and he had to get his bearings as he was *dead to the world* as his grandmother would say when he was a small boy. The Caller ID showed Debra Taylor. His phone showed 10:15 PM.

"Hello, Debra," he managed to say in the middle of a huge yawn.

"You sound like you're either drunk or were asleep. I guess asleep," she said. "I know you didn't leave the reception drunk, and you're way too tight to be getting liquor from the mini bar."

"No wonder you are a detective. And, by the way, you're the only one I've ever met that appeared at crime scenes in a two-thousand-dollar dress." Russ said.

"Well, just for your information, it was on sale."

"And why are you waking me up in the middle of the

night? I already said I was sorry about all previous mistakes, oversights, and so on."

"If you hadn't, I wouldn't be calling you. Maybe it's the middle of the night for an old Southern boy, but for the in-crowd, we are just getting started about now," she said with a lilt in her voice.

"I suspected you were in the in-crowd. So, did you get the bad guy already?" he asked.

"Bad girl, as it turns out. And she came back to the scene of the crime and confessed to stabbing her boyfriend with a letter opener. It was the only thing handy, it seems. He says he won't prosecute, so my crime scene partner said he'd take care of the paperwork, and I should go home. So that's what I'm doing."

"Good partner to have. What are you doing for a car?"

"He drives the last Ford Crown Victoria the department has. He let me take it, and I think that he secretly hopes I total it on the way home."

"I can imagine," Russ said.

"If you are not too tired, you could come over to my place. I'm not too far away, and I could pick you up. I think I have a couple of Budweiser's in the icebox. I promise to have you back before your plane leaves tomorrow."

"I'll be out front. I'll change my shirt to casual."

"You can wear your fishing shirt, if you want to. I'll be out front in ten."

Russ walked out to see the black Crown Vic pull up.

He opened the door and climbed in. Debra looked no worse for wear since they had left the church earlier in the afternoon. In fact, a closer look confirmed how striking she was.

"I believe you are staring, sir," she said. "That's considered rude by some people."

"It's entirely your fault. If you didn't look so nice and insisted on dragging me out in the middle of the night, you wouldn't have to be putting up with this rude behavior. Do you want me to get out?"

"Sorry. Consider yourself under arrest. I am a cop. You may stare, if you wish," she teased.

Her condo was next to penthouse level in a building with a doorman and a valet. Quick conclusion: this was a very expensive place paid for by her father.

She entered the code, and the door slowly opened to a beautifully decorated three-bedroom condo with a tremendous view of the city and surrounding country of Salt Lake. The rent was probably more than her take home pay as a detective. Or, she might have owned it. Poor little rich girl?

She seemed to read his mind. "You're thinking there's no way I can afford this on a cop salary. You are right. My dad bought this place for me. He bought Brad's house, too," she said as she handed him a very cold Budweiser.

"I don't get how the most eligible woman in Salt Lake is still single. Your phone must ring off the hook."

"Well, it did for a long time. There were all sorts calling me. Those that were interested in me because my father is wealthy, so they assume I am. A sugar mamma is what they want. Then there are those that really might like me, but I don't like them well enough to have more than one or two casual dates. Then, there are the ones who are intimidated by the money or the fact that I pack a nine-millimeter on my job, and they start trying to figure out if I would stop what I like doing and do what they approve of. Even my dad has quit doing that."

"I found both your dad and Brad to be a pleasant surprise. I really enjoyed being with them. Your dad and brother have accepted who you are. Let me see… how did they put it… *stubborn* and *muleheaded*," he said with a laugh.

"That certainly sounds like them. Dad put me on the payroll as a strategic planner, and I also serve on the board. He hopes to convert me, but I just like getting the checks. So far, at least. But enough about that. What have you been doing besides fishing in Florida and taking my family fishing? Catching a lot of bad guys?"

"Fortunately, there aren't many hardened criminals in Ennis, Montana. They could round up the entire population of Virginia City in about an hour and read them their rights while doing it."

"We are not a major crime center here either, but we stay busy," she said.

"I do have a question for you, since you brought up the subject of business," he said. "A lady that was involved in a case I worked on called me a few days ago. She was a former DCI agent in Montana and ended up getting shot up and almost killed, and she finally helped us get all the bad guys. She ended up serving a reduced sentence for cooperating."

He continued, "She now works as a waitress at a very large truck stop in Butte and has seen this guy coming in on multiple occasions alone and meeting someone and leaving with young girls. She got suspicious and later found out the guy is a cop in another town. She called me for advice because she is afraid she will lose her job if she makes too much of it – especially if there is nothing to it."

"We have a task force called MAAP. It really is just one person most of the time, but that officer handles the inquiries about *missing and abducted persons*. It was originally referred to as *missing and abducted children,* but it turns out they aren't all children," she said. "I have worked on it when we have an active case."

"In this case, since there is a cop involved, it could be drugs or some other undercover operation. I asked the sheriff about it, and he wanted more to go on before getting involved with the Butte and Helena agencies and maybe exposing an ongoing operation. There is little I can do as I have no standing in the matter," said Russ.

Debra responded, "I have attended a couple of workshops, and it's amazing at some of the situations that cause someone to seemingly disappear. Some kids just run away. Many are never heard from again. Maybe they are in love, and the parents don't approve of their love interest. Sometimes one or both of the parents is abusive. Small kids are abducted in child custody cases. Some end up on the streets and get pulled or pushed into prostitution or other sex-related trades. There's evidence that some go missing for body parts. That requires some planning because body parts aren't easily transferred from one person to another unless they are solid matches."

" But if you advertise on the dark web that you have a kidney or heart with match characteristics, there's likely someone out there to buy it. Some people are snatched off the street, like in the movies, but those are rare in the US. Those seem to occur more in third world countries. Although one of the most famous cases of child abduction took place here in Salt Lake with the young girl named Smart."

"Yes," Russ said. "I remember that case. What's being done to find these kids and try to prevent these cases?"

"Well, you know the basics, I'm sure. At one time faces were put on milk cartons, telephone poles, train and bus stations, and such. Now there are several internet sites that people can look for and list missing persons. Child alerts on phones and television. The problem there, if you aren't looking for a specific person, people don't visit those internet sites as a daily thing. And, children can change their appearance, hair color, tattoos, and clothing choices to make them appear so different in a short period of time. Families look through old photo albums of their small kids and have trouble knowing which one they are looking at."

She continued, "Many places put signs in public restrooms with emergency numbers to call if someone is in there and involved in such a situation. But the victim is so threatened and traumatized, maybe drugged, they are afraid to call or have no means to do so. Their phones have been taken from them and usually destroyed so that they can't be tracked. Once in that spiral, it is often only the individual that dares to break away on their own that makes it out alive."

"I've suggested the waitress try to capture a picture of the guy and the girls, but they wear caps, hoods, and never look at a camera, so identification is difficult," Russ said.

"One thing I could think of, Russ, is that since they seem to be young females, if your waitress is suspicious, and the girl should happen to go in the restroom, maybe the waitress could go in and ask her if she is okay or needs anything. She has to be careful she is not accused of child solicitation or child abuse herself."

The discussion of abducted and missing persons and selling body parts had sucked out all of the hope that Debra had for a possible romantic evening with Russ. Even a two-thousand-dollar dress, on sale, had not been enough to close the deal.

Russ might have been a great detective, but he had not picked up on a single hint or clue all afternoon at the wedding reception or now in her high-priced, decorator furnished condo.

In any case, she would stop short of dragging him kicking and screaming to the bedroom. She was saved further embarrassment and humiliation by Russ.

"Debra, I enjoyed seeing you. You really have a nice place here. I guess I should grab a cab or Uber and get back to the hotel. I don't want you having to get out to take me back."

She knew when she was whipped.

"Just push the button on the phone marked *Doorman* and tell him you want a cab. It'll be charged to my account, and no arguments, please."

The cab was at the front door by the time Russ gave Debra a hug and caught the elevator down. Debra Taylor walked to the window and watched Russ get in the cab. She thought she looked damned gorgeous in the high-priced dress. She liked the part-time fly-fishing guide who rode around in a pickup truck and lived in the rented house in Ennis.

Well, anyway, he had learned a lot about missing and abducted children and she would go to bed. Alone. Again.

In ten minutes, Russ was walking into his room at the hotel and wondering to himself if he had missed an opportunity. But she lived in Salt Lake and had lots of money and would probably not be interested in a part-time fly-fishing guide with a drift boat, a pickup truck and rented house who lived in Ennis, Montana. Yes, he wasn't broke, but compared to the Taylors he felt that he might as well be.

Chapter 15

Geraldine

Geraldine Bailey left her shift at the local hamburger chain restaurant. She had started working there in high school and had worked off and on although she was not the most reliable worker. If the manager had not been a friend of her grandmothers from church, she would have been fired a long time back.

Instead of going home, she would stop off at a local hangout and sip a little of someone else's beer since she wasn't able to buy any on her own, and there was never any at her grandmother Lois Bailey's. Her excuse for being late was always something to do with work, although her grandmother could easily check. With a look that some compared to Halle Barry; she always attracted a crowd.

The Eastdale area was her home and had always been. But life for her had not been a pleasant one. Her father was part-time at best. He was always coming and going and constantly in some scrape with the law. Money was scarce. Geraldine dreamed of the day she would be able to leave the place for good.

Her mother had battled alcohol and drugs ever since Geraldine could remember, and she had finally ended up out of a job and working as a prostitute (when she had worked at all), and eventually Geraldine's grandmother had taken her and her sister Maxine in to try and give them some stability.

Lois Bailey had worked at the post office her entire adult life and had raised three boys on her own. One was Geraldine's father, the bad apple in the lot. But Lois went to church every time the doors were opened and made Geraldine and her sister go, too. Mamma Lois, as they called her.

If there was something at school, Mamma Lois was there. Doing homework was priority. "Make something of yourself," she would tell the sisters. "Ain't nobody gonna do it for you."

But Geraldine still managed to slip away from school and hang out with other kids at the mall or some apartment and skirted trouble often herself. Calls from the school and a number of visits from Child Services were upsetting to Geraldine and even more to her grandmother. The threat of being put in a foster home or group home frightened Geraldine enough, usually, to clean up her act for a few weeks until the heat was off.

She avoided serious trouble but had a rebellious streak. And living in the environment she had grown up in had made her tough. Both physically and mentally. The other girls knew not to mess with Geraldine. And no boys dared get out of line with her either.

And Geraldine could sing. She could sound like Whitney Houston and Tina Turner rolled into one, at least that's what everyone had always told her. She had a good voice and high energy that had gotten her a gig at a local club. It paid more than working at the restaurant, and her grandmother had signed a release for her to work there. That took some practice on Geraldine's part. Practice signing her grandmother's name.

But Atlanta was where the musicians, recording studios, movie makers, and producers were. Atlanta was where she needed to be. That's where she *would make something of herself*, just like Mamma Lois had told her. Her good looks should be a help, she felt.

She could get to Atlanta with a twenty-dollar bus ticket. That would get the ball rolling.

"Maxine," she said to her sister when she arrived home. "Mamma Lois has gone to the grocery store. She thinks I'm going to work a double shift at the 'burger store and won't be looking for me until about 11:30 tonight. Give her this note about that time. My bus will be in Atlanta by then. I'll call you as soon as I figure out where I'll be staying. I have a couple of names of places I may can stay cheap, and there is a church shelter near the station if I can't get anything else."

In a few minutes, she was sitting in the waiting room about to start her one-way ride to stardom. She just needed a little break.

At the bus station in Chattanooga, a young, handsome black man came in carrying his guitar soft case. *Probably a Fender*, she thought, since most of the little bands she played with all had Fenders. He sat down right across from her.

She had to ask, "Do you play in a band?"

"I don't play for one particular band right now, but I do some fill in gigs in Georgia and Tennessee. I've played some in Florida. I've got an agent in Atlanta that's gotten me some work, and we are trying to get on regular here in Chattanooga. I came up to try out for a band over the weekend, and they have one more dude trying out. Looks like I have a shot at something with them," he said with a big smile. "I do some backup with some studios in Atlanta. Where are you headed?"

"Atlanta. There's a lot of music happening there, and I'm trying to get some work as a singer," she said. "I've done a few nights with a couple of little bands. Nothing big."

"Are you any good?" he asked.

"I think I am, and I get a good reaction from the people where I've been, but they were small places."

"So, you don't have anything lined up in Atlanta?" he asked.

"No. I looked up some names on the web and got some names from some of the guys in the little bands I've sung with up here. Hope something works out," she explained.

"My name is Dexter Brown, what's yours?" he asked.

"I'm Geraldine Bailey."

"Geraldine, you have a tough job ahead of you. There are a lot of singers coming and going, and unless you get in front of someone who's connected, it could take weeks or months. If ever. I hope you have some money or somebody you can hit up for some, or you'll end up working at some fast-food place and singing in the shower."

"Well, if I had a lot of money, I'd be driving down in my Benz, Dexter, not riding the bus. And, I see you are riding the bus, too. Are you working in a fast-food place?"

He laughed at her quick retort. "I've been getting enough work to keep me going. At least, somebody paid for my ticket up here and back," he said. "And my guy has gotten me some auditions and set me up for some audition tapes," he responded pleasantly. "Do you have a place to stay or know someone in Atlanta?" he asked.

"I don't really know anyone in Atlanta. I gotta couple of places in mind to stay that are cheap. Like you said, I may have to get a job in a fast-food place. That's what I've been doing till today anyways."

Dexter replied, "The guy that helps me is meeting me in Atlanta. He's setting up a couple of demo records for me. I will be staying at a house he has that he lets me and some others use near College Park. I could call him and see if he would let you stay there, and maybe he could talk to you about helping you get started. Would you like for me to call him?"

"Who would be staying there besides you?"

"Usually there are a couple of guys and a couple of girls coming and going. People trying to get acting gigs, modeling, and singing contracts. Can't say for sure who's there tonight. He has a guy that does security there, so it's a safe place," said Dexter.

"I guess that would be pretty cool," she answered.

"Okay. I'll step out and call him. I don't have any cell signal in here."

Might have found a place to stay tonight I'll keep you updated;
Geraldine texted her sister while waiting to hear back from Dexter
who'd stepped outside.

Dexter stepped outside the waiting room and onto the curb
and touched a number on his phone.

"Hello. Who am I speaking to?" was the answer.

"This is Dexter."

"Yeah, Dexter, have you got something for me?"

"I'm in Chattanooga at the bus station. Headed back to
Atlanta. I met up with this pretty black girl about eighteen. Wants
to be a singer. I told her I knew a guy that helped people get
started in music and that I was working for you."

"OK. I'll meet you at the station and you can stay there too.
There is another girl there and George is looking out for things
there. Does she seem to be using?"

"Nothing obvious," Dexter replied.

"See you in a couple of hours." The guy clicked off.

A few minutes later, Dexter walked back in to where
Geraldine was sitting. "You are all set," he said with that same
pleasant smile as before. "He said you can stay at the house, and
he'll see what he can do to get you started finding some work.
You are lucky. There is one girl there in and out. You might not
even see her."

"Thanks, Dexter. It was lucky I ran into you. What's this
guy's name? The one we're meeting?"

"His name is Max Johnson," he said with a knowing smile.

Geraldine sent a text to her sister: *Tell Mamma Lois not to worry
I have a safe place to stay Mr. Johnson is going to help me get my singing
career started Talk to you soon. XOXO*

Chapter 16

Russ woke up in his old bed in the new house. In the last few days, his life had seen a lot of changes and not all were to his liking. As he sat at the little dining room table overlooking the valley, he was once again alone. Sure, he had a couple of good friends including Chad Freeman and his wife, the folks at the fly shop were certainly friendly, if not real friends, and then there was Barry and Wayne at the sheriff's office.

Miriam, well, maybe she could be considered a friend, but he certainly wouldn't be hearing much from her. He still had not spoken to Nancy since she had left him the voicemail. Hardly someone to be thought of as a friend. And, most of his old friends in Marietta were never heard from anymore. Just the way the world works: no steps forward and many back. *Where to, next?*

He clicked on Google and started looking at some of the missing children and missing persons sites. More than he realized.

There were pictures, names, birthdays, and pleas from family members. Despair. Hopelessness. Tears. Over a half dozen posted just that one day.

Russ ran across a website for a group dealing with missing and exploited children. They listed the numbers of children reported missing annually in several countries. Among them Australia with an estimated twenty thousand per year, Canada with over forty-five thousand, Germany with about one hundred thousand, India about ninety-six thousand, Russia about forty-five thousand, the UK with over one hundred and twelve, and in the US a staggering four hundred and sixty thousand.

Some countries did not publish figures, and the totals in all the countries were likely not to be include all those who were actually missing.

At any rate, Russ thought, *the numbers are mind blowing, and add to those many adult aged men and women that go missing and unaccounted for, and it is easy to see why missing persons reports can seem to be not that important to a law enforcement agency when the system is bloated with reports.* Some, of course, are resolved, and the abductor apprehended when the child was taken by a disgruntled family member.

Other cases, far too many to know for sure, the victim is sold, murdered, abused, and or held against their will as a worker, sex slave, or prostitute. Some moved from state to state and country to country. They are bound by confinement, drug dependency, and physical violence. They are put on a one-way road to nowhere by people who are totally without conscience or human compassion.

Russ had to walk away from the computer, and he stood looking out the window down to the Madison River Valley below.

He was wondering what he would do if he had a child taken or lost in this fashion. He and Sarah had never had children, but he knew she would have been a wonderful mother and felt she would have made him a good father by her example.

But he shuddered at the thought of how he would react in this situation. He knew he would be a dangerous hunter if it was his child.

Could the cop in Helena with children of his own actually be involved in something as inhumane as this? And if he is, how do they prove it?

Russ typed in a text to Teresa Walker in Butte: *I talked to someone who has some experience with missing and adducted children about your concerns and one thing she suggested was that if you happened to see one of these situations again you might watch If the girl should go to the restroom maybe you could go in and ask if she is ok Be careful not to appear threatening to the girl as she might think you are a danger yourself. Especially if there is no problem.*

Russ then dialed Sheriff Steinbrenner.

"Good morning. Steinbrenner here," he answered.

"Hi, Sheriff," said Russ. "I hope I am not waking you up."

"So, you're worried after you make the call if you are waking me up?" said the sheriff.

"I guess you do have a point, Sheriff. But, since I have you, maybe we can chat."

"Chat? I don't chat. I don't think you're too good at it either. I discuss things and inform people and get informed. I don't do chatting," laughed the sheriff.

"Duly noted. I was talking to someone on this possible issue that Teresa Walker brought up related to the cop and the girls. I also looked at the information online and am just realizing how big the problem is."

"Fortunately, we don't see much of it here. We get an occasional situation where a spouse runs off with a kid, but we always have gotten them back with no serious after effects."

"I really don't know anything I can do in this situation at the truck stop unless we get something else to go on and not having any legal standing there; all I'll do is waste my time," said Russ. "I was in Salt Lake over the weekend for Miriam's wedding and saw Debra Taylor. She has had some training in the human trafficking area. She had a suggestion or two, but it all comes back to nothing to go on. And, by the way, I didn't see you and the Mrs. there."

"We got an invitation to the wedding, but we had some other family things going on and couldn't make it to Salt Lake. I hope she married a nice guy," replied the sheriff.

"From what I saw and heard, she did well on all counts. He seems like a good guy, and besides that he is doing very well financially."

"Good to hear. Well, we don't have much going on here at the moment other than the usual stuff. I'm happy to report that we have no murders, terrorist groups, or major drug operations going on. None that we know of, anyway. We are seeing and hearing about families involved in meth getting really messed up. We have seen a big increase in that activity. If we get a big case, I may be calling you," said Barry.

"I'm sitting by the phone. Can't wait to have someone shooting at me and shooting my truck up again," Russ answered.

"I know what that's like, if you remember."

"I do seem to remember something like that. I think we can both do without repeats. See, ya, Barry."

"Bye, Russ. Go fishing."

Now that's a great idea, thought Russ just as his phone lit up. The screen showed *Teresa Walker.*

"Hello, Teresa."

"Good morning. I saw your text. Nothing happening that I've seen in the past few days. But I'll watch and see if speaking to one of the girls is a possibility. Problem is, I don't know if it's one of the people Marchman is meeting until *he* comes in, and he is usually only here about a minute before he and the girl are gone."

"How about the security cameras? Any chance on getting one a little more aimed at the back area where they seem to go?

"I can try, but the manager may just reset it back how they have it. I don't know how closely they look at the monitors or the tapes."

Russ replied, "I would guess they don't look at them at all unless there is a problem reported and they are asked to check. Do they have a security person on staff?"

"I'm pretty sure they contract the security to an outside vendor. Something like Valiant Security, I believe. I don't recall seeing them going in the little office where the monitors are. It's usually always locked. May all be on some web service and no actual film here."

"Well, Teresa, I guess there isn't much else to do short of calling the local police. I can't be there on watch, myself and couldn't arrest anyone if I were."

If you get more info, you can always call me. If this guy is trafficking in young women and girls, I would love to catch him, and I'm sure you would too. Get us something to go on."

Russ poured himself a coffee and sat looking at the screen on the laptop with all the Google searches on missing kids pulled up. He could feel the pain and heartache on each of those web pages.

Chapter 17

Darin

Darin Marchman had a new package to pick up, and he was beginning to get nervous. He was going to Wayne's far too often and someday; someone was likely to spot him. Going inside had some risks, but keeping his vehicle from being spotted was important in his mind.

He had pocketed quite a bit of money. He and his wife were caught up with their bills, and maybe it was getting time to quit while he was ahead. But the money was hard to part with.

Darin always arrived early in the parking lot at *Wayne's* and watched all those coming and going. Especially law enforcement.

Once inside, he'd make a quick look around before proceeding and was prepared to turn and go without making contact. Should there be a familiar face, he would simply duck out or say hello and ignore the person with the package.

There was always a chance the package, usually a young girl, would make a scene or attract attention. But by the time they got to Darin, they had been drugged, knocked around, threatened, and sexually exploited. They had been instilled with enough fear that they did not dare to cause any problems. Their families were threatened with harm if they failed to cooperate. And, they had signed contracts. Though they probably actually had no legal standing, they served as more leverage in the game of domination and exploitation. A game where there were no rules. No pity. No consciences. These were all blocked out by dollar signs.

This trip was different, too, in another major way: his delivery was not being dropped off at some dark corner of a shopping center parking lot. He had a location in Silver Star on Montana Hwy 41. The directions were brief but clear. *Boat launch ramp parking lot on Jefferson River Montana Hwy 41 and Primrose Lane 11:30 PM Just past mining museum on left Motor Home.* It was less than forty miles away.

Darin did not like the fact that his vehicle would be visible, but the area could be easily scouted before pulling in. At that time of night there would not likely be any boaters coming and going. With only about one hundred and fifty people in the small community, traffic should be light in the town that once had two thousand miners and a hotel. His rental car would have stolen plates.

As he sat in the parking lot and watched at *Wayne's*, trucks were constantly coming and going. So were cars and RV's. Lots of people going in the restaurants and shops and restrooms. He was looking for one man with a young black woman. The young woman would probably be assisted and a little unsteady.

If anyone asked, she wasn't feeling well. He would give them a few minutes inside before going in for the handoff.

Geraldine

In the past several days, Geraldine had undergone sexual and physical abuse and drugs. Her phone had been taken away and turned off. Her driver's license and the one credit card that belonged to her grandmother were gone and she had no money. Her identity was wiped away.

The house in College Park was more like a prison with a full-time guard and boarded up windows and doors. Her new musician friend from the bus ride to Atlanta was long gone, and she was in a frantic state and afraid for her life. As it was explained to her, *open your mouth and you're dead and so is your sister and grandmother.* She was on her way to Las Vegas on Route 90 where a job paying good money was waiting, so they said. The trucker she was riding with was doing her a favor, they said. Her dream of starting a new life away from her grandmother and sister was now a nightmare.

Geraldine had been able to avoid some of the pills she had been given. She had learned a few tricks back in the old neighborhood and could pretend to swallow a pill at a party and then push it up between her teeth and cheek. She could then stick out her tongue and it would appear she had swallowed it. She was not quite as out of it as she appeared when they entered the restaurant. She had also managed to get a ball point pen from the driver's truck and hide it inside her blouse on the way out from Boston.

Once inside the truck stop, she asked to go to the bathroom.

The driver had positioned them at a table just outside the restroom doors where the tables were usually open as most people tried to avoid sitting near them. She wrote a quick note on a paper towel and stuck it in the crack of the stall divider. It read, simply:

I'm Geraldine Bailey from Chattanooga.
Being held against my will.
Taking me to Los Vegos in truck.
I'm the black girl just outside door.
Help.

Just then, she was frightened when she heard the restroom door open. and she lifted here feet so they could not be seen by anyone looking in. As soon as the door closed, she rushed out of the stall hoping someone would be there. There was no one.

Just as she returned to the table, a man wearing a baseball cap pulled low over his face walked up and said softly, "Come with me, and don't cause me any trouble." She walked out with the man holding her hand with a firm grip. She complied with his instructions. She had seen in previous days what could happen if she didn't.

Chapter 18

Teresa

Teresa Walker looked to see where the man was that had been seated at the table with the girl a few minutes earlier. The restaurant was crowded, and that was not her station, but she had seen them come in as she had been carrying an order to a table across the restaurant. Returning, she saw the girl was gone and thought that this might be a chance for her to find her alone in the restroom.

Just as Teresa opened the door, she was called to come get an order, so she only got a quick look and saw that no one was in the restroom. Opportunity lost. In another two or three minutes, both the girl and the driver were gone. She had missed Darin Marchman coming and going as it had happened so fast in the busy scene.

Geraldine

"Get in the back seat," the man said, and Geraldine obeyed him silently.

They were gone from the parking lot in a few seconds, and Geraldine was still acting as though she was in a drugged stupor. No matter where she was going, Las Vegas or anywhere else, she knew she had to try to get away and call her grandmother and the cops. She wished she had a weapon.

Geraldine laid over in the seat as though she was asleep, having no idea how long she would be in the car. She briefly heard him mutter something about a ranch.

The man drove down the quite stretch of highway. Glancing out the window, she saw a sign that something about Silver Star. On the right were huge steel wheels and rusting equipment that were relics from the mining days. Now relics in an outdoor museum.

In less than an hour, they were pulling into a lot that had a river boat ramp. A large, expensive looking motor home was parked by the ramp. Geraldine flinched – hadn't one of the girls at the College Park house warned of what happened on those things? A one-way ride to hell.

There were no other vehicles in the lot but the motorhome and none in sight on the road. The driver pulled in as his phone lit up with a message. Everything was a go, it seemed, so he pulled in. The driver seemed antsy to Geraldine. Maybe he was new at this or something unexpected had taken place that had him on edge?

She kept her eyes closed – no more peeking out the windows for the time being. Geraldine could hear the car pull to a stop.

The front door opened, and the interior light came on as the man got out to meet the driver of the motor home and get his money. He then opened the door and said to Geraldine, "Get up and get out of the car."

Geraldine did not respond but lay still on the seat.

"Get up and get out of the car," he repeated in a stern and louder voice.

She still did not respond.

He turned to the driver of the motor home and said, "She has been out since I picked her up. They must have given her too much of whatever they were using on her. I'll pick her up and hand her to you. Leave the coach door open."

The man leaned into the car and dragged her out, and as he was picking her up, Geraldine made a fierce stabbing motion toward his face with the ball point pen she had been hiding. He managed to turn his head just enough to avoid the pen hitting him in the face but not enough to avoid it hitting him in the neck and plunging in deep with a pain like he had never felt before. He let out a scream.

Startled and in severe pain, he dropped Geraldine and fell back toward the car, hitting his head on the bottom of the door frame. He let out another scream and yelled to the motorhome driver, "The bitch stabbed me with something. Help me!"

Geraldine was on her feet and running toward the highway.

Darin

The coach driver looked at the girl and then at Darin Marchman who was trying to see in the dark parking lot how badly he was hurt and if she had hit a major artery.

The guy looked again towards the girl who had already cleared the lot and was running down the road back toward the lights of Silver Star. Darin gritted his teeth up at the man who seemed to be debating with himself his best course of action. He likely felt he wouldn't be able to catch the girl now.

"Do something, you idiot!" Marchman roared.

Apparently, that wasn't the push in the right direction the man needed. Electing not to get involved with the guy lying beside a car bleeding and yelling, the man grabbed the envelope with the money and hurried towards his motor home.

"Hey!" Marchman exclaimed. "That's my money, you bastard!"

The man sped off in his motor home in the opposite direction than the girl had headed, away from Silver Star.

Marchman pulled the pen out of his neck and let out another yell of pain. He was bleeding but not like if a major artery had been cut. He managed to get to his feet and could still see the girl running and stumbling toward town. He had to stop her.

He got in the car and sped out of the lot and overtook the girl quickly. She tried to run to the right, and he came at her with the car. She made a quick move to the left toward the other side of the road, and the fender hit her a glancing blow, and she went down. Marchman stopped the car and got out holding his small .38 revolver that he always carried in an ankle holster.

The girl, bruised and bleeding, got up and started trying to run back in the other direction. One of her legs was certainly broken. Marchman fired at her twice. She fell face down on the pavement of Montana Hwy 41.

Marchman then realized what he'd done. *Oh, hell. You stupid idiot*, he said to himself.

Just as he started to go to where she was and get her back in the car, headlights appeared coming north toward him at a fast clip. It could be anyone. He had no choice. Get in the car and go. Fast. Things had gotten bad for Marchman in a hurry.

Wanda

Montana Highway Patrol officer, Wanda Carter, was doing her normal patrol run on Hwy 41. A seven-year veteran, she was one of the new breeds of troopers. Female, married, a mother, and dedicated. She had always wanted to be a Montana trooper.

She saw the car about a half mile ahead. She had not noticed it ahead on the road in front of her but really thought nothing of it until she saw what appeared to be a young woman lying in the road in a pool of blood.

She stopped and turned on her emergency lights and put the light bar on to better see, and she picked up the mike for the car radio. The Montana Statewide Interoperable Public Safety Radio System helped law enforcement cover the vast spaces of Montana where normal mobile radios and cellphones did not always work.

"This is Unit 127. I have a possible 10-57 one mile south of Silver Star. Appears to be a female victim. I am 10-78. The victim seems to be alive but is seriously injured. I need an ambulance at once!"

"Roger, Unit 127. Do you need back up?"

"I will need an accident investigation team, and we need to notify the Madison County Sheriff. There is no one else here at the scene."

"Is there any description on the vehicle involved?"

"No. I did not arrive on the scene in time to get a look at it."

"Ambulance is on the way from Twin Bridges EMS. ETA seven minutes."

The EMS truck arrived, and they set to work on the unconscious girl. The EMS was instructed to carry the girl to the trauma center in Bozeman due to the severity of her injuries. They were soon gone, leaving Trooper Carter to try and start defining the crime scene and piecing together what had happened to a young black woman on a quiet stretch of road at night. No ID and nothing to identify her. *What was she doing out here?* Just the first of many questions to come.

A deputy arrived several minutes later from Madison County.

Trooper Carter asked, "What took you so long?"

"We were all at that meth lab trailer that blew up tonight down off 278. Big mess. Explosion, fire, and we still don't know for sure how many people were hurt."

"Sorry, I didn't mean to be beating you up," she said. She and Madison County Deputy Charlie Bass set about trying to find out what happened, marking off the accident scene, and seeing if there was a handbag or any form of ID to be found.

A few more minutes in, and Trooper Carter got a call on her tactical radio she was wearing.

"This is Unit 127, Corporal Carter, go ahead."

"The EMS guys say the girl you found on 41 appeared to have gunshot wounds. Not confirmed by the hospital, yet. But that may affect how you handle the scene. May be a shooter involved."

"Understood. Madison County is on the scene, too, and I'll advise them," she said.

Deputy Bass heard the exchange. "It looks like we have a year's worth of work piling on in one night. Just great! I guess we're looking for shell casings, too."

They put out flares and warning triangles and blocked the road with their two vehicles as best they could. Looking for evidence was bad enough in the daylight. At night, it could seem impossible.

Deputy Bass called in. "This is Bass. I'm up at Silver Star with MHP Trooper Carter. We have been advised by MHP that the person she found up here is likely a gunshot victim. Please advise the sheriff. Over."

"Roger, Charlie," came the reply from Sheriff Steinbrenner. "I'm short of people right now. Can you make it for a while till I can see if I can get some help? Dunkin can't drive. I may have to get some back up."

Chapter 19

Extra deputies weren't on every street corner in Virginia City, Montana. But there was one guy who had helped them on a few cases as a special investigator. Sheriff Steinbrenner punched Russell Baker's number on his phone. It rang several times.

"Hello. God, do you know what time it is?" Russ spoke into his phone when it startled him awake. He rubbed his eyes, glancing over at his alarm clock.

Sheriff Steinbrenner's voice boomed through the phone, "I can look if you want me to. But really, I don't give a crap. I seem to remember you calling at some ungodly hour."

"I don't remember calling you at 2:15 AM, Sheriff," replied Russ. "This better be important, or I'm calling the cops. What couldn't wait till 8:00 AM once I've had my coffee?"

"Hit and run, possible shooting victim up at Silver Star by the boat launch ramp on 41. Two officers on scene. Deputy Bass and a MHP Trooper. Get that badge and your gun and get your ass up there."

"Well, now! This sounds like a job for the Super Sheriff or the assistant Super Sheriff, Dunkin."

"I have no time for small talk. I'm up to my chin in meth lab explosion victims, and Dunkin had nothing better to do than have a mower accident. He's going to be off his feet for several weeks. Can't drive. So, that leaves me having to call in some temporary help, even if it is of low quality."

"You may be a great sheriff, but you are a lousy salesman," said Russ, slowing sitting up in bed.

"I know. I'm better at about 8:00 AM, myself. But, look at it this way. At least *somebody* needs you."

"Now that hurt," said Russ, already trying to find some clothes and get dressed.

"Will you go, or do I have to beg?"

"I'm out the door. Let em know I'm coming and that I was the best you could do on short notice. I seem to have misplaced my radio."

"You don't have a radio, Baker."

Russ replied as he opened the door of his truck, "Oh. Right. Now I remember."

Russ had about fifty miles to cover. He turned on his emergency flashers and headed toward Silver Star. He figured he would not get a ticket from MHP this time.

Russell arrived at the scene in Silver Star and pulled in behind the Montana Highway Patrol car. They had blocked off the road as much as possible and strung some crime scene tape up to try to maintain control over the scene.

"You are in a restricted crime scene!" the trooper exclaimed when he crossed the tape into the area where the group of responding personnel were working. She shined her light directly in his face and snarled, "Unless you want to be handcuffed and put under arrest, get back across the tape!"

Momentarily blinded, Russ raised both hands above his head. "Whoa, there, ma'am. I'm with the Madison County Sheriff's office. Russell Baker is my name. I was sent here by Sheriff Steinbrenner to assist. Don't shoot, please. I believe Charlie Bass knows me."

The trooper glanced at Deputy Bass who gave a nod and said, "I know him. He's a part time fishing guide. Claims he was a cop in Georgia, and that's why he says *sho-nuff* and *yes ma'am*," he said with a chuckle. "How are you, Russ?"

"I was doing fine until I got a call about forty-five minutes ago. The sheriff says you've had a busy night. What do I need to do here to help?"

The trooper introduced herself as Corporal Wanda Carter and showed Russ what they had found. Not much.

A pool of drying blood on the pavement showed where the girl had fallen on the pavement. They had put some tape around the unholy mess.

"Did you get a blood sample for the lab?" he asked.

"Yes. I did two and gave Deputy Bass one," she said. "We haven't found any sign of a broken light or any car parts as of yet."

Russ asked, "You feel like it was a car that was leaving the scene?"

"Pretty sure, but I was a long way off and didn't see much of what went down," she said.

"Well, I'll bet you're correct," Russ said. "Corporal Carter, how long can you stay here?"

"I am supposed to be at the office by 6:30 AM to turn in reports and sign out by 7:00 AM. My shift is over at 7:00 AM. I can work the scene here until about 6:00 if you think you need me."

"That would help when traffic starts picking up; it will be daylight about 6:00 AM, so we can give this place a better going over. Can they send us another trooper to help until we finish here?" asked Russ.

"I'll call and tell them you are requesting one," she said.

"I think the sheriff will ask for DCI to get involved since it's a shooting, apparently. We need their crime scene people," said Bass.

Russ agreed with a nod and spoke to the both of them. "Let me ask you each, what does your instinct tell you here? Where would this woman be running from? Some place down the road, maybe? Was she in the car and thrown out or jumped out? Did the car you saw leaving have any connection to what happened, or did they just happen by?"

Russ paused and then continued, "And one other question, Corporal, do you think the car was stopped when you came in sight, and, if so, on which side of her? Past her toward Silver Star of before it got to her, back down the road."

She thought for a minute.

"If it was the car that hit her, I would think it was past her. When I came on scene, I saw her in the road and stopped before getting to her. I think most people would do that unless they swerved and went past her lying there and then stopped. If they hit her and then stopped, we might find skid marks on the pavement after where she was found."

Russ continued, "Okay. What about where she could likely be running or walking from to be here on the road?"

Deputy Bass said, "I believe the house on the corner of Primrose is for sale and is empty right now. We can check the next house after the sun comes up and see if they know anything. Maybe they heard something."

As they stood there in the eerie darkness that stretched out past the flashing lights of the two police vehicles, Russ suggested, "What if she got out of a vehicle at the boat launch ramp? There are people getting in and out of vehicles there all the time, and it's the most rational place for someone to meet up along here. Last time I checked, getting out of a stopped vehicle was more appealing than getting out of a moving one."

"That's a long shot, Russ, but what else have we got?" said Charlie Bass.

"Let's take some yellow crime scene tape and a couple of triangles and block off the entrance before some people show up at the ramp," said Russ.

"You are going to piss some people off, Russ," commented Deputy Bass.

"Well, let's blame it on the Montana Highway Patrol officer on scene. She'll be gone by then," said Russ.

"And I was just beginning to like you, Russ," said the trooper.

"Well, you lasted longer than most of my so-called friends," he laughed.

Charlie and Russ walked back down the 250 feet to the entrance to the parking area and stretched out the roll of tape.

Chapter 20

Darin

Darin Marchman had a terrible pain in his neck and shoulders from the stabbing by the young woman. He was bloody, and the driver's side door and seat were bloody. Fortunately for him, the pen had missed hitting a vital artery, but now he had a bloody mess in a rental car, a blood-soaked shirt, and somehow he had to avoid his wife or anyone from seeing the mess. And, he needed treatment for the wound. One thing was for sure: his days in the human trafficking business were over. And, the money was gone.

Tonight, he was stabbed and then he had been involved in a hit and run and shooting. Possibly a murder. His whole life was now hanging by a thread.

Marchman knew that he would be better off if the girl were dead. There were no likely witnesses to the hit and run or the shooting. The fellow in the motor home was long gone, probably, and would not be filing any reports of the stabbing. As bad as it would be, he hoped she was dead.

He had to think of something to explain the injury to his wife as she was the only person he could turn to for help. Going to a hospital was out of the question as there would be too many persons with questions of their own. Then, there was the car.

His wife would help him but not if she really knew what he had been doing and how he had gotten hurt. He decided to go home and get her to clean up the wound and get rid of the bloody clothes. Then they would clean up the rental car tomorrow, and he would call in sick.

His story to her would be that he was attacked on the security job and that he didn't want the department to know as it might cost him his job. The attacker, he would say, got away. The story would be that the car belonged to the security company, so he didn't want them to know about the incident either. She might be suspicious, but it was worth a try. So, home he went.

He got out of the car in Helena and let his garage door up with the keypad. He pulled the rental inside and closed the door quickly so none of the neighbors would see, though this was unlikely at this time of the morning.

The bleeding from the puncture wound had all but stopped with him applying pressure with his t-shirt he'd removed in the car. It had soaked up a lot of the blood. He wanted to clean up as much as possible before his wife saw the blood on him or in the car. That would only serve to make the situation look worse.

He took off his clothes and put them in a trash can in the garage. He'd do something with them later. The shower in the guest bedroom would not wake up his wife if he could slip in quietly, get cleaned up, and maybe find a good bandage. Maybe his wife wouldn't notice at all after he put on a clean shirt – it wasn't nearly as bad as he thought, so maybe he wouldn't need her help after all. But it was still hurting like hell.

There was the gun, too. It would need to be wiped clean and disposed of. It was not associated with him and could not be traced back to him. He had picked it up when he had arrested a small-time burglar who had a collection of stolen guns. Nobody had ever missed it. Not even the guy he had stolen it from.

He finally got cleaned up and wiped up some of the blood from the car. He was exhausted. It was pushing 5:30 AM when he slipped into bed. His wife roused enough to ask, "What are you doing?"

"I was in the bathroom. I'm not feeling too well, so I may call in and stay home today. Nothing to worry about. Go back to sleep."

Teresa

In Butte, the day was started as usual for Teresa Walker at *Wayne's* as she walked in to start her early shift. She would be on 7:00 till 3:00. An okay shift, but the tips were better in the evening as truckers, families, and workers were getting off for the day and were pulling off the road.

She walked in as the cleaning crew was carting out the trash from the restrooms and cleaning up the restaurant.

They would empty the large trash cans into big containers and recycling bins behind a high fence that blocked them from the customers' view.

Wayne's was a top-notch place, and they kept it clean around the clock. That was not working in Geraldine Bailey's favor.

The note she'd written asking for help had been pulled out of the crack in the stall where she'd put it hoping someone would find it. And they did find it. But, without reading it or giving it a second thought, an employee had crumpled up Geraldine's fate and threw it into the trash sack they had been carrying. Never to be seen again.

Now, Geraldine lay in the ICU unit at the hospital in Bozeman. Broken in body, mind, and spirit. Robbed of everything her Mama Lois had tried to give her. Hit by a car, shot, and discarded. Making matters worse, no one knew who she was or where she was from.

Neither Teresa or Geraldine knew how close they had come to each other. Fate or just bad luck? Really, it was neither. It was just bad people doing bad things.

Chapter 21

The sun was beginning to be seen over the mountains, and Russ and Deputy Bass were starting to feel the effects of a long night, no sleep, and no results. The light would help, but with it would come some new possible problems. Traffic would be picking up, and people would be showing up for use of the boat ramp. Mad citizens.

The MHP had assigned a new unit to help with traffic, and one of their accident investigators would be on scene from the Butte District office. They had jurisdiction for the MHP in the area.

Then there would be a DCI investigator, requested by the sheriff in maters where forensic evidence was important, and longer reach of authority was involved. The DCI could choose to assist only, and Madison County would be in charge of evidence and the chain of custody of such evidence. If DCI decided to take over the investigation, then Madison County deputies would not be in control. Russ and Deputy Bass would become errand-boys. The higher the profile of the case, and if multiple counties were involved, the greater the chance of the State taking over.

The challenge was to get as much help as possible and yet not make it appear this was a career builder case. That was tricky.

And, the sheriff was likely to show up in a while, too. Russ, the temporary and part-time investigator for Madison County, would be the lowest man on the totem pole and garner little respect from the professionals on the scene. Except, maybe, from the sheriff. He needed to get as much done as he could before all that territorial posturing started.

As soon as the MHP unit showed up, Russ said to Deputy Bass, "Charlie, would you walk down to the corner with me and around to the boat ramp? Maybe we can check it out before the circus starts. If you have any crime scene tape and evidence bags, please bring some."

The two walked the shoulder of the road back to the corner of Primrose and then down to the entrance. With the gravel lot, finding a foot print would be difficult.

There was evidence that a car had left the parking lot with its wheels throwing gravel but no way to determine the type of tread from the loose dirt and gravel mess they were looking at. It could have been a fisherman or some teenager showing off for all they knew.

Russ started on the river side near the ramp, and Deputy Bass stared at the edge of the lot nearer the road. There were numerous tracks from big wheeled pick-ups pulling boat trailers, cigarette butts, and assorted small trash items that you might would find at any parking facility.

Then Deputy Bass called across to Russ, "Hey. Can you come over here for a minute? Take a look and see if you think this is anything."

As Russ approached, Bass continued, "Some big vehicle was here. And, it made a hurried departure. You can see where the front wheels were turned to a very sharp angle and pushed up a rut in the gravel. It may be enough tread to identify. Then, take a look at this."

On the gravel, Deputy Bass had marked with an evidence bag a ball point pen, and with light from a flashlight, it had what looked like dried blood on it.

"Does that look like blood on the pen to you, Russ?" he asked.

"Great work, Charlie. Let's take some cell phone pictures of the tread and the pen. We'll leave it until DCI shows up. I think I have some emergency flares in the box on my truck we can stick in the ground to hold the tape and block off this area. May be a wild goose chase, but you don't see a ballpoint pen in a parking lot with blood on it every day. Let's hope it's not barbeque sauce."

"What do you think made these track's, Charlie?" Russ asked.

"Something with big tires, several of them a long wheel base. Could be a delivery type truck. And something else left here in a big hurry. Looks like a regular car. Maybe the one that the trooper saw. A potential witness or a potential suspect. They could have stopped to use that bathroom over there. Should we check it, too?"

"I'll flip a coin with you to see who gets that job," said Russ.

"Russ, I think I have seniority when it comes to bathroom inspection assignments."

Russ took the hint. He was not the senior man, and he was not really in charge.

"I will go check out the john," said Russ. "But at least you can buy the coffee." Then he added, "Besides, I've taken a lot of crap lately, so I'm used to it."

Bass replied, "I'll take that deal every day. Especially since there's no coffee shop close by."

The bathroom was what one would expect. Looking for evidence there was worse than looking for a needle in the haystack. Russ decided he would dig for evidence somewhere else.

After marking the area with tape and taking pictures, they started back to the accident scene just as their first fishing boat showed up trying to use the ramp. The driver got out and started to take the tape down they had just put up.

Deputy Bass, called out, "Don't take that down. You can't come in here right now!"

The driver insisted that he needed to use the ramp and had paying clients. He then made a comment about the deputy not having authority to close the ramp area. That was a mistake.

Bass walked over to him, and Russ followed. Although Russ was not armed, Bass was and was not about to take any guff from the guide or his clients. "Get back in the truck and go somewhere else or," he put his hand on his service weapon, "I will put you in that police car, under arrest, for interference with a crime scene and anything else I can think of. Your choice."

The guide quickly decided that leaving was the best option. His getting himself arrested and possibly his client too would not make for a good day on the river.

Russ decided no comment was necessary but gave Bass a thumbs up.

The DCI forensics officer had arrived as they got to their scene. She introduced herself as Agent Shirley Davis, and they briefed her on what they had found there and at the parking lot. She set to work.

Russ turned and asked, "Are you able to collect a blood sample from the splatter on the road and in that gravel lot?"

"Yes. Should be able to. Do you think there is blood in the parking lot?" she asked.

"Well, we think the ball point pen has blood on it. We are guessing. If it does, there may be some blood on the ground. Whose it is will be anybody's guess at this point. It may be on the road too if it was the same person."

Sarcastically, she said, "How many miles of road would you like checked?"

Russ responded without thinking how his tone changed, "Twin Bridges to I-90 might be enough."

"Cheeez. A little touchy there, aren't you?" she questioned.

"I was a lot nicer about nine o'clock last night. Before I got called out here," he said without his tone changing too much.

She seemed to decide it best to continue with her investigation and leave whom she considered an amateur detective alone. Russ stopped and turned, "It's been a long night. I'll tell the sheriff to look out for the blood splatter report."

She got the message. The request was official.

Blood splatter can be detected in a number of ways. Usually on TV shows, they used a spray bottle of Luminol and UV light. It could also be seen with another technique using Flourescin and special goggles and LCV could help in photographing blood evidence. The DCI people knew all the techniques.

Sheriff Steinbrenner, who had also been up all night, arrived, and after a quick update said, "Russ, you and Charlie need to go home and get some rest. We'll see if they come up with anything more."

Russ responded, "You look like you could use a nap, yourself."

"Yea, but I'm making the big bucks," he said.

"Good. So far, all I have is a promise of a cup of coffee from Charlie," said Russ.

"That's more than I've ever gotten from Charlie," replied the sheriff. "How did you manage that?"

Before Russ could reply, Charlie injected with a laugh, "Has to do with seniority."

Russ walked to his truck and headed to Ennis and bed. He made a call on the way back to John at the fly shop.

"Looks like I won't be taking any trips out for a few days. I'm helping Madison County on a case, and I don't know how long that will take."

"Well maybe you can catch a big one. Get it?" responded John, trying to be funny.

"Yes. I got it," Russ said, his tone indicating his lack of amusement. "I'm going home and going to bed."

Chapter 22

Russell could barely stay awake as he headed home. He was exhausted and hungry. He headed straight to the shower once he finally arrived. He wrapped a towel around himself when he got out and was headed to the kitchen but fell across the bed instead. He was asleep almost instantly and was sleeping soundly when the phone started ringing. *Who could be calling so early?*

He searched around for the phone and saw it was the sheriff and that it was a little after one o'clock in the afternoon.

"Don't you ever sleep?" he asked.

"Usually. But lately we seem to have some people wanting to keep us awake at night in this little county."

"You keep calling me before I have my coffee. I'm really not at my best."

"I have some preliminary information from DCI."

"The young lady they sent must have worked all night, but she did conclude that there is blood on the pen you found in the parking lot, but it is not the same as the victim. She thinks she may have found some blood on the ground and some gravel, too. They are testing the samples to confirm," the sheriff said.

"Well, that may help us. I have to give credit to Charlie Bass on finding the pen, but all we have to do is find a match from a few million possibilities," said Russ.

"Nice of you, but Charlie said he would have probably never looked in that lot for any evidence if not for you. Anyway, the girl is critical. Broken up and a glancing bullet to the head and one through the lungs."

"Touch and go and no identification. And, the gun seems to have been a .38, so we won't likely find any shell casings"

"Pocket gun or ladies handbag gun, you think? Snub nose, I'll bet," Russ said.

"Add that to your million things that need checking," said the sheriff.

"Bass is happy to have you in charge as lead officer on this, if that's okay with you."

"If you want. He seems like a competent guy," replied Russ.

"He is, but attempted murder cases are not his usual day's work."

"Lord, Sheriff, I'm a fishing guide for Goodness's sake."

"Keep telling yourself that, Baker, and you might actually convince yourself that it's true. As a fishing guide, you're at best a 7 or 8. And a detective I'd give you a 9+."

"Not a 10? I guess I need to work on that."

"Let's drop it before we get engaged. I already have a wife, Russ. What do you think we do next?"

Russ thought for a second. "I will drive back up and check with the locals and the house down the road to see if I can get a lead on who was in the parking lot or if anyone saw anything. I guess it'll be a while before we can interview the victim."

"Think you need backup?"

"I think I'll be okay today. But I will carry my service weapon in case I run into the individual with the .38. By the way, that MHP Corporal Carter was tough to hang in there with us last night. I hope Bass doesn't welch on that coffee."

"I think the trooper's father was a cop somewhere. She came with good reviews and just moved to the Butte office. Don't get any ideas. She's married with two or three kids. As far as the coffee from Bass, you can kiss that goodbye. Come by later today or tomorrow, and I'll see if I can get you Dunkin's car."

With that, the sheriff was gone. Russ wondered if he'd been home at all since last night.

In a few minutes, Russ was in his truck headed back to the crime scene. When he arrived, the crime scene tape and traffic triangles were gone. Only some spray paint and a dark spot on the road that had been left by the girl's blood remained. In a few days, no one would have any idea a crime had been committed there, much less care.

Sheriff Steinbrenner had called on Russel Baker to help out on the case because he knew Russell would care enough to find the shooter if he or she could be found. Russell couldn't help himself. He knew Russ was a very good detective and Madison County was lucky to have him.

A walk around the road scene, and the parking lot did not turn up anything new. Not one piece of broken headlight or car trim anywhere. As Bass had said, there was a *for sale* sign on the house across on the corner, and a walk over to look around there turned up nothing. Russ hoped there was a security camera there, but there wasn't a camera or even a security light. That house was about two hundred feet from the entrance to the boat launch lot. The next house down was only a little further, but the position made it unlikely they would have noticed anything, but he had to check it out.

A knock brought a lady to the door who was cautious about entering into any conversation with Russ until he showed his badge and ID. After she was satisfied it was safe, she opened the door and stepped out.

"We are being a little more careful since they found somebody shot at the corner last night," she said.

"I understand," said Russ. "That's what I'm investigating. I was up here all last night, and now I'm trying to see if anyone may have seen or heard anything that can help us."

"Don't know if we can help much. We came in from visiting my father near Missoula and got home about eleven o'clock. When we passed the boat launch lot, I was about half asleep, but my husband commented that it looked like someone was stopping overnight there in a motorhome. It was dark and hard to tell anything about it. There weren't any lights on in it, and it was off the side of the road out of view of our headlights. Don't know if that helps."

"Is that unusual for a motor home to be there?"

"No. Sometimes the fishermen meet guides there and leave their units parked there for the day. But not usually that late at night. And not overnight. There are no facilities there to hook up. There are several places in the area where someone can park a big RV, so it was really the timing that was weird."

"So, this was a big unit? What about color?"

"One of the biggest, I'd say. Hard to say on the color in the dark. Not sure."

"I guess you see quite a few of those coming through here?" Russ asked.

"Yes. And, you know, that spa down across the river has a lot of them coming and going. Lots of wealthy customers, I think."

"What place is that?"

"The Leonard Ranch. Kind of a dude ranch type thing, you know."

"I am not familiar with it, but thanks for telling me. Did you hear anything out of ordinary there last night?" he asked.

"No. I went to get a shower, and my husband turned on the TV. I guess we went to bed about twelve."

"Is he around anywhere?"

"He's gone to work and will be back about six," she said.

"I'll give you my card. If you two can think of anything else, please call me. We have a victim in bad shape in the hospital, and I'd really like to get the person responsible," Russ said.

Russ got directions to the ranch and started to leave. And, as he was leaving, he asked, "By the way," Russ asked, "Is there any place with a WIFI nearby I might can use? My cell service internet is pretty unreliable on my phone."

"My husband and I go up to the country store in Silver Star and use theirs."

"They have that fiber cable there and let people use it. Our satellite service is not always working well. They also have a couple or three computers in the corner that are free to the public if no one is using them. Gets people to stop in the store, I guess."

Russ pulled in to the country store and saw the *Free WIFI sign* in the window. He found the computers and luckily no one was using them when he arrived. He purchased a coffee and a sweet roll and started his background check on the Leonard Ranch. Russ was surprised at all of the information his search brought up on the ranch's history and the town of Silver Star.

The Leonard Cross River Ranch, or LCR Ranch and Spa as it was known by some, had been started in the late 1800's by the Leonardi brothers, Stefano and Vincenzo. They had changed their names after coming to Montana from Boston to Steven and Vince *Leonard.* This proved very useful in the days ahead as the Leonardi family in the East became more and more involved in organized crime and not many locals associated the Leonard Ranch with what was happening back in Boston.

Russ found several old newspaper articles regarding the Leonard's and how they were connected to the Leonardi family. Though they had tried to make a connection to the ranch and the rumors of criminal activity in Boston and Chicago, nothing was ever proven. But the stories caught Russ's attention.

By the time the Leonardi Brothers had arrived in the Jefferson River Valley, many of the early settlers from the Homestead act of 1862 were already at the point of giving up. Substituting reality for their dreams. Land was for sale. And with the backing of the family back east, the Leonardi Brothers, now known as Leonard, created what was now a 5000-acre ranch and spa.

It was a picture-perfect setting with the 10,400-foot Hollowtop Mountain in the distance and the very large Beaverhead-Deerlodge National Park in the mountain range behind the ranch. All near the old gold rush town of Silver Star, Montana. An area of big horn sheep, bears, mountain goats, and rams. Elk at various time and deer. Russ could see why people living in the smog and traffic of the big cities would come here.

The railroads made travel to the western states possible. The Easterners were awed by the space, mountains, wildlife, and sheer beauty. Snow on the peaks and cross-country skiing and hiking. Big game hunting and fishing.

Then came Prohibition. A major experiment in governing human behavior that had been approved by the states and the crowd in Washington. The Leonardi family was all set to cash in with night clubs and restaurants. Trucking, liquor, and produce businesses. And cash in they did. They became part of a new business category in the United States: organized crime. A grand idea to correct the moral behavior of Americans had become the catalyst for the most corruption and criminal behavior the country could imagine. Somehow, the Leonardi family seemed to stay out of the legal system and the news. Leonard Cross River Ranch took on a new significance. It was an isolated place in where liquor and gambling and prostitution could be enjoyed without anyone being the wiser. It was a place to disappear and hide out.

Tennis courts were built at the ranch. Locals and those passing by the road four miles away never saw them or the people using them.

In 1928, two 200-watt Wincharger wind turbines and battery backup had been installed. Many may have thought they were water wells, but they provided lights for the houses and barns and power to drive well pumps. Running water and indoor plumbing had been installed. Rural electric power lines were a good way off for most.

Russ could sense there was big money behind the ranch's operation. Where it all came from, he did not know.

After prohibition, money was no problem for the Leonardi's. They were now in a very lucrative new businesses: bootlegging, rum running, gambling, prostitution, protection rackets, and drugs.

Cottages were added at the ranch and then two more. The heated pool came next. Horse stables and riding. A private restaurant. All out of sight inside a fenced compound surrounded by the expanse of the ranch. All mentioned on the ranch's professional website, complete with pictures.

What the website did not show were the names of those who came to the ranch. Many were the who's who of the organized crime families, and still the locals around the area were not aware of them. They never appeared on a guest register.

Over time the place evolved, and money continued to be invested on a modern farming and ranching business with sheds and equipment and irrigation. A model ranching operation was emerging. And, the spa took shape. A house to be used for meetings and meals was built.

Ten covered stalls were built to accommodate the luxury motor homes with running water and electrical hookups.

Their occupants brought there by people like Max Johnson for the entertainment and pleasure of high paying customers.

A sign had gone up, and a new coded entry gate with security cameras and a small security office. Leonard Cross River Ranch and Spa was officially in business and even the sign looked official. The sign made it clear: Guests only. Privacy was insured by security guards.

Montana became connected, in more ways than one. Las Vegas and Los Angeles were now much more possible by car or motor home. Motor homes were a common sight. Russ's quick internet search said there are over eight million of them in the US. They were not at all unusual in the western states as people came through in droves. and people traveled in anonymity.

Once at the ranch, they were still out of sight. No prying eyes here. No ranch workers were allowed inside the fenced in area and no one was looking over the fence. After all, this was the Leonard Cross River Ranch. Successful, modern, and a long history in the area. What could be going on, anyway?

The Leonard family and their children and grandchildren eventually moved to homes in Butte. The story was that they wanted their kids to go to the Catholic school in Butte.

While many guests came for the forbidden human pleasures at the Leonard Ranch, others just came to the ranch to buy hay or livestock. No one ever suspected a thing.

Russ leaned back in the chair and tried to take in all he had just found about this out-of-the way place he had never heard of. *Is there any way this place was connected to the motor home seen at the boat ramp parking lot or the young woman lying in the hospital in Bozeman?* he thought.

The ranch was easy to find. Russ just followed the signs. It looked like any ranch type resort you'd find anywhere else. There were a number of buildings in the complex. The equipment sheds, setting a long distance from the highway, were modern and neatly planned on the long winding drive. Then, as he approached the property, a security booth and gate blocked his access. Not too unusual in resorts. Even in Florida, entrances to golf and condo complexes were gated and had security. In Montana, this was a little rarer. And, a high fence blocked the line of sight into the spa's pool and the tennis areas. Privacy for the guests was assured.

The tops of several large motorhomes could be seen parked under a huge shed similar to the ones the tractors and haying equipment were under. Russell couldn't help but wonder if one of those motorhomes had been the one spotted at the boat launch last night.

The security guard came out to Russ as he pulled up. "Sir, I need to see your guest packet and pass."

"I don't have a pass. I'd just like to look around and maybe get a tour."

"You will have to make an appointment. I can give you a brochure, and you can get in touch with the office about a visit."

"So, I can't just go in and look around? What would that hurt?" Russ was using his most charming good ole boy style.

The guard took a somewhat menacing step toward Russ and said, "I won't tell you again. Turn around and leave."

Russ held up his badge and ID and said, "Maybe you need to step back away from the vehicle and keep your hands where I can see them." His voice and demeaner changed so quickly, and with the badge in his face, the guard stepped back quickly.

"Look. I'm just following orders here. No-one allowed in without prior approval. Unless you have a warrant, I can't let you in, and I don't believe it's legal for you to force your way in without probable cause."

"Been to law school, have you?" asked Russ.

"Police academy training, smart ass," said the guard.

"I tell you what, I'll go and get a warrant and tell them that I believe a person who tried to kill a young black woman up on the highway last night is in one of those motor homes. The DCI, MHP, and Madison County will come back along with building inspectors, health department, and a whole bunch of DEA agents with dogs. And, while I'm waiting for the warrant, I'll sit at the end of the road, and we'll stop every vehicle coming and going for safety inspections. Do you think that's a better way to go? Or, you can answer a simple question, and I'll be on my way. Maybe."

"What's your question?"

"Do you log in the vehicles coming and going and the time?" Russ asked.

"Yes. But that's private information. I can't tell you that."

"Fine. I'll wait at the end of the drive and wait till the warrant comes. I'll be back in about an hour," said Russ. "We will be looking at anyone who may have been involved or has any knowledge. For example, the security guards."

The guard thought about it and said, "I guess I can answer a general question about vehicles coming in or out?"

"Let's look and see if a motor home went out or in between say ten o'clock and one AM last night. Or, if another vehicle may have come in or out. Do you have a security camera?"

"The logbook will show any comings and goings. The management has the camera files inside. Let me get the book."

A moment later, the guard handed the log book to Russ through the truck window. "Step back from the window and stand up on the sidewalk, please." Russ was addressing the guy in such a manner that he knew Russ was not kidding.

But, a quick look at the book showed no one coming or going the whole evening. No probable cause here, and Russ knew he had struck out for the time being.

"So, you log *every* vehicle?" asked Russ.

"The staff have remotes to open the gate, and they are not logged in. None of them drive a motor home. The guards go off duty at nine, but it would be a rare occurrence for anyone to come in after then. Guests are informed the gates are closed at nine. The security camera hard drives are under lock and key in the office, and you will have to ask them for any access to see them."

"Who would I need to talk to?" Russ asked.

"Rachel Wallace. But she is not here today. Some family business somewhere, but all she told me when she left this morning was that she'd be back maybe tomorrow. Some problem with one of her kids."

"Okay. I'll leave my card. Be sure she gets it when she gets back and tell her I'll be expecting her call," Russ said as he backed up to turn around.

With that, Russ left, and he knew everyone would know he had been there in a few minutes. Maybe even the governor.

He wasn't too far wrong.

Rachel

Rachel Wallace's cell rang as she sat in the orthodontist office waiting. She recognized the number as the ranch security gate.

"This is Rachel Wallace," she said.

"Ms. Wallace, we just had a visit from some detective from the Madison County Sheriff's Office. A Detective Russell Baker."

"What did he want?" she replied.

He detailed the interaction including the request for the information on who came and went the preceding night.

"What did you tell him?"

"I let him see the log book because I did not want to risk the guy going crazy and upsetting the whole place," the guard responded.

"Did that satisfy him?" she asked.

"He asked about the security camera discs, and I told him he'd have to talk to you because they were in your office under your supervision. I told him only you could deal with him on the camera recordings."

She thought for a minute. "Look at the files and see if there is anything there that we would not want them to see. Call and let me know what's on them for the time frame he's asking. Do you think there will be anything we don't need him seeing?"

"I really don't believe there will be. It was pretty slow around here last night. No one here has heard anything about a murder attempt, as far as I know."

"Call me back when you get through looking at the tapes."

She made a quick call to a number in Boston and briefed them on the law enforcement visit as she was under orders to do.

"What is your suggestion?" a burly voice on the other line asked.

"If there is nothing on the tapes, I suggest we give him a copy with our full cooperation. We'll show we have nothing to hide and are always ready to help the police. Not give them any cause to come back snooping around."

"Excellent suggestion. I will leave it to you. If there is anything we don't want them to see, we'll call in some experts. I know there was a problem out your way last night, but I don't have all the details yet. What is the cop's name that came by?"

"His name is Russell Baker."

"I'll listen for your call, Rachel."

The call ended.

Interesting, she thought. *He already knew about a police matter that happened off site in Silver Star, Montana.*

Chapter 23

After making a few inquiries in Silver Star, Russ started back toward Ennis. He made a quick call to the sheriff.

"Steinbrenner, here," said the sheriff.

"I interviewed some folks here in Silver Star. One lady said there was a motorhome there at the boat launch when they came by around eleven o'clock, but it was dark, so I got no description."

"Not much to go on there."

"The lady told me about a resort ranch near there that has motor homes coming and going. I went by, but they would not let me in without a warrant."

"What's the name of the place?"

"Leonard Cross River Ranch and Spa," replied Russ.

"Yea. I've heard of it. Some of the owners are involved in a lot of civic activities. Cattlemen's association and farm groups and the like. You think there is any connection there?" asked the sheriff.

"The only thing that bothered me was the tough-guy guard and the hardnose stance he took right off the bat."

"Could just be a prick who takes his job too seriously. Any follow-up?" the sheriff asked.

"I got a look at the logbook, but there was nothing around the time that jumped out. He says the gates are closed after nine o'clock, and no one could get in without a pass, and only employees have them. They have cameras, but he claimed he did not have access to the hard drives. He gave me the name of the lady in charge and said she was out for the day, so I left my card and asked him to have her to call me."

"What next, then?" asked Steinbrenner.

"I'll wait to see if she calls me and see where we go from there."

"Maybe she'll call, and we can get a look without a hassle. You didn't harass these fine, upstanding folks, did you?"

"I was on my best behavior."

"So, he voluntarily let you look at the log book?"

"I might have said something about setting up a vehicle safety check by the road, and I might have suggested I would come back with the DEA, DCI, and the health department. And, maybe there was some mention about dogs."

"Oh, boy! I can see my phone lighting up. But at least you didn't shoot anyone, did you?"

"Not yet," Russ said laughingly. "But then, I just started today."

"Okay. I did hear from the hospital. The young lady is not out of the woods yet, and they give her about a 50-50 chance."

"May be a while before we can talk to her. Maybe, never."

"I'm headed to the house. Did you work out anything on the car?" Russ said.

"I'll run by in the morning and pick you up, and we'll go to out to Dunkin's and get it."

"Fine. Just make it after eight unless you're paying overtime."

"Did I say anything about pay?"

"I'm pretty sure there's something in the contract about pay."

"What contract?" he said. Then the phone went silent.

Chapter 24

Russ had just finished his first cup of coffee when the phone rang. The screen showed it to be a private number.

"Hello. This is Russell Baker."

"Good morning, Deputy. This is Rachel Wallace here at *Leonard Ranch*." The voice was one of confidence, exuding a certain authority yet was somewhat cheerful for nine o'clock in the morning.

She continued, "My security officer advised me of your visit yesterday. We're glad to cooperate in any way we can with your investigation. It's hard to believe such an awful crime happened in our area. How is the person who was attacked?"

"I appreciate you calling back, Ms. Wallace. I don't have any word on the victim's condition that I can report. Besides, I am not allowed to release medical information. The hospital will do any sort of condition report to the press, probably."

Rachel Wallace continued, "I understand you want to look at our hard drive information on the comings and goings of any vehicles in that possible time frame and especially any motor homes. Is that correct?"

"Yes. Is that going to be possible without a lot of legal arm twisting, Ms. Wallace? Your security guard didn't seem too willing to cooperate yesterday."

"Absolutely. We try to insure a private and pleasant experience for our guests, but this is a serious matter. I reviewed the tapes with our security this morning, and there was one vehicle that left about ten o'clock. That was a Toyota pickup with two of our room service kitchen personnel leaving for home. No motor homes came or went yesterday after about eleven AM, and that's about the normal time for leaving. Our check out time is normally noon. You can stop by the gate, and we'll have you a copy of the discs made."

"Really? That's fast work going through a whole evening of tapes," said Russ. "I really appreciate it."

"Our cameras work on motion detection. They come on, put a time stamp on the video, and run for thirty seconds after the motion ceases. So, since there were no events, as they are called on the system, it is short and sweet. There is no continuous recording going on. We really don't need that here."

She continued, "And we can make a standard format video on a disc. I will ask them to make the disc from about eight on the night in question until the following morning. Will that be satisfactory?"

Russ responded, "I believe that will be excellent. Just curious…can I come in to see your facility? I'm not familiar with it."

"What time would you like to come?"

"How about eleven?" he asked. "I need to pick up a car before I come out."

"I will meet you at the gate at eleven," she said. "Goodbye."

Russ was about to pour another cup of coffee when his phone rang, and he saw it was the sheriff.

"Hello, sheriff. Want a coffee to go?"

"Black with no sugar," said the sheriff as he pulled into Russ's driveway.

On the ride over to Deputy Dunkin's to get the car, Russ brought the sheriff up to date on his follow-up at the *Leonard Ranch*.

"So, you feel better about the ranch since you talked to him?" asked Steinbrenner.

"Well, she seemed to be willing to cooperate and agreeing to show me around was positive. I'll see what the files show, and maybe we can scratch that off. That would be too lucky to get a resolution this fast."

They pulled into Wayne Dunkin's yard and drove around to the back parking pad where the patrol car was parked. Dunkin had rolled himself out on the patio in a wheelchair, and they all exchanged hellos and good mornings. Then Dunkin said, "Russ, I just got this new car and was hoping to drive it for a while. Looks like I've traded those nice wheels for these for a while. Sheriff, you did tell him that I am supposed to get this back in one piece?"

"For what good that will do," replied Steinbrenner.

"Are you telling people how you got hurt and laid up on a riding mower?" Russ asked.

"I can tell you in two words: stupid carelessness. But I have heard about that enough from my wife, so I'm not talking about it anymore. Any luck on the case, yet?" asked Dunkin.

"No real leads yet. Going up to the *Leonard Ranch* to see if there is a chance the motorhome we saw was headed to or from there. Do you know them?"

"I've never had a call up that way. I hear they are solid citizens, support the community, and seem to be a first-class operation. I've heard rumors that the ranch hands say they have a lot of pretty ladies and hotshot guys coming and going. Sunbathing by the pool, tennis, and riding horses. Who knows what else? Word is they are always booked when anyone calls for a spa day or weekend there."

"Well, I wish you could ride up there with me. I have been invited to tour the place."

"Maybe you can take a few pictures," said Dunkin.

"Maybe. But I suspect they would want to confiscate my camera. Concerned about privacy of the guests, they say," Russ said as he opened the door to the new Ford Explorer Police Interceptor.

"If things go bad, maybe you can call that tough lady cop from Salt Lake," Dunkin said.

"Now that's a good idea," Russ replied. "I gotta go if I'm to be there on time for my appointment."

Russ arrived at the gate at five minutes before eleven. There was a different security guard this time, and a very attractive lady, Russ guessed to be in her mid-thirties, was standing there, also. Rachel Wallace, he assumed.

The guard waved him up to the booth, and Rachel Wallace gave a wave and walked to the driver's side of the sparkling clean Explorer. "Hello, I'm Rachel Wallace," she said with a New York model smile. "I assume you are Deputy Baker?"

"That's close enough. They can't decide what to call me. I'm sort of a part time employee, and it makes the real deputies mad when they call me one. Detective Baker is just fine. Or Russ."

"If it's okay, I'll ride in with you, Detective Baker, and you can view the security footage in my office. They can't see them out here."

Russ doubted that was true. Probably more about her being in control or supporting the claim the guard had made the day before. As she walked around and opened the door, Russ sized up the security guard.

The guard was almost a carbon copy of the one he had met the day before who had said he had attended a police academy somewhere.

Russ bet the story was the same with this guy, the one yesterday, and any others they had working: Ex-military, got a job on a police force and got canned for some major infraction. Conduct unbecoming, rough treatment of a suspect, or severe personal problems. He would try not to turn his back on any of them. Maybe not their boss, Rachel Wallace, either.

"For a part time detective, you have a very nice and official looking car," she said.

"They just let me borrow it," Russ said without cracking a smile.

"What did you mean when you said you are part time, Detective Baker?" she asked as they walked into her office. "Do you have another job?"

Again, with a straight face, Russ replied, "Part time fishing guide."

She appeared conflicted to Russ – likely feeling at a loss about this random man who had intimidated a guard and worked his way into her office where, he suspected, very few were allowed to venture.

She showed the video record as she had promised, time stamps and all. "As you can see, Detective, things were pretty slow on the night in question. I'm afraid we have nothing much to offer. I made you a copy that you can play on your computer if you would like to review it anymore."

"Thank you for your help. This will probably be all I need from you," said Russ. As he spoke, he glanced around the extremely neat office. *Almost too neat,* he thought. It was as if all the papers and file folders had been put out of sight of prying eyes. Like his.

And, he noticed, no personal photos were in her office. He had been told she had at least one child by the guard the day before. No pictures. No family shots with her and the child or of her and her husband. Unusual for a family type business.

"Come and let me show you around. We won't intrude on any of the guests' activities, if you don't mind."

There were some people playing tennis. Some people by the pool. Some people who appeared to be headed to the horse stables. No one walked near them or acknowledged them. Not even a glance.

Under the big metal shed, he saw several of the large and expensive motor homes, all parked on a paved floor and hook ups like any RV park. There was no activity around them. None of them appeared to be going anywhere.

"I appreciate you showing me around. It's very nice. How long has this ranch been here?" he asked.

"The Leonard Brothers came here in the mid 1800's," she said. "Their family has run the ranch ever since. They have been running the resort and spa for many years, too."

Russ got in the car and drove slowly past the guard gate. The guard let the gate up and looked at Russ as he left but made no acknowledgement. Good riddance as far the guard was concerned, it seemed.

Rachel Wallace called the same number she had called the day before and the same voice answered.

"The detective came by and looked at the video files, and now he's gone. I did give him a little walk around, and he seemed satisfied. He says he's a part time cop. Just going through the motions, I guess."

"We did a little looking after you called. This Baker guy *is* part time, but he's not to be taken lightly. He worked in the Atlanta area as a detective for a large county police department. He was one of their top detectives. He has a lot of money and only works when he wants to. He has been in big arrests and shootouts. Don't be fooled. He may be back. Hopefully, though, we've heard the last of him. He's tougher than he looks. Best if we don't have to have any more visits from him."

She hung up the phone and looked at the business card Russ had given her. She was amazed at the resources the people in

Boston had, and now she was also amazed that she had misread this Baker guy. She hoped she'd seen the last of him, too.

Russ drove back to the boat launching site and stopped. He called the sheriff.

"This *Leonard Ranch* looks like a dead end, here. The tapes look authentic, and the lady was very business-like and showed me around the place. I had the feeling I was on a movie set," he said.

"What do you mean by that?" asked Steinbrenner.

"What I saw looked staged. Probably my imagination."

"What is the lady's name, again?" asked the sheriff.

"Her name is Rachel Wallace. I'm not sure what to think about what all I saw just yet. But I'm betting the ranch is a dead end."

Chapter 25

Marta

After several days in Atlanta, Marta Andruko had been stripped of her ID, her phone, and her freedom. She was now considered an illegal and could be deported. She had no friends and no one that knew where she was. She had been drugged, raped, beaten, sold, and threatened. There was a big man named George that made sure no one came in or went out at the College Park house. Marta could only cry and hope she could somehow get word to her father, a policeman, or someone. No one seemed to be there for her. There was no phone in the house. She would give anything to be back in Louisiana.

There were some other people in the house in other rooms. She had heard the awful sounds of their pain but could do nothing for them. How many there were, she did not know.

One morning, George threw open the door and said, "Get yourself in the shower and get dressed. This is your big day. You're going to Las Vegas like we promised."

Marta hoped this was good news. In any event, she did not argue. Being punched in the stomach or ribs by George was far too painful. They always hit her where it would not show. Mustn't spoil the merchandise.

A large motorhome pulled into the driveway. Marta heard it, and she could see through a small crack in the boarded-up window. She had never been on one of the big bus-like vehicles before.

As she watched, George took two other girls, one at a time, out to the big RV. They appeared very shaky, and George was having to help them to the vehicle. She could see Max Johnson reaching out to help get them inside. They appeared to be heavily sedated. With the high, overgrown fence next door and the size of the RV, it was not likely anyone would see the girls going out.

George came in and opened her door. "Get your suitcase. We're going. I need you on that bus. Keep quiet on the way out and don't try to attract any attention. You're getting your big break now, and if the cops come, you'll get shipped out or put in jail."

"Are you really taking me to Las Vegas?" she half whispered.

"That's what the big man says," answered George.

Marta did not know whether the move was a good thing for her but prayed it wouldn't be any worse. She cried as she stepped up in the unit and walked toward the back and was directed to sit at the vehicle's dining table.

There was a bathroom and shower, flat screen TV, and some fast-food breakfast items on the dining table. There was a refrigerator, cooktop, and microwave. It was nicer than some houses that Marta had been in. And, there was a woman sitting in the passenger seat of the RV that she had not seen before. The woman did not speak or acknowledge her as she came in.

There were two sleeper sofas, and all the way in the back was a bedroom that could be closed off from the rest of the unit. In a few minutes, the woman moved over to the driver's seat; Max Johnson sat in the passenger seat, and George was in the big recliner. The door closed, and the home on wheels got underway.

Anyone passing by would see what looked like a husband and wife enjoying a nice vacation in their motor home. It was plain to Marta that the woman was some sort of professional driver as she moved the big RV out on to I-85 in heavy Atlanta traffic. From what Marta overheard, it sounded like the plan was to stop somewhere in Virginia that night. Petersburg, maybe?

The RV made the work of Max Johnson convenient. Somewhere around a 250-gallon fuel tank would allow them exponential travel without having to stop for fuel. The large cabinets in the dining area were supplied with plenty of food. The bathrooms meant no bathroom break stops. They would be on the road with no way out for some time, it seemed. It was George's job to keep the passengers quiet and prevent anyone from leaving the coach or attracting attention. Drugs or fists or both were at the ready. Compassion was not on board.

The trip to Boston was uneventful, and they arrived at a truck stop outside Boston. Marta had managed to quietly ask one of the other girls her name. "I'm Maria Torres from Cedar Creek, Texas," she had responded. "What's yours?"

Whispering, Marta replied, "Marta Andruko. Please remember that if you get a chance to tell anyone. I was living in Louisiana, but I'm from Ukraine. They say I'm going for a job in Las Vegas."

"Yea. Well, you'll be doing it on your back, I'll bet."

"What are you going to do, Maria?" Marta asked.

"If I get the chance, I'm going to kill Max Johnson."

Marta looked into the eyes of Maria Torres. Maria wasn't kidding.

"Where are you going, Maria?"

"Don't know," she replied.

George had been dozing in the chair and saw them talking. He jumped to his feet and shoved them apart.

"If I see you talking again, I'm going to hurt you both. Bad."

They didn't speak again.

Trucks were coming and going, and Maria and the other girl were taken off one by one. Then, Max Johnson came and got Marta. He walked her over to an old Kenworth truck where a man named Manny Misinco was standing.

On the way over he said, "I know we've been a little rough on you, but you need to be tough to make it in this world. The job in Vegas is a big opportunity for you, and they have all the papers you need and an ID. You will be able to do anything you want. You'll need to work for them for a while first."

"What kind of work?" Marta asked, though by now she suspected exactly what this was she was involved in.

"Whatever they tell you. Keep your mouth shut while you're with this driver. All he does is drive a truck and is taking you across the country for us. If the cops pick you up, you'll be back in Ukraine or jail."

Manny Misinco opened the door of the old truck; she climbed in, and her one-way ride continued.

Maria

Maria Torres was sedated and put in another truck. They hoisted here into the sleeper cab and closed the curtain. The driver was given several syringes and instructed to give them to her as needed to keep her quiet. She had been a fighter from the start. She, too, was on her one-way ride. But she would be traveling on I-80 with a load of medical equipment bound for Sacramento, California. Her final stop was to be San Francisco. Her future? Unknown.

She did not remember being put in the truck, but she was awakened by the engine and braking noise as the truck pulled into a truck stop in what she finally realized, from a sign at the truck stop, was probably Toledo, Ohio. The driver opened the curtain that was used to close off the sleeper compartment, and she pretended to be asleep. He shook her to see. There was no reaction from Maria.

The driver fumbled with the syringes and then decided she was out, so he would not need one now. He closed the curtain, and there was a small space that Maria could see through. She could see him pull a seat cushion forward on the nice air ride seat he sat in to drive. It appeared there was a flat leather pouch under the cushion, and he got some money out and put it back. The lights were off in the cab of the truck, and he looked around to be sure no one was watching.

The driver climbed down out of the cab and locked the door. Maria was partially alert, but her body ached and she was starving and thirsty. She desperately wanted to get out of the sleeper and the truck, but climbing out of the truck did not seem like a possibility. She fell back on the sleeper bed and was back semi-conscious when the driver returned.

He shook Maria. "Do you need to go to the bathroom?" Maria did not answer.

"If you need to go, you'd better do it now. We won't

be stopping for a long time, and if you mess up my sleeper, I'll bust your face"

She said, "Okay. Maybe I can get up."

Maria thought if she could get outside, she could get free of this guy or get some help.

He partially pulled and lifted Maria, and she got into the passenger side seat. The driver ran around to her side and lifted her out. They were in the last parking spot and away from any other rigs. There was no one to help.

"You do your business right by that tire. No tricks. I was told you might try something funny."

Maria did as she was told.

"Get in the seat. Here is a burger and some fries. I got a water, a cola, and a milkshake for you. Don't make a mess in my cab."

Maria was too hungry and thirsty to risk making this guy mad.

And, she did not want a needle. They had used them on her in College Park and on the big bus coming up to Boston to keep her under control. They had used them on her during her stay and during her so-called *training* at the house.

Maria had felt pain. She had been abused and forced to do things she had never thought could happen to her or anyone. She was embarrassed, ashamed, confused, and powerless. All from trusting a man she knew as Max Johnson.

But what Maria was feeling more than anything else was rage. Something she had never experienced before was boiling inside of her, and it was ready to explode. But she had to play it smart and wait. She had to be smarter than this driver. She had to get some food in her and feel stronger. And wait. She had a score to settle with someone. And the drugs and withdrawal were making it tough to think and plan.

It was a long ride, and the driver had to get sleep and keep his logs up. Most of the logs were being done by satellite. She found him in the sleeper with her more than once. She did not really know if he had assaulted her or not.

The driver got concerned that she might be planning something and without warning, at some point, he held her and pumped a syringe into her thigh. She tried to resist, but he was too big and too strong, and she was too weak.

At a truck stop on the outskirts of Salt Lake City, the driver at last made a mistake. He shook Maria to see if she was awake or might need another shot. He seemed afraid that too much of the drug would be fatal. The last thing he needed was a dead girl in his truck.

She did not respond when he shook her, but instead went

completely limp. After trying several more times, he muttered, "To hell with you. I'm getting something to eat and a shower."

He climbed down, locked the door, and walked at a fast pace toward the big trucking plaza. Maria watched through the opening in the sleeper curtain, and as soon as he went in, she started climbing down. There was an access door from the outside, but they had not been using it. Instead, she had been forced to climb up and over the seats.

Maria looked around the cab, and the small overnight case she'd had since leaving Texas was on the floor board. She managed to weakly get it and found a way to unlock the door. Then she remembered…

The driver had some money under the seat cushion! Could she find it?

It took some effort and pulling on the cushion, but she finally found how it was placed and pulled it out. Without taking time to look, she put it in the overnight case and started the process of getting out of the cab.

She missed the step and fell with a jolt on the gravel. She wasn't sure she could get up.

After trying a couple of times, she grabbed something on the truck and made it to her feet. She had to get away from here fast.

Maria moved behind the rigs, some so close to the fence she could hardly squeeze through. She finally came to a place where some trailer had been backed into and through the fence. There was an opening that she could get through, and in the darkness, Maria Torres started a walk to freedom.

The driver returned to his truck with a sandwich and drinks

and walked around to the driver door. Finding it partially open, he panicked. The girl was nowhere to be seen. He ran up the row of trucks and tried to look where she might be. When he found the place in the fence, he realized she was gone for good.

The driver's only thought then was to get away as fast as possible. It would only be later that he realized his money was gone. What would he do about the package he'd lost? He had to figure something out before Sacramento!

The constant forced use of roofies (benzodiazepine) the Rohypnol drug; cherry meth; scoop and goop (GHB); cat valium, k-hole and purple (Ketamine), plus the sedatives had brought Maria to a sad state physically. She made it to a nearby apartment complex where she collapsed beside the trash dumpsters. She managed to crawl to one side out of sight of the parking lot and leaned up against the bin. She had gone as far as she could for the moment.

She had the awareness to look in the overnight bag at the pouch she had taken from the truck driver's hiding place to see what was in it. Even in her condition, she found something to be happy about: almost nine hundred dollars in cash as well as a Visa credit card with the driver's name. She had enough money to go home. But it wouldn't be tonight.

The lining in her overnight bag had a zipper that allowed it to be removed. It was designed, apparently, for cleaning, but it wasn't obvious unless you took everything out. Her mother had bought it for her to use in school trips and weekends. Maria managed to unzip the lining and slide the pouch in and close the case. That was the last thing she did that night.

When Maria regained consciousness, she was in the ICU of

the University of Utah Medical Center. The Level 1 Trauma Center had admitted her after a 911 call had come in about an unconscious female from a couple who had just finished cleaning a vacant apartment at the complex and were dumping the trash. Fortunately for Maria, they had not ignored her and had not taken any of her things. They probably had saved her life.

She was checked in as a Jane Doe:
Unidentified Hispanic Female.
17-20 years of age.
Drug addicted.
Sexual Assault.
Condition, Critical.
Maria did not yet know how lucky she was. She was in one of the best facilities possible for her condition. They were providing her the best care available.

Maria could not talk as there was a tube in her throat. At first, she almost panicked, but a nurse came in and calmed her down with a soothing, almost motherly, tone. Maria was alert enough to know none of her tormentors were present. They were aware enough to know that she had been subjected to severe trauma and abuse. Bruises, needle marks, and malnutrition convinced the staff that the authorities needed to be called in to determine her status and investigate the reason she was found abandoned at a trash dumpster. The appearance was that she had been dumped there for dead.

Debra

A call came in to the sex crimes unit at the Salt Lake City Police Department from the Medical Center. The case was assigned to Detective Debra Taylor. Debra headed over to get what information she could and to try to talk to the victim.

She first met with Dr. Stephen Devereaux and the patient representative. Maintaining the patient's confidential information was a concern.

After a quick introduction, Debra asked, "What can you tell me about her condition, Dr. Devereaux?"

"The patient has severe trauma to the vaginal area, severe bruises about her torso that would indicate she has received numerous blows over an extended period. She has been taking or administered several drugs. Some were obviously injected by someone other than herself judging by the point of injection. She was in a state of malnutrition, not uncommon in this situation, and dehydrated. She was unconscious when brought in and non-responsive."

"Can I talk to her, now?" asked Detective Taylor.

"I doubt it, but you can go in and see if she responds. She hasn't responded to any of our medical team, as of yet," he replied. "Most we've gotten out of her is a first name. Maria."

"What is your best guess about her situation?" Taylor continued.

"Traumatized by whatever she's been through. I can tell you she comes from a different background than this."

Curious, Taylor asked, "How can you tell that?"

"She has perfect teeth. At some point she had major orthodontic correction done. She also had an old injury, probably when she was small, with a broken heel and foot. No real guess as to the cause but could have been a sports injury, bicycle, or car wreck. It required pins and screws. A superb orthopedic job. She had someone that cared about her once."

"Are the pins and screws still there?"

"No. These were removed ages ago, but the marks are there."

"I'm going to keep this between us and not get immigration involved until I know more. I don't want her having to deal with that if it becomes an issue," Taylor said.

They took the detective to the unit and to Maria's bedside. Looking at her, Debra Taylor had to take a deep breath to control the anger it caused to see this young woman in this condition. Abused and abandoned at a trash dumpster.

Maria saw them come in and turned her head away.

"Hello, Maria. I'm Detective Taylor with the Salt Lake City Police. Can you answer a question or two for me? Maybe you can just shake your head or give me a sign with your hand? Do you feel up to that?"

Maria did not respond.

"I am so sorry that this has happened to you. I can't imagine what you've been through. I want to find out who did this to you and put them away so that they can't do it again. Will you help me?"

Debra could see the tears in the young woman's eyes. She knew the girl was understanding some of what she was saying.

But she did not respond.

"I will leave my card here, and I'll come back tomorrow. If you feel like talking to me, let them know so that they can contact me. Anytime. Okay?"

No response.

"Does she have any personal belongings here?"

"There is a small overnight bag. We couldn't find anything with a name or phone number. No ID anywhere."

"I'll check back in on her tomorrow. When do you think the tube can come out?"

"As soon as she can start eating something."

For the next two days, Debra Taylor stopped in to see the young woman. On the second day, she was sitting up and eating in the bed. A major improvement.

"I'm so glad to see you improving. Do you remember me?"

Maria shook her head to indicate she did not.

Taylor looked for another of her business cards. The only one she had left had a small lipstick smudge, but it would have to do. She put it on the tray in front of Maria. "I'm Detective Debra Taylor with the Salt Lake Police. I'm trying to find out what happened and who did this to you. Do you feel like talking to me?"

Maria did not answer but shook her head to indicate, "No."

"Okay. Can you at least answer one question? Are you a US citizen? Nothing is going to happen about that here, but I need to know in case other people want to get involved with your case. If you are a citizen, they can't get involved. It will just be you and me. Are you a citizen of the US?"

Maria seemed to be considering whether to answer. She simply nodded.

"Great. Can you talk?" No response.

"You just don't feel like talking to me, is that right?"

Maria nodded again.

"You know, for me to find the people who abused you, I will need your help?"

Maria nodded again and turned away from Debra.

"I'll try to come back tomorrow," Debra said.

The nurse commented, "We'll probably be moving her to a private room tomorrow. She should like that better. Check when you come in to see where she's moved."

The next morning, Debra was called out on another case and did not get by to see Maria. It was two days before she was finally able to return.

She asked at the nurse's station for the room and asked how the patient was doing, showing her badge and ID. The nurse behind the desk said that the young woman had improved remarkably and was eating like a horse. "I'll walk down with you, detective," she said.

The door was closed to the room when they entered. The bed was empty. The nurse tapped on the bathroom door, "Hey, sweetheart. Are you all right in there?" the nurse asked.

No response.

Detective Taylor stepped up and opened the door, expecting the worst.

The bathroom was empty, too. The young woman was gone. Detective Taylor ran into the hall as the nurse called for security and sounded an alarm. People were scurrying around all over the hospital trying to find her.

Detective Taylor asked, "Is her overnight still here?"

It too was gone. Maria wouldn't be answering any questions today. Maybe, never.

After a frantic search, security cameras revealed she had gotten dressed, taken her bag, and left the hospital on her own power, alone, out the front door. She was not under arrest and was not compelled to stay against her will. Everything was gone including the two business cards Detective Taylor had left her. Maybe she would call. Maybe. Debra Taylor could only lean against the wall completely confounded by the turn of events.

Maria

Maria Torres had only one thing in mind: getting back to Cedar Creek, Texas. And out of Salt Lake City.

She got a cab outside the hospital and asked that he take her to a Walmart. She went in and bought some personal items and a prepaid phone. Using the self-checkout, she tried the credit card from the driver's leather folder. To her surprise, it worked. She stepped outside and made a call to her mother's cellphone.

"Hello, who is this?" her mother answered, and Maria's heart swelled.

"Mama, this is Maria." They both started crying.

"Maria, we've been so worried. Where are you? Are you alright? Please come home, or we'll come get you."

"I'm doing okay, Mama. I'll tell you all about it when I get there. It will be a few more days."

"Do you need money? I can send some to you."

"No. I have money. I lost my ID, so that would probably be a problem. But tell Daddy I'm okay and I'm coming home soon. I'm so sorry, Mama."

Maria Torres was on her way.

She asked a lady coming out of the Walmart with two kids if she knew where the Greyhound bus station was. She did. "Do you need a ride?" she asked Maria.

The last time someone offered her a ride, it had not turned out well. But this lady with two small kids in tow seemed like a safe bet.

"If it's on your way, that would be great."

"Going home or just taking a trip?" the lady asked.

"Going home," said Maria, the words feeling almost too good to be true.

The lady at the Greyhound window selling tickets was having her own problems on a personal sounding phone call when Maria walked up.

"What can I get for you?" she asked as she stopped talking for a moment on the phone.

Maria told her what she wanted. The lady said, "That will be $285. How are you paying?"

It had worked once, so she thought she'd try again. She handed her the credit card, and the lady asked her to sign the screen. She did. She used the name *Maria* but used the last name on the card. The lady handed her the ticket and went back to her very important personal call.

The bus was leaving soon.

Chapter 26

Things had not progressed much for Russell Baker on the case of the unidentified young woman found hit by a car and shot. One bullet from the .38 had hit a glancing blow to her head, and she was suffering from Traumatic Brain Injury. The TBI had caused severe swelling of the girl's brain. That had required surgery, and she was not yet awake to be questioned. They could find nothing about her on missing persons or any alerts. They were stuck. They could only wait.

Russell decided to make another stab at finding a witness around the Silver Star area. On the way up, he called the sheriff.

"Hello, Russ. How are things this morning?" asked Sheriff Steinbrenner.

"I was hoping you would have some news from somewhere. I'm fresh out, myself," said Russ.

The sheriff responded, "No. Nothing from anywhere. The state crime lab has some blood traces but not the bleeder. They believe the pen must have been jabbed in pretty deep, but that hasn't helped yet. Nothing new on the young lady. She appears to be our only witness. Have you talked to the trooper anymore to see if she has any new thoughts?

"No," Russ said, "but I'll give her a call. I'm on my way up to the country store in Silver Star. I thought I might hang around there for a while and catch people coming and going there. Any more ideas?"

"Oh, I meant to mention that I ran a little background on the Wallace lady you interviewed. You said she was trying to appear helpful but felt that she might have been putting on a show."

"Really? What did you come up with?" asked Russ.

"Turns out that Rachel Wallace is her married name. Or, in this case, her divorced name. She has one twelve-year-old kid. And, she grew up in Butte. She attended the Catholic School in Butte and UCLA. Has a master's degree in business. Got married in first year of college. Her maiden name was Leonard. Ring any bells?"

"So, she is more than an office manager it seems," said Russ. "I wonder why she didn't mention that she's part of the Leonard family who owns the ranch?"

"I think her brother is over the Ranch, and she's over the Spa part," said the sheriff. "And, there's something else very interesting, Russ. They pop up on the FBI's radar from time to time. I found this surprising. I couldn't believe I'm just hearing this: the family name is actually Leonardi. At least, it was, before they changed it. Bad relations. That's an old organized crime connected family back in Boston and Chicago."

"I did see some mention of that when I was looking them up online. Does it appear they are still connected?" asked Russ

"According to my source at the Bureau, they are. But they just haven't been able to pin anything on them. They have always been too smart." the sheriff said.

"Are you making the assumption there is some connection here?" Russ asked.

"You know about assuming, Russ. Let's watch and see. Probably just a cop with no clues trying to find some."

"Gotcha. I'm almost to the country store. I'll let you know if anything turns up here."

"Maybe an RC Cola and a Moon pie. Huh, Russ?"

"What a great idea. See ya."

Russ pulled the Explorer onto the store's parking lot and went in. A throwback in time, and it reminded him of some of the few remaining stores like this in North and South Georgia. It was worth the trip even if he came up empty.

Russ followed the sheriff's suggestion and got himself an RC, and much to Russ's surprise, it was made in Montana. He was looking out the window when he saw Rachel Wallace pull into the parking lot. Her eyes lingered on the patrol car, and Russ was sure she recognized it, and she seemed bothered knowing she was about to bump into him.

He walked to the rear of the store and kept his back to the front when she came in. Cat and mouse was at work. Unless she was purposely looking for him, she'd not be likely to see him.

But, see him she did. "Hello, Detective," she said as pleasantly as she could manage.

Acting surprised, Russ turned around to see the very attractive Rachel Wallace standing there, and she still was wearing her New York model's smile.

"Hello, again, Ms. Wallace. Nice to see you."

"Do you usually shop here?" she asked.

"No, can't say that I do. But I'm finding myself up this way more recently."

"Such a nice day. I'm surprised you're not fishing."

"Well. In a way, I am," he said.

"Did you do a lot of fishing in Georgia?" she asked. "I don't know if policemen fish much."

"A fair amount. Never enough," answered Russ. "Do you ever go yourself?"

"Not since I was small and my dad took me. Any luck on the case you were working on?" Suddenly the woman bit her bottom lip. She had made a critical error, and Russ knew that she realized her mistake. So had he.

He had not told her he had been a cop in Georgia, so she had gotten that information somewhere else.

He smiled, not responding to the comment so as not to make her aware that she had been caught. "Not too much luck so far. Anyway, not anything I can talk about."

"Oh, sorry. I didn't mean to be nosey. I'm sure you have to keep some things to yourself until the case is closed," she said.

"We all have our secrets, Ms. *Leonard*."

That startled her. He had now put her on notice: she wasn't the only one with sources of information.

"Well," she said, trying not to look frazzled. "Do have a good day, Detective. I must be off."

Russ nodded farewell to her and watched her scurry out of the store without so much as a glance around. He spoke to several customers as they came to the store and talked to no one that had seen anything. He started back toward Ennis as much in the dark as he had come.

He called the sheriff as he pulled out. "Just leaving Silver Star. No one here admits to seeing anything, and I think that is probably correct. But I did have one interesting conversation. Albeit a short one."

"Interesting *and* short? That's usually an oxymoron for you," said Steinbrenner.

"I was standing in the store drinking my RC, just like you suggested, when who do you suppose pulled in?"

"The fellow that hit the girl and shot her came in and confessed?" the sheriff replied somewhat sarcastically.

"That's a real good guess, and I wish it was true. This police work is messing up my fishing. But, no, it was a very nice-looking lady in a shiny SUV named Rachel Wallace."

"She probably stops there all the time, wouldn't you think? It's not far from the Leonard Ranch," the sheriff suggested.

"You'd think so, but when she left the lady behind the counter commented on what a pretty lady she was, and I asked if she stopped in a lot. She said she'd never seen her in the store before."

"So, what do you make of that?" the sheriff asked.

"Did she see your car and was so impressed with the handsome and charming fishing guide that she just had to come in and speak? Maybe looking for a date?" the sheriff said with a slight chuckle.

"I wish. I think she saw my car and wanted to come in and speak to the detective who had been at her place investigating an attempted homicide. I think she wanted to see if we had come up with anything," replied Russ. "Really got my curiosity up."

"Now, Russ. You're not a conspiracy theorist, are you?"

"As a matter of fact, yes. I wonder if we had cell phone records if we would see a call made from the area to her, from her or to someone in, say, Boston, on the night it happened."

"Detective Baker, don't run off the rails on me, now. You know that would require more evidence than we have now to get that information. In fact, it would likely have to be a federal case. Can you make it a federal case, and do you want to?"

"Not at this time. A lady stopping at a convenience store won't do it, I suppose."

"Not even if she's pretty," replied the sheriff. "And, not even if she was the shooter. This is our case. These are cases, that when we solve them, we get our picture in the paper and get reelected."

"But I'm not running for office, Sheriff."

"Good. But, I am. The next guy here might not put up with some super cop from God-knows where getting all the police vehicles shot up."

"Just a reminder. That was my car," Russ said.

The sheriff chose to ignore the comment

The sheriff continued, "I did get a call from the hospital. They think the victim's improving. Signs are better. Maybe we can talk to her in a day or two. They say she has old bruises and signs of severe sexual abuse."

"That brings up a lot of possibilities. Wow. Kidnap victim, prostitution, or maybe spousal abuse." Russ said.

"Yea, life's peachy. Ain't that what you guys say in Georgia?" said Steinbrenner.

"That's a phrase I've heard. They also say that life's a bitch, sometimes," Russ added.

"That's probably how this young woman would describe it right now. Let's see if we can find the SOB who did this to her."

"I'll be happy to oblige, Sheriff. Talk to you tomorrow," Russ said.

"Be careful driving back, Russ. They may stop you for driving under the influence of an RC."

"Well, I know one trooper personally. Maybe if it's her, she'll let me off.

"Yea, right. She was awestruck." The phone went dead.

Russ had nothing to do, no one to call, and no one waiting at the house. He had a brief urge to call Nancy, but it passed quickly. *Move on*, he thought.

There was a time he would have called Miriam. That was no longer an option. The only other remote possibility of someone to call was Debra Taylor in Salt Lake. Maybe he'd do that tonight.

Rachel

Rachel hurried from the store after her encounter with the deputy, her head spinning slightly as she thought back on her little slip up. And, he apparently had been making inquiries about her, too. Why? As she pulled out, she called the back east number again.

"I ran into that detective again. He was up here hanging around the little country store. He knows that I am part of the Leonard family."

"That's not too earth shattering in itself, is it?" the voice on the other end replied.

"I guess not, but I let it slip I knew he was a cop in Georgia. He picked up on that, I'm sure."

"Well, that's not exactly a secret either. We'll keep an eye out, but they don't seem to be looking at the ranch right now. He took that off the list after coming up and visiting you. I think you did well. They have made no connection to the ranch and the lady they found in the road."

"I didn't know there *was* a connection; did I miss something?" she asked.

"She was one of our transfers, apparently, and we had arranged to have her picked up there to keep the customer from knowing too much. The ranch was not to be involved. It's a mess. And, on top of that, we had another screw up in Salt Lake. Another of Max Johnson's packages slipped out on the ride and is gone. We are trying to find out what happened. That prick is two for two right now."

He's going to have to watch who he brings on for his projects in the future."

"Are we still safe using these phones?" she asked.

"They are encrypted. As safe as they come," was the reply.

Still voicing concern Rachel asked, "Are we still on for next week? There are a lot of people coming, and we're going to need a lot of diversions."

"We have some extras in Las Vegas that we will send up. Things are a little slow down there. I'll get the arrangements made. Just keep alert for any strange activity. I believe the ranch is still off the radar, and there is no connection between the ranch and these two incidences that the police could possibly find." The man sounded very confident.

"Okay. What about this Georgia cop?" she asked.

"If he gets too close, we may have to react. I don't want to arouse any more suspicion, though, so we'll pump the breaks on that for now," he responded.

"All right. I have to go. I'm picking up Jessie; they have a play tonight at the school."

"Hope it goes well. Goodbye, Rachel." With that, he was gone.

Chapter 27

Russ made himself a cold sandwich and sat down with a bottle of water. *Man*, he thought to himself, *this is the life*. Self-inflicted sarcasm may be the worst kind.

He had flipped the TV on but had thought better of it and switched it back off. He picked up the phone and found Debra Taylor's number.

"Well, if it isn't Russell Baker from Montana. To what do I owe the pleasure of your call? You just running down the list of the poor ole girls in Salt Lake you can call and cheer up?"

"Now, if you are going to be mean, I may have to hang up. But the fact is, I only know two girls in Salt Lake and neither would be classified as poor. One just married a guy with a bundle of money."

"The other was born with plenty of it. I hope I'm not interrupting anything."

"Ha. That's so funny. I haven't had a date since you left here, and I don't know that we actually had a date. Did we?" Debra joked.

"Let's say we did. Because otherwise, I've also had a really long dry spell," Russ answered.

"That's a deal. That's our story. We had a date, and it was great. I remember now; I had on this nice designer dress, got called out on a stabbing, you came by and left early with me standing there and not a word since," Debra said somewhat sarcastically.

"My goodness. How come every time I talk to you, I have to apologize for my poor behavior?" he questioned.

"I love busting your chops, Russ. But I love it that you called. How are things on the river?" she asked in a much softer tone.

"Been a few days since I was there. Thinking today I should put some gear in my car and stop when I see a spot. I was asked by the sheriff to help on a case."

"Not another group of terrorists, I hope?"

Russ answered, "I don't know what we have, yet. The only clues we have are a bloodied ball point pen and a young woman that had been hit by a car and shot, and we don't know her name."

"Well, that's a bad day in anybody's book." Debra sounded genuinely concerned.

"How about you, Debra. Anything happening in Salt Lake?"

"I did have a similar situation. We think someone dumped a young Hispanic woman by a dumpster maybe thinking she was dead. She was on drugs. She started improving but refused to talk to me. Lots of signs of abuse: physical and sexual. Then, she walked out of the hospital, and we haven't seen her since. No ID. No nothing."

"Maybe someone from across the border?" he suggested.

"Doctors say she had once had expensive orthodontic work and some orthopedic procedures in the past. Maybe a runaway," replied Debra.

"Hard to imagine a kid with everything running away."

She responded, "Oh, I had thought about it a few times, myself."

"So, you've got nothing to go on?" Russ asked.

"She wouldn't talk except to nod that she was a citizen, so I didn't get immigration involved. Thought I could coax her to talk to me. Went in, and she was gone."

"Our victim has been unconscious. We're hoping to get something from her in a day or two," Russ said. "They say she has been abused sexually and physically as well."

"Well, enough shop talk, Russ. Seriously, why did you call? Are you calling to invite me to come go fishing?"

"That's a standing invitation," he said.

"Do I have to bring my father and brother?"

"No. They can come on their own. I'll call you when I get a break in this case. And you can come for as long as you want."

Without thinking how it might sound, she blurted out, "Maybe I'll just stay."

Before Russ could think of what to say, she tried to correct the mistake. "I guess I shouldn't have said that. Now you won't ever let me come."

"I'll willing to risk it, Debra," Russ said.

They did small talk for a few more minutes, then Russ said, "I'll call you about that fishing trip as soon as this works out here."

"I'll keep a bag ready. I'll be listening for your call."

They both ended the call wishing they had handled it differently.

Russ enjoyed his cold sandwich more than he thought he would. He didn't know why.

After a good night's sleep, Russ got his coffee and sat at the table to look at what bills had come in the mail the day before. Not many. He had no debt and only had the local bills. The Montana Northwestern Energy bill was there, and the Ennis water and sewer bill. Not even a bill from American Express. Well, it was there, but hardly anything on it. The same with the gas credit card. Russ preferred cash. He was old fashioned. His trip expenses to Atlanta and Florida had all been paid by his father-in-law. At the man's insistence, of course.

The phone ringing broke his boredom.

"Good morning, Sheriff. Well, you screwed up. I've already had my coffee."

"Damn. I must be slipping."

"Looks like it. What's up?"

"I got a call, and we may can talk to the victim after about ten this morning. They are doing some tests, but then she'll be back in the room. Iffy, at best. But she's coming in and out of consciousness right now."

"I can be there by ten. Do you want to go, too?" asked Russ.

"Thanks for asking. I think I will. I'll meet you there at ten. I have a dentist appointment, so I'll drive up on my own."

The sheriff, as was his custom, did not wait for a reply. He hung up.

For some reason, Russ was in a great mood. The best since he had gotten the goodbye message from Nancy. He couldn't help but look in the mirror of the Silverado pickup and ask himself why. Talking to Debra was nice. Could that be it? Or the fact that the young lady looked to be out of the woods and that they may start to make some progress.

The sheriff was standing at the nurses' station talking to the doctor when Russ arrived. "Looks like a false alarm, Russ. She was awake for a while but has gone out again."

"That's too bad. Is there any chance she said anything that could be of help to us, Doctor?" asked Russ.

"The only thing we got from her was what sounded like a name. Jerry? But we are not certain. Then she said something like Mack. Again, those were slightly above a whisper. Sorry we don't know what those have to do with her."

"That could be her name, the name of the persons who assaulted her, or both," said the sheriff.

"Doctor, please put my card on her chart. Call me anytime – day or night. I'll be here as fast as I can from Ennis," Russ said." "I really want to get my hands on these people."

The doctor looked at the card. "I'll be happy to," he said and then looked at the sheriff. The sheriff's only reaction was to give a little nod of the head and a wink. It was sort of a *this guy means it* affirmation of what Russ had said.

"What now, Russ?"

"I'll buy you a coffee."

"No. I have that dentist appointment here in town. My local guy in Ennis referred me to them for some special root canal thing."

"Sounds serious." said Russ.

"Yea, it is. About $3500 serious."

"You said you make the big bucks just the other day," Russ reminded.

"Thank goodness for my military retirement and insurance."

"I'm going by the fly shop and say hello. And, I think I will call the MHP trooper and bring her up to date. She might like to know. Unless you have another avenue to explore. The possible names don't seem to be anything we can chase after right now."

"I agree." The sheriff turned and walked away toward the car, and the two men went their separate ways.

It was nice to stop at the fly shop and talk to the folks working there. Busy, busy, busy they said. Sure could be using his help, they said. *Nice to be wanted*, he thought.

But he knew, down deep, that what would make him happiest right now would be to arrest the person or persons who had left that young woman to die in the middle of the road. More than a thirty-inch rainbow. Maybe more than an eighty-pound tarpon. She would have likely died had it not been for the sheer chance arrival on the scene of the MHP trooper.

He scrolled down and called the trooper's number. "Corporal Carter," she answered.

"This is Russell Baker. I just wanted to bring you up to date on the young woman you found in the road. No doubt, if you hadn't shown up, she'd be gone."

"I'm glad I was able to help," Corporal Carter replied.

Russ filled her in on what he knew. She thanked him for calling.

"Anymore thoughts on what went on there?" he asked.

"I've been back by there on my shift. I stopped and tried to visualize what was going on. The only thing that makes sense is that the car that made the track and the motor home were meeting up. Drug deal gone bad, maybe. Maybe the girl or someone was switching vehicles. The pen, to me, is an improvised weapon. No one shows up at a dangerous situation armed with a pen."

"That's a great observation, Corporal. I really hadn't thought of it in quite those terms."

Corporal Carter continued, "If the girl was there against her will, she may have defended herself with all she could get her hands on. If she'd had a gun, she'd have done the shooting."

Russ thought for a minute.

"Are you there, Detective?" she beckoned

"Sorry. I think you are on the right track. Maybe she was shot in retaliation to the stab with the pen," answered Russ. "The person in the car ran her down. Then wanted to shut her up for good when she tried to run."

"Sounds reasonable. But, hey, it's anybody's guess. Thanks for calling, Detective."

The call was over. Where did the injured girl fit in? Figure that out, and the case would be close to being solved.

Back to Ennis. Back to the cold sandwich. No calls or voicemails. No calls at all. He wondered what Debra Taylor was doing.

Chapter 28

Marta

Marta Andruko had not made it to Las Vegas, as promised, except for a night here and there. When extra help was needed in a hotel or casino party to cover the requirements of those wanting an escort or prostitute, they would send a van or limo load of women and men to cover the demand. Most of the time, Marta was being kept in a large home that was an unlicensed bordello in Nye County where prostitution was legal. While prostitution was pervasive in Las Vegas and all other large cities in the US, it is illegal nearly everywhere except eight counties in Nevada. Nye being one of those counties.

Marta had been provided fake ID's and passports. She even had a Nevada driver's license. She also had the threat of deportation and retaliation against her family for failing to cooperate. Like the other young women, she had been knocked around, physically assaulted, and drugged and battered to make her comply. A handler accompanied the women to insure they stayed in line. They never had money or cell phones. Nor were they to be seen using one. It could have a serious or fatal outcome. The women each earned the people running the businesses thousands of dollars a month, and they saw very little of it.

She was removed from the regular weekly rotation and put with five other girls. They had their hair done. Manicures. Extra fine treatment was being provided, and a rumor was being circulated that they were headed out of town for a big week with big, high paying clients. Many from out of the country.

All the girls were blue eyed, fair skinned, and white with blonde hair. Just the look desired by the customers coming in. Marta fit the requirements perfectly.

Marta was constantly trying to figure a way out. But the slightest hint of someone planning a rebellion was dealt with painfully and swiftly. But she kept looking for any crack she could slip through. It had not happened yet.

While most of the counties required prostitutes to be 21, two counties allowed workers at 18. Marta had ID showing her to be 21 and a US citizen. She was tested for STD's and carried a certification but had never been asked by anyone to see it.

Demoralized, embarrassed, and ashamed of what had happened to her, she had reached the same dreadful place all of the young women were in who had been lured and forced into this world. She wanted to go back to her family, and if that meant Ukraine, it would be better than this.

The women were destined to go to a big assembly taking

place in Silver Star, Montana. She did not know the name of the place yet. Silver Star was a little over eight hundred miles away. All they could piece together was that they would go on a motor coach and be required to service the whims of the attendees. Remote and hidden from view, and there would be no one to hear them cry or scream. There would be plenty of chemical concoctions to put them in the right frame of mind, also, if needed.

For a few days, Marta was getting some much needed rest and recuperation time. She wanted to talk to the others to see if she could get support for trying an escape, but everyone was watched and afraid to talk. Marta decided she'd have to go it alone if the opportunity came. Maybe not discussing it with the others would be best?

Marta had decided at some point that she could not fight them every day and survive the abuse they could dish out without losing. The better way was to appear to have caved in and given up. Do as she was told. And wait. Wait until someone let their guard down. Wait until she appeared cooperative.

She saw the upcoming work assignment out of town as a possible chance for someone to make a mistake. She would not know what that would be, but she needed to stay alert, off their medications and sex drugs, so that she would spot the chance when it came. She would have to endure some more humiliation and abasement, but in the end, she planned to prevail. For now, that meant cooperation so that she didn't get the needle. So that she could keep her head on right. So that when the opportunity presented itself, she would be able to take it.

Chapter 29

Russ had some voicemails from people wanting to go on float trips, but that wasn't something he could take on at the time. Chad Freeman had also called and had invited him to dinner at his house. They were grilling out. And, no, Nancy was not invited.

That reminder of Nancy didn't hurt as much now. Maybe he was getting over her. That should be a good thing, he decided. He dialed Chad.

Chad's wife answered his phone. "Hey, Russ. Are you calling to say you're coming to the barbeque?"

"I'm calling to say yes, but with the sheriff department stuff, I could be a no show. But it would have to be something major to keep me away. I haven't had a hug from a pretty girl in a while."

"Well, I'll try and slip you one, but I think Chad's getting suspicious."

In the background, he heard Chad's voice, "Suspicious, my ass. I see it as plain as day. Tell that guy to quit calling here."

"Russ, I think we've been found out. He wants to talk to you."

"Listen, Baker, sheriff or no sheriff, you better not be messing with my wife," Chad warned half-heartedly once he had hold of his phone.

"Believe me, Chad, if she dumps you, I'm going the be the first to call. But, somehow, I think you're safe. Why, though, is a mystery to me."

"I can give the list of reasons, but it's too long to do on the phone. You coming to the barbeque?" questioned Chad.

"Wild horses and all that jazz. See you Saturday," answered Russ.

"Bring a date," added Chad.

"Sure," Russ said. "Maybe the sheriff or his wife will come as my date. That's about all the people I know to ask. I did meet a very nice state trooper. Her husband might be like you, though. And I did meet a nice divorcee up in Silver Star at that Leonard Cross River place."

"You talking about Rachel Wallace?" Chad asked.

"Yeah. How do you know her?"

"I have taken her and her former husband on some float trips. And, she has booked some of her clients with us," Chad explained.

"I guess I hadn't thought about them doing that, but it makes sense."

"Her brother that lives in Butte has been on trips with us as well as her other brother, father, and uncle. I think they live in Boston or some place. Do you want me to invite her?" Chad asked.

"It's your barbeque, but she probably won't come if she knows I'm coming," Russ said.

"Man, give me some credit. If I called her, she would come."

In the background he heard Chad's wife, "She'd better keep her hands to herself if she comes."

"What's good for the goose, sweetheart," Chad said laughing.

"I think you better listen, Chad," Russ said.

They both said "Bye" about the same time.

How about that? Russ thought.

He envied Chad. Chad and his wife had what he would have had with his late wife. He might never be able to have that again.

He figured it was a good time to call Teresa Walker in Butte to see if she had had any more activity at the truck stop.

She answered on the third ring. "Hello, Detective. How are things where you are?"

"Plodding along here in Ennis. I have a new job since I last talked to you. I'm back working a case for the Sheriff's Department."

"Yes, I do remember Ennis. Not all good memories, either. So, you can't give up being the detective?" she asked.

"Well, it's sorta in my blood, I guess. Anything happening at the restaurant lately? Thought I'd check in on your little case."

"I haven't seen much, and the other waitresses aren't helping much. Don't want to get involved, you know? There was a fellow that I think was a truck driver in a few days ago who had a young black girl with him. I say young… she might have been in the 18 – 20 range. At first glance, she looked like one if those movie stars. Can't think of the name. I noticed them come in, and she was wearing a baseball cap pulled low, and they sat by the restrooms."

"Unfortunately, we were swamped, so I couldn't pay too close attention. I looked and noticed she was gone, so I took a chance she might have gone in the restroom. So, I went to look. I got a call for a pickup for my table that was in a hurry, so I only got a quick look, but there didn't seem to be anyone in the restroom or in the stalls."

She sighed and continued, "The next time I looked, they were both gone. I asked one of the other waitresses if she had seen them, and she said the girl left with some other guy but that she didn't think anything of it. Like I said, we were very busy at the time."

Russ asked, "You did say it was a black girl? Not a Latino, perhaps?"

"I'm pretty sure she was an African American."

Russ's mind was racing.

"Would you recognize her if you saw her again?"

"As I said, I probably could not make a 100% positive identification that would hold up in court, but she looked like, oh I don't know, Halle Barry. Why the interest?" she asked.

"Well. Damned. I'm asking because we have a young black girl, can't say if she looks like Halle Barry or not, but she was hit by a car and shot up near Silver Star. If you remember that little community."

"Is she dead?" asked Teresa.

"No, but she's a mess. In and out of consciousness in the hospital in Bozeman. Lots of injuries and TBI. Any chance you could come and take a look at her?"

"Why do you need me to look at her?" she asked.

"We have no identification on her – nothing. They have her as a Jane Doe; I'm dead in the water on this. It's probably a long shot that these things are connected, but it's not like I've gotten any new leads."

"I have the late shift tonight," she said. "I could come now and be there by about ten. Will you pay for my gas? I hate to ask… but with my mom, things are tight."

"Gas. Coming and going and lunch. And a hundred for your trouble."

"That won't be necessary, Detective," she said.

"Never turn down cash, Miss Walker."

"I guess that's good advice. See you at ten. That's at my old hospital, right?

"Right. Just down the hall."

Teresa Walker arrived just at ten as promised. Russell Baker was pacing like an expectant father at the thought of maybe making some progress in a case that had so far stumped him.

The nurse overseeing the floor was to meet them and accompany them down to the room of the unidentified woman. The patient was still not able to converse in any lucid manor although she was more alert to her surroundings.

The nurse came up and introduced herself to Russ and Teresa Walker. She said, "I remember both of you." Looking at Teresa Walker, she said, "I was the nurse on your section when you were brought in all shot up. I hope you are doing well. You look great."

"Thank you. I owe this place a lot."

Russ said, "We're hoping Miss.Walker can help us identify our Jane Doe, and we can move forward in catching whoever did this to her."

"Well, don't expect too much help from her. She has no memory of how she got here and hasn't been able to tell us her name," responded the nurse. Not at all what Russ wanted to hear.

They entered the room, and the girl looked at them with a vacant stare. They all said hello to her. She said nothing.

Teresa Walker walked over to the bed and gently put her hand on Geraldine's arm. "I was once here just like you. They didn't think I would make it back, but I did, and you will, too. I am so sorry that this has happened to you. Do you understand me?"

There was no real response to the question, but she looked from Teresa to Russ. There became a look of panic in her eyes. Teresa Walker knew that look from personal experience.

Teresa stepped back and took Russ's arm. Softly she said, "You don't need to be afraid of this guy. He's here to find the people who did this to you. Do you understand what I'm saying? They are the ones that need to be afraid. He wants to catch them really bad."

The girl looked at Russ and back at Teresa. Teresa stepped back to the edge of the bed. "Has anyone ever told you that you look like Halle Barry?"

That seemed to hit a nerve, but she still did not speak.

Teresa looked at Russ. "Russ, I can't be sure, but it could be her. I would say a 60/40 chance."

Russ slowly moved toward the patient, and they could see she seemed to recoil from his approach

Russ spoke in a low voice. "I promise you that we will get the folks that hurt you."

She turned her head and seemed to stare at Russ. She seemed to be saying, *I'm holding you to that.*

Thanking the nurse, they started to the door. The girl made some sound that none of them could understand. She held out a hand. Russ walked back over and took her hand in both of his. She looked at him, and he leaned down and whispered something in her ear that neither the nurse or Teresa could here. He gave her hand a gentle squeeze and turned and walked out.

Teresa and the nurse were dying to know what he had said.

"That's just between the two of us," Russ said.

At lunch, Russ was somewhat heartened by the fact that Teresa Walker thought that there was a chance this was the girl she had seen. 60/40 was good odds but not a sure thing. He wanted a better hand to play.

"When you get back, can you ask the fellow in charge if we can look at the video records for that night? What's his name, again?"

"His name is Chuck Renfroe," she said. "He runs a good operation. He may say we need a warrant."

"Well, ask and see what he says. Tell him that we only have suspicions and that we want to just take an informal look. We don't need to take the drives or tamper with them. And, we prefer not to get Helena, Butte, and Madison County people all in stint until we think there is good cause. If we have a cop involved in something like this, we have to pull out all the stops. He can call me and ask any questions he might have."

"I'm not sure if he'll be there tonight. If not, I'll drive over in the morning when he comes in. I think I should talk to him in person and not on the phone."

"I agree. Call me when you know something. And, here's the gas money and the hundred I owe you."

"Just keep the hundred," she said.

"A deal's a deal," Russ said, as he put the hundred-dollar bill in her hand.

Now, they would have to wait and see what happened next.

Chapter 30

Teresa Walker showed up for work at Wayne's to find Chuck Renfroe had the night off. She made a call.

"Detective Baker, it's Mr. Renfroe's night off. He'll be here in the morning, I guess. I'll talk to him then," Teresa's voice came through the phone.

"Thanks for letting me know. I'll be listening for your call."

Then, something unexpected happened. Russ had just hung up after checking in with his in-laws in Atlanta when his phone rang again. Debra Taylor's number popped up on his cell. Russ heard a familiar voice in his ear.

"Good evening, Mr. Baker. How are things over in Ennis, Montana?"

"Same old same old here. And you?" he asked, surprised to be hearing from her.

"Well, to tell you the truth, I have some plans for the weekend, for a change. I'm not sitting home all weekend or spending it with my folks. You'd think that I'm old enough to not have my brother and parents involved in my every weekend, wouldn't you?"

"You certainly seem old enough to me. Who's the lucky guy?" he asked.

"I'm not sure how lucky it is for him. It may not be to his liking, seeing as how he doesn't know about it yet."

"Well, that is an unusual circumstance, I'd say, Ms. Taylor. Did you meet this guy on some dating site?" he asked.

"No, I met him at work. In fact, I showed up unexpectedly at his job once, and all hell broke loose."

"Maybe you need to reconsider. Maybe a weekend with the folks is not such a bad idea. Are you calling to gloat or asking for advice from an expert on adult relationships?" asked Russ.

"Neither. I am calling to see if you can pick me up at the Bozeman airport tomorrow at about one o'clock. I'm coming to spend the weekend with you in Ennis. If that's okay with you, that is."

"I think that's okay. I do have some social commitments for Saturday, though. Do you like barbeques and cookouts?" Russ asked.

"I love 'em as long as I'm not having to host and cook."

"What airline?" he asked.

"I'm coming on my plane," she said.

"Your plane? You have a different plane from the one your dad flies in?" Russ asked.

"No. It's the same one. Bombardier Challenger 350. But I own 24%. So, it's mine too."

"Oh. I see."

"Brad owns 24% and Dad owns 52%. He's the boss, you know."

"Does he know you're using it to come to Bozeman to see a fishing guide for the weekend?" Russ asked.

"It was his suggestion; he's trying to lure you to come to work at the company, remember?" she said with a laugh.

"He's using a helluva bait."

"Hmm. I guess that's a compliment, or were you talking about the plane?" she asked.

"You're the real detective; you figure it out."

"See you tomorrow, Russ. You have until about ten in the morning to change your mind," she teased.

Russ was astonished, to say it mildly. And, he had just learned Debra was a lot more than a casual employee at her father's company. She was a partner. And she was coming to see him.

Russ didn't sleep too well. He really needed to clean up, put up, and generally make the place ready for company. That would mean a trip to the grocery store. Maybe a stop at the *Family Dollar* for some supplies and new sheets for the guest bedroom. He didn't want to take anything for granted. But a set of $700 sheets from some fancy place wouldn't happen today.

Then Russ stopped for a moment and realized: he was acting like a kid on his first date. And it was, in a way. Well, anyway, he didn't have anything to lose except maybe a friend from Salt Lake. If that happened, it was her fault for calling.

It was about eight the next morning when Teresa called back. Russ was busying himself with last minute cleaning in preparation for Debra Taylor's arrival.

"Mr. Renfroe said if you want to come up and see the tapes, come on," Teresa said proudly.

"That's great. So, he didn't give you any trouble about a warrant or anything?" asked Russ.

"No. He said he has two daughters and a step daughter plus a son. He couldn't imagine anyone doing anything to one of them and nobody being willing to help. He liked the informal approach."

"I'll be out of here in a minute. It's about ninety miles up 287 and I-90, so I guess it will be about an hour and a half from me to get there."

"You can have lunch with us too, if you want to. Food's pretty good here," Teresa suggested.

"I won't have time. I have a friend coming in at the Bozeman airport at one o'clock, so this will have to be a fast trip. Maybe he will let you find the spot on the tape that shows us them coming and going, and let's be sure and get the time stamps. Maybe take a cell phone picture."

"I'll get on it," she replied.

"One other thing, Miss Walker."

"What's that?"

"Thanks."

They hung up, and Russ exhaled in relief.

Russ couldn't help but think out loud, *At last. Something is going right, but why does everything happen at once?*

Russ would have to put some preparations for his guest on hold. Maybe she wouldn't notice. But he was off and running to Butte to watch some security videos. Hopefully.

Teresa was on the lookout when Russ came in, waving him down the moment he walked in the door. "Hey, Detective. Come on back. Mr. Renfroe is expecting us," she said.

The door was opened to Renfroe's office, and when he saw them, he motioned for them to come in. He stuck out his hand to Russ.

"Hello. I'm Chuck Renfroe. I'm the general manager here at *Wayne's.* Teresa tells me you are trying to make a connection with this young woman you have in the hospital that may have come through our restaurant."

Russ shook his hand and responded, "I'm Russell Baker. I work as an auxiliary deputy for Madison County, as I'm sure Ms. Walker told you. And you're right, there may or may not be any connection, but we hope can get a clue to who she is and who might have put her in the hospital. I really appreciate you allowing us to look at the video files. We don't not want to put you in an awkward position."

"Where are you from, Detective?" Renfoe asked.

"I grew up in Marietta, Georgia."

"I thought you sounded like a Georgia boy. I lived in Cobb County for many years."

"How about that?" Russ replied. "I was a Cobb County Detective for several years before moving out here."

"I still have family down that way, and we get back as often as we can. My wife has family and lots of friends there as well," Renfroe said.

Teresa commented, "I know you have to get back, so Mr. Renfroe and I have about three or four spots we looked at. It does appear that the girl was here that night and came in with what looks to be a truck driver. She then went into the bathroom. Then, it gets weird."

Renfroe moved the images as they talked, and he said, "It shows Miss Walker going and opening the door to the ladies' room and looking in. She says she did not see anyone in the restroom. But, in a moment the guy goes to the door, opens it slightly, and it looks as though he may have called to her. The girl comes out just as a guy walks up wearing a baseball cap pulled low over his face."

"So," Russ said. "When you looked in there and did not see anyone, she was actually in there."

"Yes. So, it would appear. I didn't search the place, but I did lean over and did not see any feet and legs in any of the stalls," Teresa said.

"You feel sure this is the same girl?" Russ asked.
"As you can see, it is not a full image, and not all that clear, but that looks like her to me," Teresa said, sounding more confident than she had that day in the hospital.

"I mentioned that she looked like Halle Barry," said Renfroe. "And Teresa said she had made that same comparison when she saw the woman in the hospital."

Russ thought for a minute and said, "Those observations are too specific to be just coincidence. I think we can place our Jane Doe at your restaurant on the night she was injured. Now, how about the guy that picked her up?"

They scrolled to the brief video of the man who had walked out with the Halle-Barry-lookalike.

"Well, hell, we won't get any arrest warrant on that," said Russ in a frustrated voice. "You're right, Ms. Walker, that guy knows how to come and go where there are security cameras. Cap and sunglasses at night."

"I've taken a number of photos of the videos with my camera, and I will send them. Maybe we can play around with them and see if we can get a clearer picture," said Teresa. "The cap doesn't have a logo, either. He's smart."

"I'm curious, Mr. Renfroe, do a lot of people come in acting like they are high or doped up? Do these people not stand out and attract attention?" asked Russ.

"Unfortunately, no. They don't stand out. It's fairly common with as many people as we have coming through here. All ages, sexes, and colors. Our company policy is not to interfere or refuse service as long as they are not abusive or acting dangerously," replied Renfroe.

"Not unusual, then?" commented Russ.

"Sadly, no. And if you need this, you can take it," said Renfroe, waving towards the security disks.

"How about you keep it safe and in your possession? I would like to get it picked up by the local police or DCI. If they see it, it can help in getting an arrest and conviction. We can have an official chain of custody that can't be challenged in court," said Russ.

"Please remember that I have not touched or handled the equipment if you are ever asked."

"You think this guy is local?" asked Renfroe.

"At least nearby," Russ said.

"We will look over the outside camera footage over the next day or so and see if there is anything there. There are several, but the quality of detail is not always great," added Renfroe. "I've always thought I might like being a detective."

Russ noticed a picture on the wall of a truck and Airstream Camper rig. A woman was smiling and waving from the door. "Is that Mrs. Renfroe?"

"If it wasn't, I wouldn't have it in my office," he said with a laugh. "That's Jenn. She's also my camping buddy."

"My folks went, and I went camping when I was small. We had a much smaller camper that my dad pulled with the car. My mother hated the thing, but she went along every time," said Russ. "He never went anywhere without her."

Russ thanked Renfroe and Teresa for their help, said goodbye, and headed out the door.

"He seems like a really nice guy, MS Walker. You met him on the job, I suppose?" asked Renfroe.

"Yes. I met him on the job when I was working for the State on Montana," she replied.

"So, you worked on a case with him?"

"I was the case. Or, part of it." She answered. "He arrested me and I went to jail. I told you about that."

"Oh. Yes, you did," was his startled reply. I don't know if I would be so forgiving."

"Yeah, well. On top of that, he killed my former boyfriend."

Renfroe was speechless.

"Of course, my former boyfriend had shot me and put me on life support. I'd better get back to work or you'll be asking me to leave." Teresa turned to walk away.

"I have just one question, Miss Walker."

She turned and said, "Yes, sir?"

"Do you have any more boyfriends that might be dropping by?"

"Right now, I think Detective Baker is about as close to a boyfriend as I have. I've had coffee and lunch with him and invited him for lunch today. He turned me down."

As she turned and walked away, she asked, "Do I still have a job?"

"With boy friends like you have, I'd be afraid to fire you," he said with a smile and motion waving her to go back to work.

It was going to be close getting back to Bozeman before Debra Taylor arrived. He hoped he would avoid the MHP between Butte and Bozeman.

It was close. Russ did not see a familiar face in the Jet Aviation lobby. He walked over just in time to see a plane rolling up. On the tail was Challenger 350 in big letters. *That must be it.*

His phone vibrated, and he saw a text: *Arrived in Bozeman. Are you here?*

Yes

As the plane rolled to a stop, the stairs were lowered, and a fellow walked by and stopped to watch.

By the door on the side of the plane was a small sign:
Taylor Development
Salt Lake City

The fellow commented as Debra came down the stairs. "Taylor Development. Wonder who that gorgeous lady is coming down the stairs."

"That's Miss Taylor," said Russ without looking at the man. "Okay," he said. "So, you waiting on her?"

"Yes." This time he gave the guy an unmistakable look that suggested he might should mind his own business.

The man turned and walked away and said, "Lucky guy."

The woman walking across to the entrance would never be mistaken for a tough cop. She had on cowboy boots. The expensive kind. A dress befitting a singer or movie star. The expensive kind. And a hairdo that spoke of a visit to the best hair salon in Salt Lake. No doubt, the expensive kind.

She had a small bag and one of the crew was carrying some other bags and sacks. Russ walked over to the door.

"Hello, Debra. You are Debra, right?" Russ was not too good at clever quips.

"Yes. That's me. You don't recognize me without a gun, I suppose."

Russ, without thinking about what he was saying said, "You are a killer with or without a gun on your hip."

With that she gave him a hug and a kiss on the cheek. "You sure know how to make a girl feel welcomed."

They walked out, and the crew member was walking with them."

"Randy is going as far as your car, if you're wondering. I asked him to help carry this stuff I brought. I knew you wouldn't have any good things to eat at your house, and I figured we might need to be prepared. I hope it's alright."

Russ smiled and gave a two-shoulder shrug. "I think that's terrific."

"And, wow, you picked me up in a police car. What a start to a lovely weekend."

Russ wasn't too sure if that was meant to be funny or sarcastic. But, for once, he thought he had a good comeback.

"Only the most important visitors get a police escort. Movie stars, country music singers, rock and roll idols, and the like," he said.

"Which am I?" she asked.

As he started the car, he looked at her with a new appreciation. "My beautiful friend from Salt Lake."

She smiled, reached over and touched his arm. "Now you're getting somewhere."

They had no sooner pulled out of the lot toward Ennis when his phone rang. He started to ignore it.

"Go ahead and answer it, Russ. It's probably one of your girlfriends."

"They all call on my special number," he said with a smile.

It was Sheriff Steinbrenner. "Russ, any luck with the security videos?"

"Yes and no. We are pretty sure the victim was in the

restaurant the night of the incident. Mr. Renfroe and Teresa Walker both had the same reaction to her. She was there and, in the restroom, when Teresa Walker went to look but for some reason was not where Walker could see her."

"I wonder if she was purposely trying to avoid anyone seeing her?" queried the sheriff. "What about the people with her?"

"The driver had on one of those hats that do a good job of cutting out a view from the cameras. No useful info there. And the guy that came in looked like he was right out of a Marlon Brando movie: sunglasses, cap and collar pulled up. They're going to see if they spot anything on the yard security cameras, but they weren't too optimistic."

"Why wouldn't someone notice a girl like that if she is all doped up and having to be helped in and out?" asked the sheriff.

"I asked Mr. Renfroe, the manager there, that question. He's being very cooperative, by the way. He said it's an almost daily occurrence. Men, women, boys, girls – every race, creed, and religion. They come in high on something and as long as they don't cause a disturbance, they don't try to interfere. Sometimes it's a couple, and sometimes it's one person with someone else. Commonplace, is how he described it. They have so many people coming and going in that place it's unbelievable."

"Okay. Where are you now?" the sheriff asked.

"In Bozeman, on the way back."

"Would you like to come have dinner tonight? My wife suggested it."

"Ordinarily, I would never turn down a date with your wife for dinner, but tonight I have other plans. Thank you, though."

"Anyone I know?" the sheriff asked.

"It's a secret. It's a cop from Salt Lake."

"Oh, I see. *Undercover* work, I assume."

"You are on speaker phone, Sheriff."

"Not my fault," he countered.

Debra spoke up, "Sheriff, this is Debra Taylor. I'm on special assignment."

"Hello, Debra. And, goodbye, Russ." The line went silent.

They both burst out laughing.

"Did we embarrass the sheriff?" she asked.

"Not likely."

Marta

Marta Andruko was in one of the cottages at a Montana ranch. She had been carried there as soon as they had arrived from Las Vegas, and they had put her to work entertaining some big, heavy-set man who was speaking in a foreign accent and who wreaked of cigar smoke and sweat. She wanted to find a way out, but she didn't know where she was.

The man got up and walked out yelling something about getting a drink. It was about two o'clock in the morning. Marta sat up on the edge of the bed. She needed to go to the bathroom but had been sedated to the point she had trouble getting up.

She finally made it to her feet and stumbled to the door. It had a dead bolt of some kind, and she could not get the door open. The cottage had a security man that had seen her abuser leave and had locked the door from the outside. She was a prisoner.

Marta headed for the bathroom and sat down on the toilet with her head in her hands, sobbing. She took a deep breath and looked in the mirror of the lavatory sink. In the mirror, she almost didn't recognize herself. She had bruises on her face, her lip was swollen, and she ached all over. And, then, she saw the cell phone on the sink with some money and keys.

Frantic, she picked up the disposable phone and finally got it turned on. She knew the man could be back any minute or one of the security people. If they saw her with the phone, she would be in serious trouble. She started to call home but knew they would not be able to help her where she was. So, she dialed 911.

"Madison County 911," the voice said. "What is your emergency?"

"I am being held prisoner. I need help!" Marta was trying whisper and yell at the same time.

"What is your name, please."

"My name is Marta Andruko. I'm from Louisiana, but I'm being held…Oh, God, he's coming." The phone went dead.

Chapter 31

Russell Baker was nice and cozy in his bed under the covers and couldn't figure out the noise he kept hearing. Trying to wake up, he thought he was dreaming when he heard a very strange sound. It sounded like a very muffled woman's voice. Not a happy one, at that.

"Baker, will you please answer that phone? It has been ringing over and over. Must be an old girlfriend or someone really important. I'm not awake, and I don't know where the phone is."

As he was trying to find the phone, he remembered whose voice he was hearing in his waking up reality: it was Debra Taylor with her back pressed up against his. How could he have forgotten that? He found the light.

The phone had stopped ringing and had gone to voicemail. As he tried to read the name in the caller ID, it started ringing again. He said out loud, "It's Steinbrenner."

"This is a new record, even for you, Sheriff," Russell said with a slight growl.

"We had something come up, and it struck a nerve. We had a 911 call this morning. Came in about 2:00 AM. The woman said she was being held prisoner and gave us a name, but she got cut off or hung up before we could get a location."

"Okay, Sheriff, what do you think I should do about that? As you may remember, I'm on an undercover assignment."

"Aw, Baker, I forgot about that. Sorry."

"You said it struck a nerve?" Russ asked, rubbing the skin between his eyes in an attempt to wake himself.

"The cell tower that we think it came from is in Silver Star."

Russ sat up, pulling the cover off the undressed Salt Lake Detective, making her most unhappy. She grabbed the cover and pulled it back over her.

"You thinking there's a connection to our victim in Bozeman and this woman, Sheriff?" Russ asked.

"Strange coincidence, don't you think?"

"What do we do?" Russ asked.

"It's been pointed out to me that the cell tower up there is what's known as an extended range tower and is at a high altitude. So, the area it can serve is a larger foot print. We certainly don't have enough information to take any action," the sheriff growled.

"What is the name you have?"

"It's Marta Andruko – and let me tell you, it was hell trying to figure that out. The call was shotty, but you know Frankie. When I set her to it, she figured it out for us."

From what the sheriff had always told Russ, he liked Frances "Frankie" Willingham. She was a no nonsense, take no crap fifty-five-year-old who had been married for a few years, once, and that was enough for her. She and her two dogs got along just fine. She had been a nice addition having worked in the New York Police Department at one time.

"What do you know about the woman?" Russ asked.

"18 years old. And she's a Ukrainian national living in New Orleans with her father until recently. I'll text you a picture and her name and details. She had left home on her own but then the family couldn't get in touch with her. They reported her missing a short while back. We haven't made contact with her parents yet. Don't want to get their hopes up since we're probably chasing a goose at this point, but I've got a hunch about this one, Russell."

"Your hunches are rarely just hunches, Sheriff. What do you want me to do now?" Russ asked.

"You can go back to the undercover assignment for now."

"Sheriff, why did you call me, then, at this time of the morning?"

"I didn't want to be the only one having a good time," the man replied.

"Sheriff, I have been having a good time. And, I'm going to be in Bozeman at a barbeque this afternoon. Please refrain from sharing anymore of the joy unless you really have something I can act on. Okay?"

"You're bordering on insubordination, Baker."

"You can fire me, I guess."

"Not until you clear up these cases. Then, buddy, you're out. Till I need you again." He hung up.

"Mr. Baker, you are so much fun to spend the weekend with," came the muffled voice from under the covers.

Russ did not respond verbally. He sat on the edge of the bed for a moment, reminded of these kinds of moments when Sarah was alive and they were always together as much as their lives would allow. Those warm feeling came rushing back. But instead of sadness, now, he had learned to smile happily at those memories.

He couldn't believe that this beautiful, rich woman who could have guys standing in line, was sleeping in his bed in Ennis, Montana. He climbed back under the covers, and she nestled back against him. Just like Sarah used to do.

Chapter 32

Russ had been amazed at seeing Debra Taylor exiting the plane at Bozeman. She could have been a TV star, a movie star, or a pop singer. He had never really appreciated how beautiful she was.

Russ had commented on the ride to Ennis, "I thought that dress you wore to the wedding was nice. But this outfit is gorgeous."

"Well, it's nice to know you at least noticed the outfit," she'd responded.

"Oh, I get it. Now you've taken up fishing too?" he had said with a laugh.

"Looks like the only way I'm going to get a compliment from you," she had said.

Russell had come up with a great comeback. At least he had thought it was.

"I could not think of the words to describe how lovely you are, Debra. The words escape me."

He had looked at her and she had returned the look with a smile. "Mr. Baker, you surprise me. That's about as nice a thing that has been said to me lately."

"Well, maybe you should wear your gun less and that outfit more." She had punched him in the shoulder.

Debra had brought everything for a meal for the evening. Food packed in dry ice with all the trimmings. And she had set about improvising with Russ's limited assortment of cooking utensils. Many of which had been left from the previous tenant.

She had made a gourmet meal, and they'd had a great evening. He had commented to her about how great it was, and she had said she wanted him to know she was more than a pretty face, with a laugh. He had said he'd noticed that already.

A great meal, and a great night. It had been wonderful until he had gotten that call from the sheriff at around three in the morning.

She finally sat up at about eight o'clock and asked, "Do you want to get in the shower before me, after me, or with me?"

"If you're giving me the option, I take the last one," he said. And away they went.

Later, they made it to the kitchen, and Russ asked, "Are you doing breakfast, or are we doing cereal and toast?"

"Cereal and toast. We have a barbeque today, don't we?"

The phone rang. "Oh no. It's the sheriff, again," Russ said.

Answering his phone while trying not to groan out a "Hello?" He put the phone on speaker and sat it down on the counter, deciding to prepare their makeshift breakfast while talking it out with the man.

"Is this a good time, Baker?"

"Better than three in the morning," Russ said.

"My apologies to the undercover operative you have there," said Steinbrenner.

Debra was listening. "Sheriff, you're so far in the doghouse with me, you may never get out."

"Russ, you have to stop answering my calls on speaker. I may actually say something important sometime."

"Well, we're both waiting," Russ said.

"Nothing new to report. We got a communication from the New Orleans PD, and they say the girl didn't want to go back to Ukraine and thought she might get into the movies in Atlanta. Apparently, they are doing a lot of movies in Georgia. She left some messages, and then her phone seemed to be cut off. The father's visa has expired, and they all need to leave the country. ICE will be looking for her, too. There is some indication she met up with someone in Atlanta that offered to help her."

"And, nothing new on our Jane Doe victim here, I suppose?" Russ asked.

"Nothing."

"Debra and I are going to a barbeque at Chad Freeman's house up in Bozeman. Call me if anything comes up."

"Russ, I never call at a bad time. Just when bad things happen."

Russ and Debra headed toward Bozeman and the barbeque.

"We're not going empty handed, are we Russ?" she asked.

"Thanks for mentioning that. There is a small convenience store on the way to his place. I'll pick up some beer, water, and some soft drinks. Sound okay?"

"Sure."

Once again, Debra looked like she was going to a photoshoot. Even in blue jeans and some fashionable boots, she was glamorous.

Russ pulled into the store, and Debra got out also. They picked up the items and started out the door just as an SUV pulled in on the opposite end of the lot. The two of them were laughing and carrying on as they made their way towards the truck.

Russ only glanced over in time to lock eyes with Nancy Freeman staring at him from that SUV. He imagined she knew he was on the way to her brother's barbeque, and Russ knew she had not been invited. For a moment, he thought about saying hello, but she slowly backed out of the parking lot without ever getting out.

"You good, Russ?" Debra questioned.

He smiled. "Yeah, let's get the booze," he said, and he meant it. He really was good for the first time since arriving back in Montana.

There was a nice gathering at Chad's by the time they arrived, and he and his wife were greeting and making people welcome. Russ and Debra approached them with the drinks, and Russ locked eyes with Alise as they crossed the lawn. There was a nervousness about her, and she slapped Chad and whispered something to him.

A number of the guides and their wives were there swapping fish stories, and in some case, just plain lies. All in good fun. One of the guides saw Russ and yelled, "Baker! Did you really threaten to put a guy and his wife out and make them swim back?"

Debra looked at him with a raised hand as if to say, *"You did what?"*

Russ was getting better at little quips, he felt. "No, I didn't say anything about swimming. Just told them they weren't riding back in the boat with me." The group burst into laughter.

Another said, "Baker. Are you going to introduce us to that beautiful lady?"

"No." Again, they all laughed, but Debra Taylor walked over and introduced herself.

"Where are you from, Debra?" one asked.

Before she could reply, Russ said, "She is my friend from Salt Lake and works in her family business."

Debra sensed that Russ did not want to discuss her being a cop. He appreciated her noticing.

In a short time, another SUV pulled in, and Rachel Wallace got out. Russ frowned as Chad and Alise pulled him aside.

"You're going to kill me, but I didn't know you were bringing a date… I thought it might be nice to invite Rachel Wallace… she knows several of the guides here," Chad muttered, nodding towards the SUV.

"Smooth move, matchmaker," Alise scowled in Chad's direction. Now Russ knew what Alise had been slapping Chad frantically about earlier – she had noticed Russ had brought a date. "You might as well have invited Nancy," she scorned.

"Heck no," Chad snarled at his sister's name.

"No problem, Chad," Russ assured him, and he thought for a minute and continued, "I'm surprised to see her, though."

Rachel spotted Russ, and she seemed to be contemplating whether or not to go on the offense or defense. After a moment, she seemed to decide on the proactive approach and go on the offense. She walked over to Russ and Debra.

"Well, Detective Baker. Nice to see you here. Do you work with Chad?" she asked.

"I help John out at *The River's Run* when he gets overbooked. I'm part time. Chad is their top guide. I would like to be as good as he is someday."

"So, you are a part time fishing guide and a part time detective. You don't have a full-time job?" she asked.

Russ could tell that she didn't intend to sound as condescending as it came out. He was unbothered. "No. I don't need one," he said.

Debra's eyes narrowed. Russ wasn't sure if the look Debra had on was due to some sort of cop instinct or instinctual feminine rivalry. She seemed to instantly disliked Rachel Wallace.

"Hi," she said to Rachel Wallace. "I'm Debra Taylor, from Salt Lake. Part time girlfriend."

Russ wasn't sure about what had just happened. But the two women had a clear understanding. Rachel did not like Debra, either.

Rachel asked, "Did you drive over from Salt Lake?"

Debra said, "No, my father let me use his plane."

"How nice."

"Detective Baker, have you found out who was responsible for the person found up on the road?" Rachel asked.

"Not yet. But we're still working on it,"

Rachel excused herself and mingled on.

Debra looked at Russ and said, "Females can be asses too."

Russ decided no comment was best.

Then, it happened. Russ's phone rang. Steinbrenner, again.

Russ let out a deep sigh. "Who is it?" Debra asked.

"Guess."

"Go ahead and talk to the sheriff. Maybe he's lonely," Debra said with a groan, clearly growing tired of the interruptions.

"Baker, here."

"Russ, the victim is partially awake. Can you go over there now?" the sheriff asked.

Debra was giving him the thumbs up and nodding.

"On the way." He hung up.

They said goodbye to Chad and his wife and trotted off. This did not go unnoticed to Rachel Wallace.

Rachel

Rachel Wallace had counseled with her people in Boston as to whether or not she should go to the barbeque, especially with the crowd at the ranch. The conclusion had been that it would help her see what information she could pick up about the girl found on the road. Anyone that might be interested in the ranch or her would see her being there as a normal activity. Go ahead, accept an invitation from a company you do business with to a barbeque. Blend in. Act normal.

Rachel continued to mingle with several of the guides, after who Russ and Debra departed.

Many had worked float trips for the ranch's clients. Eventually, she found her way to the party's host.

"Well, Chad, the detective left in a rush. I hope it wasn't anything I said," she began as a polite attempt to get some information.

Chad did not understand the comment, of course. "Not to my knowledge, Rachel. He got a call from the sheriff. Don't know what it's about."

Rachel couldn't help but wonder if it had anything to do with her and the Leonard Ranch. She was still on edge ever since Russ had paid them a visit. So far, things appeared to be going well on her end, but it still had her nervous.

She thought briefly about Marta and the other girls she had locked up at the ranch at the moment. She needed to play it cool; they didn't need any more unwelcomed visits from people like Russ. *Easy, Rachel,* she told herself. As far as she knew, the girls were all locked up safely in their rooms with men who were paying big bucks for the privilege of being there.

"I guess he's a good cop for them to call on him part time on a big case," she said.

"Wouldn't want him after me," Chad said.

"Nice girl he's with," she said.

"I don't know her. Never seen her before," responded Chad. "Not going to lie to you, Rachel, I was hoping to try to set you two up. Didn't expect him to show up with a date, though."

Rachel smirked. The last thing she needed to do was to start dating a cop. "I think I'll be all right. Thanks for thinking of me, though, Chad."

Chapter 33

"Do you want me to come in or stay outside, Russ?" Debra asked as they pulled into the hospital parking lot.

"I think having you there will be very important. Hopefully, she will be more comfortable with you in the room and may be more comfortable with you asking questions."

They approached the nurses' station, and the doctor was there as promised. He was not very optimistic.

"The patient has regained consciousness but is still suffering some brain trauma, and as a result she has memory loss. This will likely subside but whether it is one day, ten days, or months, we don't know at this time."

"We can still talk to her, though, right?" Russ asked.

"Certainly. I just want you to know that she may not have a clear picture, and she may not be able to connect the dots and could be confused on specifics."

They walked down to the room. The same room he had visited with Teresa Walker a few days before.

Geraldine looked at them but did not speak. Everyone said hello and waited. No response.

"I came by the other day to see you. You seem to be better. Do you remember me?" Russ asked.

No response.

"I am the local detective working on your case and this lady is my friend and colleague. Her name is Detective Debra Taylor. We want to find the people who did this, and we need your help."

She whispered something they could not understand. "I'm sorry. But I didn't understand. Can you speak a little louder?" Russ asked.

She spoke again. The doctor, the nurse, and the two detectives could hear it a little better this time. *"She has on pretty clothes."*

Debra Taylor stepped forward and took the girls hand. "That is so nice of you. Do you know who you look like to me?" she asked in a soft voice.

The girl made a little head shake that seemed to say *no*.

"Everyone says you look like Halle Barry." The girl made a brief effort at smiling.

"We need to know your name. Can you tell us your name?" Debra asked.

No response.

"Is there someone we can call and let them know where you are. Someone must be missing you."

She whispered, "Lois."

"Is Lois your name?" asked Debra.

"*I don't know*," she said in a raspy tone.

"Okay. We'll just talk a little. You can talk whenever you want. Detective Baker is more familiar, so let's let him talk first."

"We think you were at a truck stop in Butte with a truck driver who brought you in. You went to the restroom. Do you remember that?"

A nod of yes.

Then she said something that sounded like *"A note."*

"Did you write a note to someone?"

A nod of yes.

"What did you do with the note?"

She shook her head *no*.

"Do you remember the man you left with? Is he the one who hurt you?" Russ could see a glimmer in her eyes. It looked like fear.

"There's nothing to be afraid of here. We are not going to let anyone hurt you," Debra said and squeezed her hand. "Did the man that you left with hurt you?" Debra asked.

A nod of yes.

Russ asked, "Did you stab him with a ballpoint pen?"

Again, the flash of fear in her eyes.

Russ asked again, "Did you write a note with the pen and then stab the man with it?"

Debra leaned over and said, "You are not in any trouble. If you stabbed the man that was hurting you, he deserved it. Did you stab him with the pen?

A nod of yes.

"What is your name?" she asked again.

"Lois," she said, her voice a tad clearer.

"Where do you live, Lois?" Debra asked.

"Chattanooga," she said.

"Do you know the name of the person that hurt you?" Debra asked.

"Max."

Then she turned away, and the doctor said that would have to be all. Russ had recorded the short interview on his phone.

They thanked the doctors and asked if they could try again tomorrow. The answer was, probably.

"Well, Debra, we didn't get too much out of that, but at least it was something."

"You got Lois and Chattanooga and someone named Max. Maybe the sheriff can piece something together," Debra said. "And it appears she wrote a note for someone and stabbed the attacker with the ballpoint pen. Something else, Russ. That girl reminded me a lot of the girl I had that ran out of the hospital in Salt Lake. I'm not sure why. Something about their eyes. The looks."

Russ gave her a surprised glance. "Well, so far we have nothing to link anyone to anything. No note and no one reporting a stab wound with a ballpoint pen."

Russ called the sheriff and filled him in. "We'll get started on the FBI and the NamUs sites. Frances is good at coming up with ideas. Maybe we can get lucky and get a young woman missing recently in Chattanooga with the name of Lois. Are you going back tomorrow?" the sheriff asked.

"That's the plan for tomorrow. And, by the way. Guess who was at the cook out?"

"Garth Brooks?"

"Goodness. I did not know you were into country music," Russ said, shaking his head. "Great guess, though. No, it was Ms. Rachel Wallace."

"How did that come about, I wonder?" asked the sheriff.

"I think Chad has done business with them and thought he might fix me up with her."

"I guess that went over well with Debra Taylor?"

"It didn't go worth a damned, Sheriff," Debra said.

"Russ. You have to keep me off the speaker. Where are you headed now?"

"Gourmet meal at Perkins," Russ said, smirking.

"Geesh, Russ. Is that the best you can do?" the sheriff prodded.

"It is, unless Debra's buying. She cooked last night."

"Hmmm. I could take that one of two ways."

"Goodbye, Sheriff," Russ said and hung up.

After dinner at Perkins, they headed for Ennis and watched the last of the sun go down beside the Madison River.

Debra Taylor really liked being with Russ. And Russ had not felt this way in a long time. Now if she could just do something about his phone, the evening might go very well.

Meanwhile, the Madison sheriff's office team set to work trying to run down a missing person named Lois from Chattanooga. They found one, but she was 55 years old. No luck. No Max, either.

Sheriff Steinbrenner decided to let Russ and Debra have a quiet evening with no calls.

Rachel

Rachel Wallace reported in, "Didn't learn anything at the barbecue except that the detective was there. He works his fishing through *The Rivers Run* shop. He had some girl from Salt Lake with him. Very pretty and rich, too, it sounded like."

"What's her name?"

"Taylor. Debra Taylor."

"Why do you think she's rich?"

"When I asked if she drove over from Salt Lake, she told me she came over on her father's plane," Rachel explained. "Anyway, I have to go. We are super busy, and we have a couple of heavy drinkers here slapping some of the ladies around."

"Can you handle it?"

"What do you think?" Rachel questioned, almost insulted.

"Call you tomorrow," the voice said.

Night had come to Montana.

Chapter 34

Russ and Debra finally made it to the kitchen and got their morning coffee. "Russ, I have to get back this afternoon. I am on call for the evening and have to be in court tomorrow morning on a case."

"Debra, this was a very nice weekend. It could have been even nicer if not for this mess we're trying to clean up here. Sorry about the calls and interruptions."

"Russ, I'd like to do this again. Soon. Maybe you can come to Salt Lake where they can't find you. I'll send the plane for you."

"That sounds wonderful. And, remember, I owe you a trip on the Madison. Any excuse to see you will work just fine with me," he said.

"Do you really feel that way, Russ? I was afraid that if I invited myself out here, you might want to run in the other direction."

"I'm so happy you called. So happy you came. Thanks for helping with the hospital visit yesterday. Maybe, soon, we can schedule getting together?"

"My dad said to tell you that job offer is still good," she said with a slight grin.

"Well thank him for me. Right now, I think that is a stretch for me. But I'll come to Salt Lake to see you. Or, maybe you can move to Ennis and get a job with Steinbrenner."

"I would need a little more than a job with Steinbrenner to get me here permanently, Russ, but I can think of a couple of reasons I might move here."

"And they are?"

"You're a detective," she said with a slight glimmer in her eye. "You figure it out."

"When is your plane scheduled to leave, Debra?"

"It leaves when I get there and get aboard."

"Of course. I forget what it's like to have a plane and two pilots on call," he said.

"Did you ever have a plane and two pilots on call?" she asked.

"Sure. I call Delta, buy a ticket, and go get on the plane. Almost like what you do."

She walked up to Russ, leaned up, and gave him a kiss on the cheek. She patted him on the shoulder and said, "Not quite the same."

"Will you be willing to drop by and see the girl in the hospital with me on the way to the airport? She responded to you well, yesterday."

"

Sure. I'd love to do that. Anything I can do to help."

Almost on cue, Russ's phone rang. "Good morning, Sheriff," said Russell.

"Just to let you know, we got nothing back so far on the names and the Chattanooga reference from our work last night," he said.

"Debra has to get back to the airport and get back to Salt Lake, but she's going to stop back at the hospital with me on the way there. The girl responded to her well."

"Okay, let me know if you get anywhere. And, Debra, I know you're listening; I really appreciate your help."

"No problem, Sheriff," she said.

"What airline do you use from Salt Lake?" the sheriff asked.

"Taylor Aviation, LLC," she said.

He started to say something like he did not know that airline, then he said, "Well, of course."

He hung up.

In a few minutes, they were headed toward Bozeman. They were both quiet most of the way. Russell was wondering if this was something serious for Debra or was it just a whim. Something to do for a weekend. Getting too involved and then being brushed aside hurt too much. Time would tell, he supposed.

The nurse checked the room to ask the girl if she would like visitors, and though it sounded as though she didn't recall having any previously, she eventually agreed.

Russ and Debra stepped inside the door, and to everyone's surprise, the girl reached out in a welcoming way toward Debra.

Debra walked over, and the girl embraced her in a big hug.

"I'm so happy to see you again," said Debra. "Are you feeling better today?"

"Yes," she whispered.

"My name is Debra. This is Russ. We're both with the police, and we're trying to find who did this to you and put them in jail for a long time. Is that okay with you?"

"Yes," she whispered. "Can you tell us your name?"

"My name is Geraldine."

Debra and Russ, as well as the nurse, all looked at each other in shared surprise. The girl was incredibly responsive now, and she was obviously starting to remember things.

"What is your last name, Geraldine?"

"Bailey."

"Who is Lois, Geraldine? Yesterday you mentioned Lois," Debra explained.

"My grandmother."

Russ just watched as Debra continued the dialog with Geraldine, soaking it all in.

"What is her last name?"

"Mama Lois Bailey," she said.

"Where does she live, Geraldine?"

"Eastdale."

"So, she doesn't live in Chattanooga like you?"

"We both live in Eastdale. My sister lives there, too."

"What is your sisters name?" Debra asked.

"Maxine."

"Where is Eastdale?" Debra asked.

Geraldine become noticeably irritated. "I told you we live in Eastdale. Eastdale's in Chattanooga."

"Sorry, now I understand. Yesterday you said Max was the one that hurt you. Were you talking about your sister, Maxine?" Debra asked.

Again, Geraldine reacted angrily, "Maxine is my *sister*. She would never hurt me. The man was Max."

"Do you feel like talking just a little more?" Debra asked, picking up on the girl's irritation.

"A little."

"Do you remember going to a restaurant and going in the bathroom?" Debra asked.

"Yes. I left a note in one of the stalls," Geraldine said.

"What did the note say?"

"*Help*. I put my name on it."

"How did you get to the restaurant?"

"In a truck."

"A big truck or like a pickup truck?" Debra asked to clarify.

"Big truck. Had a bed in the back."

"Where did you get on the truck?"

"Not sure. Came from Atlanta with Marta and another girl, but I didn't learn her name," Geraldine explained.

Russ almost jumped out of his shoes. Marta was the person who had called 911. They were connected, after all.

"Where was Marta going; do you know?" Debra asked.

"Las Vegas."

"Where were you supposed to be going?"

"I can't remember."

With that, the unknown girl had a name, a grandmother, and a sister. Russell had something to go on at last. But they knew they would have to wait for another chance.

But there was a connection. Something bigger than one victim. But what was it?

Outside, in the hall, Russ gave Debra a hug and a kiss. Debra was startled by his affectionate display.

"You police people work a little differently. Here we just do high fives and pats on the back," the nurse teased as she too stepped out into the hall.

Debra said, "We are a close-knit organization," laughing. But she was happy too.

They walked to the truck, and Russ was calling the sheriff. The news was both helpful and alarming.

"So, you're saying this victim is somehow connected to the other possible victim from Louisiana?" the sheriff questioned.

"So it seems; Debra did a masterful job of talking to the girl, but she eventually tired out and quit talking to us."

The sheriff replied, "I'll contact the DCI and see if they want to get the FBI involved. Sounds like someone moved the girl against her will. We at the very least have kidnapping. Maybe, Human trafficking and the Mann Act Violations."

"What about her grandmother and sister? Will someone let them know?" Russ asked.

"I'll call Chattanooga PD and let them contact the grandmother. Maybe she will want to come and make a confirmation. If so, we may get some useful information from her, too."

"We'll keep digging for a connection to her attacker. I'm taking Debra to the airport. I'll be back in a couple of hours," said Russ.

Soon, Russ was standing and watching the Challenger jet stairs lift and close. The plane's engines rolled up, and the plane started down the taxi way. In a few seconds, it was sailing down the runway, nose up, and away. Russ thought he might should pinch himself. Had this weekend really happened? Suddenly, he found himself missing her. This could be a problem. A good problem, for a change.

Russ spoke in to the blue tooth phone in his truck: "Call Teresa Walker."

"Calling Teresa Walker," came the female artificial voice.

"Hello, Detective Baker."

"Hello. You know just plain Russ is okay, Ms. Walker."

"If you'll call me Teresa. I'm not a suspect now, hopefully."

"Not that I know of. I wanted to share some news. Our young lady victim has regained consciousness. We have a name. Geraldine Bailey. She is from Chattanooga, Tennessee. She was being transported against her will, drugged, beaten, and sexually abused and exploited."

"Poor thing. What about her family?"

"A sister and a grandmother. The sheriff's working on notifying them now. I think they will be happy to hear from her. And, she named someone that we had just gotten a 911 cellphone call from saying she was a prisoner and needed help. She was cut off before we could find her location. We're still looking."

"Do you think that person came through *Wayne's*, too?" Teresa asked, sounding stunned.

"No way to tell. This is our first bit of information indicating a larger scheme."

"What's your gut reaction to all this, Russ?" she asked.

"I believe there is a connection locally, but that's all I can say for now."

With no prompting, Teresa said, "You know, when I was with DCI, there were suspicions about that Leonard Ranch over near you having girls and boys brought in, but nothing was ever proven. Do you know the place?"

Russ was jolted by the news. "How extensive was the operation that was looking into them?"

"Can't really say. It was handled at the highest levels and was hush hush. I was not ever briefed on it."

"Does the name Rachel Wallace mean anything to you?"

"No – should it?"

"I'll let you know if we get a break. You do the same, okay?" he said before hanging up.

Russ had more to think about now.

Then he got a text: *Loved being with you. Miss you already.* ♥ *DT*

The same here, he replied.

"Don't read too much into this," he said out loud to himself.

Chapter 35

Max - Trey

The Max Johnson that Maria, Marta, and Geraldine had encountered did not show up on any google searches or country club lists. Why? Because his real name was Martin Thelston Montgomery, III. His family called him Trey. He was junior partner in the law firm of *Montgomery and Montgomery and Associates.* They were a big firm and worked with big clients. Trey had yet to make it to the top level and handled the less important clients.

But Trey's firm handled a major client named Maxwell (Max) Johnson. A successful builder and developer. The real Johnson had country club memberships, a Buckhead address, and was a pillar of society. But he had a couple of personal weaknesses: gambling and prostitutes. And, he needed a way to hide the gambling money, trips to Vegas, and money spent of other pleasures from his family and business associates.

The real Max Johnson and Martin "Trey" Montgomery had met at a party, and Johnson had too much to drink.

He had let it slip to Trey Montgomery that he liked to go to Vegas and Reno. Gambling and womanizing. Realizing he'd said too much, he had cautioned Trey about saying anything.

After more discussion, the real Max had asked if Trey could help him figure out a way to hide the money, flights, and hotel bills from his own company and his family. Trey had come up with a solution. One that would benefit Max Johnson, and of course, himself.

They would set up a shell company, one that would look like a business connection to Max Johnson. Money, bills, correspondence, and anything related to the Johnson's extracurricular activities would go to that company, and all the expenses would be billed to Johnson's company as business related expenses. The shell company would be called *Accurate Engineering, LLC*. Supposedly, a Civil Engineering firm.

Trey Montgomery had set up bank accounts, created a letter head, invoices, and a mailbox address for the company. A credit card had been set up, and everything from then on out was handled by Trey, and he was paid a salary from the shell company. An accounting went to Max Johnson privately. For a while, things had worked great for both men.

Then, unexpectedly, the real Max Johnson had died. There had been a funeral, the will read, and the estate settled. But the only person who knew about *Accurate Engineering, LLC* was Trey Montgomery, who by now, had learned a lot about the world of gambling and prostitution. A world he had seen as full of opportunity for himself.

A few calls and a few dollars later, Trey Montgomery had a driver's license, passport, photo ID's, and a new identity for his outside business venture: Maxwell Johnson had been reborn anew. Things had gone exceptionally well for a long while.

The *new* Max Johnson had experienced some setbacks lately, however, and had missed being paid on some of his human merchandise. But, then, he was in the clear. No connection to link him to anything and none to Martin Thelston Montgomery who lived on Blackland Road in Atlanta. One in the same.

The solution was to collect some more merchandise and get it out in the marketplace immediately to make up for the losses. There was plenty of demand and customers with money. He would recoup his loses quickly.

Max was out scouting for prospects when he made his usual look around at the bus station in Atlanta. He always stayed outside, and no one ever saw him in the terminal. Stay away from clear camera images that might be in use. He was in luck.

Outside on the sidewalk was a blonde girl in jeans and cowboy boots; she appeared to be looking for someone. The sunglasses in the twilight were a nice touch, he thought. She was trying to look cool. Worth a shot.

Max parked the car down the street and walked back. He started in with his usual line.

"Hi, young lady. I work up the street and saw you standing here. I hope you have someone coming to pick you up. It's not safe to be out on the streets alone here at night."

The girl backed away a little. To Max, she looked like any one of a dozen or more girls just like her.

About five foot seven and 125 pounds, she would bring a good price in his marketplace. So, he pressed on. "If you are waiting on someone, I'll be happy to wait until they come. I really don't want to leave you here." *What a nice man*, he thought amusingly to himself.

"I don't really have anyone coming, and someone stole my wallet at the bus station. So, I have no money," said the young woman. "Is there a homeless shelter nearby?"

"I'm sure there may be, but if I left you here like this, my wife would kill me. Look, let's go to the Waffle House. It's just down the street. Then I know a motel nearby, and I'll pay for you a room for tonight. You'll be much safer. Then you can figure something out in the morning."

"I don't know how I'll get any money to repay you," she said.

"Don't worry about it. We'll figure all that out tomorrow. Do you want to come to the Waffle House or not?"

"I guess that would be alright," she replied.

"What is your name? My name is Max Johnson."

"Gabrielle Sanchez," she said, keeping her head down as she spoke.

"Where are you from, Gabrielle?"

"Originally Mexico, but we came to Austin a long time ago."

"Do you need to call anyone and let them know where you are? You can use my phone."

"I'll call tomorrow," she said.

Max smiled. This girl was going to be an easy grab.

They walked to the black Mercedes, and he clicked the door locks. As he pushed the button to start the car, the girl said, "This is a nice car. You don't have to use a key to start it? How does that work?"

He thought it was cute she didn't know the answer. "Well, the key fob that opened the door is connected to car wirelessly. The car knows when the fob is present, and then I can start it."

"Oh. That's really cool."

They ate at the Waffle House and halfway through their dinner he said, "I'll run you over and drop you off at the motel. I need to be getting home, my wife will be looking for me." That wasn't true but was said to make the girl feel safe. Appearing off the market and concerned for 'the Misses' always put these girls at ease.

It was an old motel that had seen its best days several years before. The sign outside said $39.

It was the old style that all the rooms opened to the outside, and hers was to be on the second floor. Paid for by Max Johnson.

"Okay. You're all set."

"Mr. Johnson, this is very nice of you. Could I ask you to walk with me to the room? I'm a little scared to be out there by myself."

Max took her bag, needing to keep up the charade of the kind and friendly do-gooder, and they went to the room. He opened the door and walked over and put the bag on the bed. She closed the door and followed.

"Can you turn on the air conditioning. It's sort of stuffy in here?" she asked.

Max Johnson walked to the air unit under the window.

Suddenly, the first thrust of the ten-inch hunting knife went deep into his back on the right side. He tried to scream and turn around to see what was happening, and the second thrust hit him in the left side.

Max Johnson fell on the floor on his back and tried to scream, but the young woman put her hand over his mouth. She raised the hunting knife, and with all the effort she could muster, drove it into his chest.

Max Johnson was dead.

The young woman sat and leaned against the bed for a minute, trying to see if she was going to vomit or go to shaking or scream herself. But she was totally numb. She felt nothing. No sick reactions, no tears, no nothing.

After a minute, she went to make sure the *Do Not Disturb* card was hanging on the outside of the door. A quick glance, and no one seemed to be around. She closed the door and went to work.

She put on a pair of cheap cloth work gloves she had brought. She could not leave any finger prints.

She washed the hunting knife under hot water and wiped it clean. It went into a small plastic bag. She took off the clothes she had worn in and put them in the sink They had a small amount of blood on them. She would wash them and put them in the bag.

She went through the dead man's pockets and got his wallet and car fob. He had an ID that said Max Johnson and a credit card with the same name. The photo ID was clearly the man on the floor. His wallet had about $450 dollars in an assortment of bills, which was great. She'd be needing that. She got his phone and turned it off.

All the clothes she had worn in went into the plastic bag. They were wet, but she would not leave them behind.

She reached in the suitcase and unfolded a cloth type travel bag. When unfolded, it was larger than the suitcase. She then removed the blonde wig that she had bought at Walmart. The same place she had bought the hunting knife. A present for her father, she had told the person that had sold it to her. In a way, it was. The green fake contacts were removed and carefully put in the bag as well. She might need the wig and contacts again. She put on a different outfit and shoes and then she put on a brunette wig. No one would know she was the same girl that had just checked in.

After putting everything into the cloth travel bag, she checked the room, under the beds, and wiped doorknobs and bathroom handles. The towel would go with her. She was ready.

She thought it might be a couple of days before anyone looked in the room, and that would give her plenty of time to cover her tracks and leave town. She had given her plan a lot of thought.

Johnson had parked the car on the street since even cheap motels sometimes have security cameras, and he had wanted to avoid being seen with one of his prospects as much as possible. His choice was now working to his killer's advantage.

Living in a rural community growing up, the young woman was a good driver, although she had not driven much recently. But Johnson had shown her how to use the key fob, and she had gotten the car started and left the area.

Finding Peachtree Street, she headed north toward Buckhead. She found a side street that said 15th Street, and it was fairly wide and dark with a lot of old residences and apartments. She found a place to park on the street and sat for a minute before starting to look through the car. She wanted to see what was in the trunk.

She had trouble figuring out where the trunk release was. It finally occurred to her to look at the key fob, and there was small button with a trunk lid on it. With a small click, the trunk opened, and she got out and looked inside.

There were two briefcases. Both had some cash, credit cards, three cell phones, all off, and files and one had a thumb drive.

The files, two of the phones, and the thumb drive were in a case that had the ID for Maxwell Johnson. The man that was now dead in the cheap motel near downtown. There was a small notebook with numbers that she did not recognize.

The other had an ID for a man named Martin Montgomery, III, and looking at the picture, she knew it was the same man that was lying dead in the motel. It had cards for a law firm, one phone, and some case files. Between the two cases was a total of $1250 dollars. She now had enough to finance her remaining expenses.

She removed all the contents and put them in her bag, making sure the phones were off. She got out of the car, making sure there was nothing left that could trace her to the car, and she walked the dark street back up to Peachtree and started back toward downtown. She tried several times before getting a cab to stop, and he wanted to be sure she had money. "A little," she said.

"Where to?" he asked.

"I need a cheap motel for the night. Someone stole my ID, so I need a place cheap that won't ask a lot of questions."

"Can you pay me twenty-five dollars for the ride and $49 in cash for the motel?" She pretended to count her money. "I can come up with that, I believe."

He drove her to a motel very similar to the one Max Johnson had used. He stopped and went in with her. The driver and the clerk both appeared to be of Middle Eastern backgrounds, and the clerk motioned for her to sign in and give him the $49, and the driver wanted his money which she already had in her hand.

She signed in as Gabrielle Sanchez, got the key, and went to her room. She locked the door, put the chain on, and she used the rickety desk chair to block the door. She put the ten-inch hunting knife on the nightstand, climbed in the bed under the worn and tired bedspread and sheets and went to sleep.

It was about eight AM when she woke up. It took a minute to get her bearings and remember all that had occurred last night. Had she missed anything?

She still had to get a bus and get out of town. That would be the next item.

She placed the brunette wig on the counter and got a shower. Afterwards, the young woman put the brunette wig back on and dressed as she had been when she had come in. She walked down to front desk, gave the man the key and five dollars and asked him to call her a cab. She had two more important things to get done to complete her plan.

When the cab arrived, she said, "I need to go to the Greyhound bus station."

At the station she asked for a ticket to Austin, Texas. "Leaves at eleven thirty," she was told, and she gave the agent the cash. She made herself as un-noticed as possible.

She had checked in her planning and knew there was a FedEx shipping center a half mile up Forsyth St. She would walk up and get the things she needed. Small shipping box for overnight delivery, a small roll of packing material, tape, and pen. She would find a seat on the long bus ride to pack up the items to be shipped. She would get a guy she knew in Austin to ship the box.

The guy she knew in Austin didn't have a problem with ID's: he had several and could make you one if you needed one. For a price, of course.

When she stepped off the bus in Austin, she found a cab who would take her to Cedar Creek.

"It will be expensive to carry you to Cedar Creek," the driver said.

"It'll be worth it," she said.

Gabrielle Sanchez had boarded the bus in Atlanta, but she never got off and was never heard of again.

"Where are you headed?" the cab driver asked.

Maria Elena Torres smiled and said to the taxi driver in Austin, "I'm going home."

Chapter 36

Russ made a trip back to see Geraldine Bailey. The nurse was a little hesitant but said she would check as Geraldine had company. She walked down and looked in the room. She then motioned for Russ to come down.

Geraldine Bailey was much improved, talking better, and smiling. "Where is the lady that was with you?" she asked. Russ explained that Debra had to return home because she worked in Salt Lake City.

"This is my grandmother Lois and my sister Maxine." There were greetings and introductions all around. "My grandmother wants to talk to you."

"I'll be happy to talk to her. But I really need to talk to you and get everything down on tape, if you feel up to it?" Russ said.

"Okay."

"Does my granddaughter need a lawyer, Detective? Before she starts answering any of your questions?" Lois asked.

"Your granddaughter is not considered a suspect in any crime as far as my department is concerned. You can get a lawyer if you feel the need."

"Mama Lois, I don't want a lawyer. I want to talk to the detective," Geraldine assured her grandmother.

"Let me point out, you're likely to have the State DCI officers in here and maybe the FBI. It's highly possible that what happened to you is part of a larger criminal activity and maybe federal laws have been broken in your case. If they feel you should have legal counsel, they would have to read you your rights and offer you that chance.

I'm not reading you your rights because, to me, you're the victim," Russ explained.

"As far as my interviewing Geraldine," he continued, turning to Lois, "she is not considered a juvenile and can choose to answer me privately or have you present. It's up to her. She may not want to burden you with the details."

"Whatever will help you catch these people, Detective," said Lois Bailey.

Once they got started, it was a mixture of tears, hugs and more tears. The grandmother was a tough woman, but there were spots she had to leave the room. Russ felt that way too. He now had information about a young man in Chattanooga, a man named Max Johnson in Atlanta, a house somewhere, a large bus or motorhome, a trip to Boston, and truck drivers. There was a note left in a stall in the women's restroom at *Wayne's*. Then, there was the man that picked her up in a car in Butte and drove her somewhere. She did not know where. The number of people involved in this operation made Russ's stomach churn.

She told of stabbing the man with the ballpoint pen. "Where did you stab him on his body?" Russ asked.

"In the neck." She pointed to show where she thought the pen had managed to land. Then she had run. She remembered nothing after that.

"What was the person riding in that was there to pick you up?" Russ asked.

"One of those buses like what Max had."

Russ sat for a minute in silence, trying to control his anger and frustration.

Lois Bailey said, "I believe you're as angry as I am, Detective."

"You might be right, Mrs. Bailey. You just might be right." Russ turned to the girl in the hospital bed who had just bravely shared her tale with him. "Geraldine, would you recognize the man who took you in the car, ran you over, and shot you if you saw him again?"

"He had on a cap and sunglasses. But if he talked, I just might. His voice – I'll remember his voice."

Russ said goodbye, took his recorder, and headed out the door. "Detective. Can I ask you something?" It was Lois Bailey. She had stepped out of the room to follow him.

"Sure."

"Do you think you will ever get this person?" the old woman asked.

"It's my only job right now, Mrs. Bailey. If I don't get him, it won't be for the lack of trying."

"Thank you. If you don't know what to do with this guy and the one in Atlanta, just let me know. I'll think of something."

She turned and walked back into the room.

Russ spent the entire time back to Ennis on the phone. First to Sheriff Steinbrenner. Who was Max Johnson? Where was he? Who was the guy in Chattanooga? Who was the driver? Who was the shuttle driver in Butte?

More questions than answers. Where was Marta Andruko? Was she part of this, too? What was the

connection, if any, to the Leonard Ranch? Russ couldn't get the ranch off his mind. Perhaps it was just instinct – or perhaps he was losing his touch?

Then he called Debra and Teresa. They were all pleased that Geraldine was getting better. Maybe they would find Max Johnson in Atlanta. There were a lot of people working on this thing from different angles. There was a chance they could bring some of these creeps to justice.

Chapter 37

Rachel

"Hello. This is Rachel."

"Are you in your office?" the voice asked.

"Yes. I can talk. What's up?" she asked.

"Have you heard from our guy in Atlanta?"

"No."

"We can't seem to find him, and it looks like both of his phones are off. He was supposed to have some replacements for us and has disappeared."

"Is it possible he's been found out?" Rachel questioned.

"My sources don't have anything on it, if he has. But I did check on the lady friend that was with the detective that has been bugging you."

"I'd love to hear," said Rachel.

"She's a rich lady, alright. Her father's very successful, and she and her brother were both given a piece of the company. But she is also a detective on the Salt Lake City PD. I don't know if her visit was purely personal or if there is any connection to the girl we lost in Salt Lake. She is known as a tough officer inside the department."

"Should I be worried?" Rachel asked.

"Not at this point. They have no way of connecting you to anything."

"We have a full house here for the next several days, so I'll have a lot of money to move next week.," she said.

Debra

Debra Taylor was at her desk at 3365 South 900 West in Salt Lake when the front desk officer on duty walked back to her with a FedEx package. "This has your name on it, Detective. We did screen it for explosives. It seems clear."

"*Seems* clear? Well, how reassuring. Who and where is it from?" Debra asked, not making eye contact with the guy as she was nose deep in some paperwork.

"Looks like Victor Pasqual. San Antonio. But it was shipped from Austin, Texas."

"Well, I don't know anyone in San Antonio, and I don't know Victor Pasqual," she said, glancing up at the guy in confusion.

"Another of your many secret admirers," he said as he walked away.

She took an opener and had to work to get the several layers of tape off. Finally, inside, she was taken back by the contents.

She put on some latex gloves and started removing everything.

"Detective Ellis, can you come and help me with the contents of this box?" she called. "A camera would be nice. And some evidence bags."

"What's up here?" asked Ellis.

"Not too sure. Two wallets and three cell phones. A key. A thumb drive and a notebook. So far. Might be more under all this bubble wrap."

She called the section's administrative assistant over, Clara Wilcox, and asked, "Please handle the FedEx box with gloves. I need you to check out the address on the shipper to see if you can find out anything about the person who sent it. Almost looks like someone is sending us some evidence on a case."

They moved into a conference room and started laying out the contents of the wallets.

And, there he was: Max Johnson, or Maxwell Johnson as the Georgia Driver's License showed. She had heard that name from the hit and run and shooting victim in the hospital in Bozeman. She couldn't believe her eyes. There was an insurance card and a spa membership card tucked inside the first of the wallets. Maybe real. Maybe phony. But they all had an Atlanta address.

Then she opened the second wallet. A wallet belonging to someone named Martin Montgomery, III. Blackland Road in Atlanta, Georgia according to the driver's license. Only one problem: the picture in both wallets were the same.

The two phones would take some time. Locked, unlocked, encrypted. Who knew? She would get a team on it.

But there was one problem: they had no case associated with this man in Salt Lake. Not as as far as she knew.

She continued removing items. The thumb drive was next. Again, careful handling was called for. As she removed the last of the packing, a small card fell out on the table. It was a business card. It was Debra Taylor's business card identifying her as a Salt Lake City Detective. It had what looked like a lipstick smudge.

She stood in silence. "That's one of your cards, Debra," said Ellis.

"Yes, I believe it is. In fact, it has my name on it," she said. Then she added, "Sorry, I didn't mean to be a prick."

The administrative assistant came back with some rather unexpected news. "The address used by the shipper is a vacant lot in San Antonio. They are about to build something on it. I looked on Google Earth. Nothing on the shipper so far."

"Thanks, Clara. I expect that name is as phony as the address," Debra said.

"How do we find out who shipped it?" asked Ellis.
Debra said, "I think I know who shipped it. She was a Jane Doe in the University Hospital and skipped out. I left her this card, and it was the only one I had left that day. I remember the lipstick smudge. We'll keep that quiet for now. And I can't help but wonder if Mr. Johnson or Mr. Montgomery, whatever is name is, may have run into her somewhere?"

"What do we do with this stuff, Debra?" asked Ellis.

"I'll talk to the chief about this. As of right now, we seem to

have been sent what might be evidence… but technically, we have no crime…and, I need to make a call."

Chapter 38

Russ's phone showed that it was Debra calling. He decided to answer in a professional manor. "Detective Russell Baker, Madison County Sheriff's Office."

"Good morning, Detective Baker, this is Detective Debra Taylor with the Salt Lake City Police Department. I'm here with my colleague Detective Ellis. It came to my attention that your office is involved in a case where you have been looking for one Max Johnson. Possibly from Atlanta. Is that correct.?"

Russ frowned. He had been hoping to joke with her with the professional sounding tone, but now it sounded like this really was a work call. But if she knew something about Max Johnson, he was all ears.

"That's correct. Max Johnson has been implicated in the abduction, rape, and possible false imprisonment of multiple women. We have been unsuccessful in locating him."

"I received today, from an anonymous source, a package with Mr. Johnson's wallet, ID, and telephones. We don't have a specific case linked to Johnson here, so I wanted to contact you and see if we could assist in your investigation by sharing what we received."

Debra went on to describe all they knew so far from the package's contents. She left out the business card detail.

"This is fantastic news, Detective Taylor. I'll get with the sheriff, and he'll notify Atlanta and the FBI right now, I would think. Can you get us a copy of the picture ID's? And, what about the phones?"

"Our office is sending the photo's now. We haven't done anything with the phones, yet. Do you think we should send them to the FBI?" asked Debra.

"Can your folks look at them there? We don't have the forensics capabilities here that you have. It may turn out that you did have a crime there and need the information, and we know we have at least one local victim and maybe two. If we get this drilled down, we can turn the cases over, but I'd really like to get these guys ourselves. And once you look at the thumb drive and phones, we'll know more about who needs to be involved at the State and Federal levels."

"I'll check with my chief. If he's willing to hold back on a little of the info, I'll let you know. There is also the notebook which we haven't looked at to see what, if anything, it contains," replied Debra.

"Great, Detective Taylor. I'm calling the sheriff right now. I'll be in touch," Russ said, hanging up and promptly getting to work.

The Atlanta PD was notified and the ID's sent. The Salt Lake forensic lab would go to work on phones and detailing what info might be on the thumb drive.

Before handing the thumb drives and phones over to the lab, Debra Taylor and Detective Ellis put the drive in Debra's laptop to see if they could open it. What they saw was a list of names, phone numbers, and dollar transactions with dates and places. The sales figures and data for a criminal enterprise dealing in human lives. Debra Taylor was speechless. She called Russell Baker.

"Hello, again," said Russ, surprised at how quickly he was hearing back. He'd just gotten off the phone with the sheriff informing him about the package.

"You won't believe what we have on this drive. I have copied it to my computer. I'm going to quietly put this on my Dropbox and send you a link so you can look at it. Russ, we may have these bastards. I don't want any chain of custody problems, so let's see what we have, and then we can get formal disclosure and share with the FBI as necessary. I'll get my boss involved."

"When will I have that?" Russ asked.

"Sending the file and the link now."

"I'm going to get with Steinbrenner at the office. He may want to talk to your chief. Please send that contact info, too."

Russ immediately called the sheriff after getting off the phone with Debra. Things were starting to feel like they were moving fast.

"Steinbrenner, here," the sheriff said as he answered Russ's call. "You must be reading my mind."

"Probably ESP. Do you want my news, or do you want to give me yours first?" asked Russ.

"Well. Atlanta was interested in the two ID's showing the same person. The first guy, Maxwell Johnson, died some months back at his home in Buckhead in Atlanta."

"You've got to be kidding!" replied Russ.

"Afraid not. So, you won't be arresting that Mr. Johnson and neither will they. It seems that Martin Montgomery, III was actually the person on the ID's. His ID was the valid ID. The fake ID was Johnson's. Montgomery was using the dead guy's information,"

"So where do we go to find Montgomery?" asked Russ.

"That's more of the good news I have to share. They found him already," said the sheriff.

"I don't think I'm going to like this, Sheriff," said Russ.

"Neither did his wife. They found him a couple of days ago in a cheap motel in Atlanta. Dead. He had three rather deep stab wounds."

"He had brought in a young, pretty blonde girl, according to the clerk, who registered as a Gabrielle Sanchez. Johnson paid for the room. Apparently, he paid to put young women up there a lot as Max Johnson. When they did not check out as planned, the hotel manager went looking," Steinbrenner explained.

The Sheriff continued, "The police came and were trying to find out about Max Johnson with no luck. Montgomery's wife finally reported him missing. When we sent over the ID's, a sharp Atlanta PD Detective put the two together. They are posting a lookout for the blonde. So, Detective. Can you top that?"

"I really wanted to arrest Max Johnson, Sheriff."

"Yea, me too. Someone else got to him first," the sheriff said.

"If you'll wait there with Ms. Willingham, I may have some info we can work on, and we'll need the High Sheriff involved. There is going to be a lot of cross jurisdictional issues, probably," Russ said.

"Okay, Russ. What do you have?"

"Debra Taylor opened up the thumb drive and is making a copy available to us. It has names, dates, phone numbers, and monetary transactions. We need to see who we have involved and then you can decide who you want to pass the info along to."

"Get over here to the office!"

Chapter 39

Russell Baker pulled up to the sheriff's office in Virginia City. He was armed with his laptop as he entered. As they found the link and opened the file, the scope and scale of the operation was revealed.

Names and phone numbers of people involved. Names of victims and partial addresses. The dollars involved and the dollar value that young men and women had been reduce to were shown.

"Why would he keep such incriminating material on a file like this is beyond me," said the sheriff.

"Maybe it was protection. He had this in case they decided to cut him out or do away with him," responded Russ.

They ran through the names and numbers. Several jumped out from the recent entries.

There was Marta Andruko, the girl that had called for help and had not yet been found. A notation said New Orleans, Ukraine and Las Vegas, and there were some numbers that seemed like a code.

There was Geraldine Bailey. It said pretty, black, Chattanooga, San Francisco – and another code.

There was one that said Maria Torres, Cedar Creek, Vancouver and the same type code.

They had two names they recognized and one of them was still lost.

Russ's phone rang. It was Debra Taylor from Salt Lake.

"Russ, I am on the line with my chief. We have been able to open one phone so far, and we have the small notebook. You may want to get the sheriff in on this."

Steinbrenner said, "Well Ms. Taylor, for once, I'm the one listening in on speaker."

After a quick introduction of the two officers in charge, Debra said, "We have contact numbers that show calls to the Leonard Ranch, calls to Rachel Wallace… and, Russ, there are calls to the cop in Helena. A one Darin Marchman on the date in question for Geraldine."

"I think we should put together a raid on that ranch at once," said Russ. "I believe we will find some of these women there, and I believe we'll find Marta Andruko there. It's the only thing that would make sense now."

"If I were a betting person, the girl we had out here as a Jane Doe was part of this list of victims," said Debra.

The Salt Lake police chief said, "Can you guys wait till later today or tomorrow? We have our best people working on the other phones, and if we get them cracked, maybe the whole thing can be brought down."

Russ said, "I would like to get the sheriff to contact the Helena Police Chief and let's see what we can do about getting an ID on the cop there from our young lady at the Bozeman Hospital. She's likely to be going home in a day or two. If we can get that, we can see about getting a DNA swab and blood sample from him. If we could match him to the blood on the ballpoint, we might start shaking that tree. I would really like to nail that guy."

"I'll make that call right now," said Steinbrenner.

Russ added, "And, with the photo IDs on Johnson slash Montgomery, we can also get Geraldine to give us a positive ID on that guy linking all his activities to her. That should give the FBI and Atlanta PD, maybe even the IRS, some probable cause to tear into that situation."

The Salt Lake chief asked, "What do you guys want out of this?"

Steinbrenner said, "We want the person or persons who attacked the young woman in our county. We want any and all persons connected with her movements in our county. And, if this Marta Andruko is in our county, or was when she called us, we want to find her and whoever is responsible for her situation. As far as the young lady in Salt Lake, if she is part of this, we will render any assistance we can to you. That's not our case. And, we will assist Atlanta PD, the FBI, DCI, or whomever in getting those in Atlanta or other cities. Bringing this whole organization down will have to be at the Federal level, and we aren't trying to outdo the FBI."

"Detective Taylor has been a big help to us, again, and if you can spare her to help with the young woman and the ID'ing of our suspect, that would be great. She's got a rapport built up with the girl from what I understand."

"We will make that happen," the chief said.

Steinbrenner looked at Russ and smiled. Russ gave him a *I can't believe you did that* look.

After the call ended, Steinbrenner said to Russ, "See. I look after my people."

"Much appreciated, Sir," said Russ.

Russ called Teresa Walker. "We're ready to get a positive ID on your policeman. Will you sit in with us if they want a face to face in Helena? This will be a bitter pill for that department to swallow."

"Yes. I may need your help letting Mr. Renfroe know what I'm doing. Will you want me to come back to Bozeman to see the girl too?" Teresa asked.

"Would you like to? I know her grandmother would like to see you. I warn you: expect a hug like you ain't ever had. How about in the morning?"

"That will be worth coming for. It's been a while since I've had a good squeeze – I'll take a grandma hug any day," she said.

"Teresa. Stop being so hard on yourself. It's time to move on. It took me a year and a half to realize that myself."

He hung up. The ball was rolling.

By the next morning, a group of photos were assembled. Included were pictures of Max Johnson, the girl named Andruko from the New Orleans police, and Darin Marchman. Russ, the sheriff, a DCI agent, and Teresa Walker were allowed to use the hospital conference room since Geraldine had not been dismissed.

After all were assembled, they explained to Geraldine that she was going to look at pictures with no prompting to see if she recognized any out of the twenty-five or so they would lay out. Just as they were about to start, there was a tapping on the door.

"May I come in?" a familiar voice said.

Sheriff Steinbrenner smiled said, "Glad you could make it, Debra."

The pictures were laid out on the table. Lois Bailey had wanted to be right next to her granddaughter but was persuaded that Geraldine needed to make a decision about the photo without any influence. She was allowed to stay in the room, but she needed to remain aside and quiet.

Russ said, "Geraldine, when we show you these pictures, please understand, the people we are looking for may not be here. If you don't recognize anyone, then we'll just keep trying. Okay?"

"Okay."

Slowly, she looked at each picture. Some she picked up and put down two or three times. In about ten minutes, she pushed two pictures out from the rest.

With tears streaming and in a voice in almost a whisper, she said, "That man raped me and held me prisoner in Atlanta. He put me on a bus and hauled me to some place. I think it was Boston. I was put in a big truck and then this is the man took me from the truck place. He's the one I stabbed with a ballpoint pen –" and she pointed to her own neck "– right about here. There was a lot of blood. Then I ran, and he hit me with his car. I tried to run, but my leg hurt so bad, and it wouldn't work. I guess that's when he shot me, but I don't remember that part much."

The room was silent. The female DCI agent, Debra Taylor, Teresa Walker, and Lois Bailey were in tears. It was all Russ could do to hold back himself. The feeling he was experiencing was difficult to describe. Max Johnson, or Martin Montgomery, was dead. *Good riddance.* Darin Marchman made Russ sick to his stomach and angry.

"I think you should know Max Johnson was not his real name. We know who he actually was. He was found murdered in a hotel room in Atlanta. He had been stabbed three times," Russ said.

Lois Bailey yelled, "Thank you, Lord. Thank you, Lord. Now I won't have to do it!"

No one doubted that she would have, if given a chance.

Then, Russ turned to Teresa. "Can you identify anyone in these pictures? The DCI may be interested in your identification for later evidence."

"Yes. As I have previously stated, *that* man —" she pointed to Marchman "—was in our restaurant on several occasions and left with young women. I did not actually see him leave with Geraldine. I saw him working another time when taking my mother to the doctor in Helena. He pulled me over for speeding. I recognized him from being in our restaurant."

Sheriff Steinbrenner stepped out of the room and made a call. He came back in moments later.

"The Police Chief in Helena, his name is Larry Berger, will meet with us at their place in two hours. He'll have the suspect there. He is one upset guy right now," Steinbrenner said, shaking his head. Russ imagined that had been a difficult call to make.

Chapter 40

Teresa said goodbye and headed back to Butte. Lois and Geraldine were taken back to Geraldine's hospital room. Russ and the others were off to Helena.

The trip to Helena was fast. Steinbrenner had lights going and passed everything in sight. The DCI agent had to work to stay caught up in her car. No one said a word until they were almost there. Debra said, "I really do like flying." Everyone laughed.

When they walked into police station at 406 Fuller Street, they were met by Chief Berger and escorted to a conference room. "You'd better have something really good if you are going to interrogate one of my officers. We have a great department with great officers," the chief said, clearly fighting off a snarl.

Before anyone else could speak, the DCI agent said, "Sheriff, I don't need your permission to interview this suspect."

"As a courtesy to you, Sheriff Steinbrenner wanted to call you so you would not be blindsided. Do you wish to sit in and do it here, or do we need to pick him up and carry him back to Virginia City?"

There was no mistaking that she meant it.

"Tell me what you have first. Please," the chief said, quickly changing his tune.

By the end of the update, the chief was saddened and angry. "He's supposed to be in my office. I'll go get him."

When Darin Marchman came in the Sheriff, Russell, and the DCI agent were all standing. A sizable look of force. The sheriff gave the nod to Russ to start out. He pulled no punches.

"Officer Marchman. I am Russell Baker, detective with the Madison County Sheriff's Office. That's my boss, Sheriff Steinbrenner. That lady that met you at the door you know as a DCI agent for the State of Montana. That is Debra Taylor, a detective with the Salt Lake City Police. The FBI allowed us to take the lead in this case due to the local nature of some of the offenses. They will be around later, I'm sure."

"What the hell are you talking about? What offenses? I'm not going to sit here and listen to this BS." He stood up as if he was going to leave.

Russell Baker stepped up, almost touching him. "Get your ass back in that chair *now*."

Marchman complied. Part of the air had left his sails.

"You should be happy to know that we have enough on you to put you away for a while. Assault with a motor vehicle, assault with a deadly weapon, transporting a person across the country for sex, and false imprisonment and identified by the victim."

Oh, I was about to forget, we have a ballpoint pen with your DNA and blood. Man, that must have hurt… and from the blood at the scene, she got you good. And, she did survive, by the way, and is really eager to testify.”

Steinbrenner added, “I guess you've figured out we have Max Johnson, too. Your supply of sex workers and the money are cut off. I imagine he'll be selling you out for a plea bargain.” “I want a lawyer,” Marchman said, his voice sounding dry and airy.

“Great. We are placing you under arrest, and you will be transported to the Madison County jail. You can call your lawyer from there,” said Steinbrenner.

Darin Marchman was put in handcuffs and walked out through the police department to the shock and dismay of those fellow officers there. He was put in the sheriff's car and headed to jail in Virginia City. Russ sat in the seat beside him, and he saw that Marchman was crying. Russ had no sympathy for him.

“Can I at least call my wife?” he asked. “I need to tell her I won't be home for dinner.”

“I'm thinking you're going to miss dinner for about the next twenty-five years,” Russ said.

“Go to hell,” said Marchman.

They rode in silence.

They set about booking Marchman and gave him chance to call his wife and start trying to get a lawyer.

After he got off the phone with his wife, he announced, “I'll tell you everything I know. I can't drag my family though this.”

The sheriff said, “You requested a lawyer up in Helena. Are you waving your right to a lawyer?”

“Yes. I am.”

Russ and the sheriff sat down in the conference room and turned on the video camera and tape. And after an exhausting hour, they had names, procedures, and contact systems for a group that was operating a human trafficking, money laundering, drug smuggling, and prostitution business all across the country.

Then, Debra Taylor's boss called her. They stepped out from the interrogation and put the man on speaker.

"Detective Taylor, the forensic folks, with some FBI assistance, have gotten into Max Johnson's other phone. We've got a massive number of calls and texts; a lot were encrypted, and we're still working on those. We are sending the sheriff over a file on their email with a lot of info from their area. Helena, Butte, and a place called Leonard Ranch. There may be some people there now, according to what we're seeing."

After some discussion, they decided to do simultaneous raids in Boston, the Leonard Ranch, and a couple of other places that included Las Vegas. The FBI were to be contacting the sheriff there soon.

The call came immediately. After some conversing with the agent on the phone, the Sheriff Steinbrenner asked Russ if he wanted to add anything. "Yes. Can we wait to enter the Leonard Ranch until we are sure Rachel Wallace is there? I don't want her skipping out or being able to say she wasn't involved."

"Okay," the agent on the phone said. "But we won't wait forever. We will send an FBI SWAT crew by helicopter from Butte. With the local support, you'll have from Bozeman and Butte, we should be able to sweep that ranch with minimum resistance. We have enough warrants to choke a whale. The same back East."

Chapter 41

Russell and Debra, along with two other county cars, were parked at Cemetery Road at the mining museum in Silver Star. They could watch the road for Wallace to pass going to the ranch. There were two other cars just down the road. The helicopter was just 5 minutes away. At ten o'clock, Rachel passed them.

"Madison Unit Two to all units. The subject is driving into the ranch now. All units move in," Russ said into his walkie-talkie.

As Rachel Wallace approached the gate, Russell had caught up with lights and sirens. Other cars were arriving along with a black helicopter with FBI written on the side. The chopper was sitting down in the open field before Rachel knew what was happening. The guard wanted to stop Russ, but there were two deputies pointing weapons at him from one of the support cars. In a moment, the guard was face down and handcuffed.

Russ followed Rachel to the office parking area. By this time there were officers at all the motor homes, ordering the people out.

Rachel Wallace was enraged. She was screaming at Russ, "You have no authority to be here. I'm calling my lawyer!"

Debra Taylor grabbed Rachel Wallace, spun her around into the wall. Russ read her rights to her as Debra put the cuffs on. "Calling a lawyer would be a good idea, Ms. Wallace," Russ said.

"My family will nail you bastards to the wall!" she screamed.

"They may have a few of their own problems right now," said Russ.

"Now, where is Marta Andruko?" asked Russ.

"Never heard of her," Rachel hissed.

A female officer from Silver Bow County Sheriff's office took Rachel Wallace to area around the pool where everyone was being assembled. One of the motor homes tried to leave but thought better of it when two FBI SWAT officers pointed their automatic weapons in the driver's face.

Russ and Debra passed some rooms where officers had entered and were removing the men and women. They came to a locked door. Russ banged hard on the door. "This is the police. We have a search warrant. Open the door."

A voice inside, speaking in a foreign language, yelled back. They did not understand what he said.

"Open the door, now," Russ said again.

A female voice called back, "He doesn't speak English. He has a gun." She sounded scared.

Russ yelled back, "Go get in the bathtub. Do it now!"

Russ thought the door might could be more than he could handle, so he asked Debra to run get one of the officers carrying a battering ram.

As soon as Debra turned the corner, the door flew open.

A large man with a big belly was there carrying a semi-automatic pistol.

"Drop the gun. Drop the gun, now!" ordered Russ.

The man responded by pointing his gun at Russ and yelling. A fatal mistake.

Russell Baker fired two rounds at the big, heavy man. He was dead before he hit the ground.

Debra came running back along with two other officers, guns drawn.

"Cover me, Debra." Russ entered the room. It was clear. He tapped on the bathroom door.

"Are you in there? I'm a police officer. The man with the gun is gone."

"Is he dead? I heard shooting," was the weak reply.

"Not sure, but he won't be bothering you again, sweetheart," Russ said.

"I'm scared to come out," she said.

"Hello in there. My name is Debra. I am also a police officer. Can I come in?" Debra said from behind Russ.

"I guess so. Are you going to take me to jail?"

"We are just trying to make sure you're okay."

Debra opened the door, went in, and closed it back. Then she called out. "Detective Baker, would you mind stepping out for a minute? She needs to get dressed."

In a couple of minutes, Debra said, "Coming out."

She stepped out with a frail and frightened young woman. "Russell Baker, meet Marta Andruko."

Russ stepped forward and said, "I am so happy to meet you. I'm sorry it took us so long to find you, Marta. I heard your 911 call. Good job. That was very brave of you."

Debra and Russ walked her to an ambulance that was on scene. Debra said, "Marta, we're sending you to the hospital so that they can take care of you." She told the ambulance driver that this was a hostage and victim.

"I'm afraid to go," said Marta.

"Russ, I guess you'll have to go home by yourself. I'm going with Marta." And with that, the door closed, and off they went.

The Leonardi Family criminal enterprise had just had a bad day.

Chapter 42

Most of the police work was done, so it was now paperwork, lawyers, district attorneys, and attorney generals. Russ thought he might could go fishing soon.

"Hello, this is Russ," he said when his Bluetooth started to buzz.

"Are you coming get me in Bozeman, or do I need to get a cab?" asked Debra.

"I'm actually on the way. ETA 10 minutes. Then, how about breakfast? And, I called Teresa Walker and thanked her for her help. How is Marta?" asked Russ.

"She has been through a lot. But maybe she'll get a chance at a decent life now."

"Well, they arrested a number of people in Boston, Las Vegas, and some more places. Some warrants are out on others".

"Are you okay Russ?"

"Yes."

"What next?" she asked.

"I think I may need a day or two off after the paperwork is finished. I wish we knew who killed that Johnson guy… or whatever his name was."

"Well, at least that's not your case or mine. We'll leave that to someone else," said Debra.

"You're right. And, I doubt Atlanta PD is too concerned about him after all we've found out about him. They're probably happy to be rid of him."

"Russ. I have a thought. Marta Andruko gave me the name of one girl, and I think it might be the unidentified girl we had in the hospital. Her name is on those documents in the material we got in the stuff from Johnson. I want to go to Austin and look her up. Will you go with me? We'll go to see Austin City Limits and tourist stuff for a couple of days."

"Does she live in Austin?" Russ asked.

"No, but not too far away."

"That seems like a lot of effort on your part to check on a runaway. Are you sure you want to go?" he asked.

"I'm positive. It's something I have to do. No questions, okay?"

"Okay. Let's go. Is this on the Taylor Airlines plane?" he asked.

"Afraid not. This will be on the Russell Baker credit card."

"I may want to reconsider," he teased.

"Too late. You've committed."

The next afternoon, the plane landed in Austin, and a short time later, their rental car pulled into a neat little house in Cedar Creek, Texas.

Debra walked up and knocked on the door. A woman came to the door with a name badge on and appeared to be just coming from work.

"I'm Debra Taylor, and this is Russell Baker. We're friends of Maria's. We wanted to surprise her. Is she home?"

They were told she would be home in a few minutes from her classes at the community college in Austin.

"Would you like to wait inside?" the woman asked.

"We'll just wait here in the swing, if that's okay," Debra said.

In a few minutes, a Honda Civic pulled in. The driver seemed hesitant to come all the way in the yard. Debra gave a friendly wave.

Marie Torres walked slowly toward them. Debra and Russell stepped down to meet her.

"Hi, Maria. I don't know if you remember me. I was the investigator on your case in Salt Lake City," Debra said.

"I remember you. Sorry I ran out on you. Did you tell my mother about that?" she asked.

"No. We told your mother we were some friends of yours."

"Are you here to arrest me?" Maria asked.

"As far as I know, you have not committed any crime in Salt Lake City. Russell is from Madison County, Montana. Russ, do you know of any crime she committed in your county?"

"I do not," said Russ.

"How did you get my name?" Maria asked.

"From Marta Andruko and some files we came across. We arrested the people who were holding you and the man that picked you up at the restaurant in Butte Montana."

"How is Marta?" Maria asked.

"She's recovering and will be going home soon."

"Good. Thanks for telling me," Maria said.

"I wanted you to know that Max Johnson in Atlanta is also dead. I believe he was responsible for your abduction."

Without batting an eye, she said, "Yes, he was the one responsible. That's good news that he's dead."

"Well, we're going sightseeing. But I have a small gift for you to remember me by."

Debra reached into her small designer purse and took out a little plastic bag. From it, she removed one of her business cards that said Detective Debra Taylor, Salt Lake City Police Department. It had her phone number and the address of the police headquarters. It also had something else.

In the corner of the card was a lipstick smudge.

"Call me if you're ever out our way again and need anything," said Debra.

Russ was a little confused about what had just occurred. As she and Russ walked away to their car, Maria called, "Wait."

She ran to Debra and gave her a big hug, and, sobbing, she said, "Thank you."

As they drove away, Russ said, "I've never seen a person so happy to get a business card."

"That one was special, Russ."

"Because you gave it to her?" Russ asked.

"No. Because it was the one item that I had that connected her to the box of evidence that was taken from the dead Max Johnson in Atlanta. It put her at the scene. I knew it was the one I had given her when she was in the hospital because it had a lipstick smudge."

Russ gave a startled look at Debra, "You think she killed Max Johnson?"

"Marta Andruko asked if Maria had killed Max Johnson when I was with her at the hospital the other night. I said I didn't know and that wasn't my case. She said the last thing Maria told her before they were separated was that she was going to kill Max Johnson."

It all was clear to Russ why Debra had wanted to come to see Maria, now. After a moment, he responded, "Not my case."

Debra echoed his statement. "Not my case."

Russ said, "I wonder who all will be performing at Austin City Limits tomorrow?"

"Better yet, who's performing in room 3721 at the Fairmont Hotel tonight?" Debra asked.

"Checking here, I believe that's us." replied Russ

End Of The Road